KU-466-662

THE SLIDE AREA

Scenes of Hollywood Life

Gavin Lambert

A STAR BOOK
published by
the Paperback Division of
W. H. ALLEN & Co. Ltd

A Star Book
Published in 1977
by the Paperback division of W. H. Allen & Co. Ltd
A Howard and Wyndham Company
123, King Street, London W6 9JG

First published in Great Britain by
Hamish Hamilton 1959
Penguin edition published 1963

Copyright © Gavin Lambert, 1959

Printed in Great Britain by
C. Nicholls & Company Ltd, The Philips Park Press, Manchester

ISBN 0 352 39633 4

This book is sold subject to the condition that it shall
not, by way of trade or otherwise, be lent,
re-sold, hired out or otherwise circulated without the
publisher's prior consent in any form of
binding or cover other than that in which it is published
and without a similar condition including this
condition being imposed on the subsequent purchaser

Contents

THE action begins just before Christmas 1956 and ends two years later.

Most of the episodes cover several months in time and they take place simultaneously, so do not be surprised if a character who dies or disappears at the end of one section turns up again in part of another one.

As they say in the movies, all characters are fictitious and any resemblance to actual persons, living or dead, or to actual firms, is purely coincidental.

Acknowledgements are due to the *London Magazine*, in which the first and third episodes appeared.

G.L.

The Slide Area
February 1959

The Slide Area

ABOUT this hour and season, four o'clock in the afternoon and early summer, I find myself looking out of the window and wondering why the world seems bright yet melancholy.

I am sitting in office 298 of a Hollywood film studio, working on a script and thinking that the film Cliff Harriston is going to make of it won't do either of us much good. This morning I noticed a truck parked outside one of the shooting stages. Scenery was being unloaded, the walls and furniture of a living-room carried into the empty stage where camera, lights and the high crane are already waiting. There is no stopping it now, I thought. Later, imagining the reality being hammered and painted and wheeled into shape over there, I looked at the pages on my desk and found them more unreal, more impossible than ever. Tomorrow there will be more arguments with executives. We shall plead our cause and discuss what is truth. I would like to start work on the novel I am hoping to write and pretend is already under way.

Office 298 is small and square and rather dim, because there are venetian blinds across the windows and heavy faded curtains that cannot be pulled back far enough. I have tried letting up the blinds, but the heat is unendurable. Better to be cool and slightly depressed. There is a desk with a telephone and typewriter and stack of paper, a tray full of finely-sharpened pencils and a calendar with leaves you are supposed to tear off each day. It doesn't seem worthwhile to tear off the leaves. Let time stand still or move back, it doesn't matter.

There used to be pictures hanging on the walls, coloured sketches for the sets of a recent production laid in ancient

Rome. Another sketch was labelled *Costume for Mr Victor Mature*. The designer had autographed them all with a grave flourish in the lower right-hand corner. I took them down my first day here and hid them behind the filing cabinet. No one will take them away, although I have asked the office cop several times and once in desperation left a note for the cleaners.

I glance at the cabinet and know they are *there*. About twice a week this obliges me to leave the office early. It always happens at the same time. From my swivel chair at the desk I face this cabinet and the door leading into the corridor; the dim light is strange and enervating, it reminds me of an unoccupied house swathed in blinds and dust-sheets. Swivelling, I look out of the window across the parking lot with its rows of shining two-toned saloons and convertibles, and the neat flower-beds dustily brilliant in puce and yellow. The sun is climbing down the sky. In another hour it will be cooler.

As I leave the building, the cop silently notes my early departure in his little book. He has already noted my late arrival this morning. A friendly ritual that we do not even bother to talk about.

Two men are staring at the newspaper rack near his desk. Both are plump and clean and perspiring, and wear white nylon shirts with sleeves rolled up. They have familiar anonymous executive faces.

For once a political event, though it was later found not to have taken place, occupies the front page headlines. With no kidnappings, aeroplane crashes or sex crimes blocked out in huge letters anywhere, I feel for a moment that something has gone wrong. So do the executives, as they gaze at each paper in turn and find no escape from REDS INVADE BURMA!

Their faces are solemn, sweat pours down. They scan the pages like people trying to find their bearings. Then, his eyes narrowing, one turns to the other. 'It says Bobo Rockefeller's got herself arrested.'

With sighs of relief they move on.

A white Lincoln shoots past, I glimpse a woman in a white sleeveless dress at the wheel, green silk scarf fluttering out of the window. She pulls up with a squall of brakes at a STOP sign, two feet from a weakly handsome young man in a beige tussore suit.

'Hi, Julie! Trying to kill me?'

She laughs loudly. 'Yeah, but I changed my mind.'

This is Julie Forbes, a famous star. She has been in pictures for thirty years and everyone is always saying how good she looks. The young man is an actor recently arrived from Broadway and placed under contract to the studio.

He leans charmingly on the window of the car. 'How about dinner this week?'

She shakes her head. 'I'm busy every night.'

'Next week?'

'Call me over the week-end and see how I'm fixed.'

He looks disappointed. She pats his hand. 'And pine for me, loved one.'

She drives away, scarf fluttering.

The studio is like a large country estate. Haphazardly ranged buildings are white and clean and look entirely uninhabited. What to do? I put a coin in the automatic Coca-Cola machine, the bottle slides out on a tray and I place it under the automatic opener. I don't like Coca-Cola much, but drink a little and pass the smiling Negro shoeblack at his stand.

'Hi, how are *you*?'

'I'm fine. How are *you*?'

Back lots with permanent exterior sets occupy most of the grounds. The residential street of white frame-houses with sprinklers on the front lawn, a nice replica of anywhere in the more modest stretches of Beverly Hills, has as much and perhaps more reality than the real thing. So has the small-town square: well stocked drugstore, a bank and a school, a church and an empty green. The windows of the bank are still shattered from a robbery scene staged there last month.

In the western town, the St Louis Midland Express is always standing at the railway station. The Last Chance Saloon is empty except for silence and a few chairs broken and overturned from the last brawl. The main street turns a corner and is suddenly a footbridge across a dried-up stream. Beyond it lies something that began as a medieval French village and has been altered here and there to suit the centuries as a corner of Italy or Corsica. A rotted pulpit leans across the entrance to Our Lady of the Fields.

Further away the ground slopes up, then down again to an abandoned harbour town, slightly Dutch with its moored barges and rosebrick warehouses along the quayside. It is watched by an artificial canvas sky, shaped like an immense blue panoramic screen, bluer than the thing above my head. Spotlights are standing by, ready to reinforce the sun.

Then comes the point of no return. The great open air scene dock is like landscaped bric-à-brac. Derelict pioneer wagons left to flake and lurch in the dry grasses; a huddle of chipped classical pillars; an early ranch house with no glass in the windows and one wall missing and the stains of fire; an old stockade, a Chinese palace arch, a tall unhinged door fallen across a wheel, a rowing boat propped up against a castle watchtower, and a staircase winding to the sky.

Here it sleeps in the sun, this neglected litter of the past.

Time and heat make their inroads a little more each day. A
ruined secret world more real than practical avenues and
boulevards, the only place you can be certain that ghosts
walk.

What to do? In the parking lot, hidden among princely
roadsters, stands my fog-grey seventy dollar 1947 Chevrolet
with the battered front I refuse to have mended. As I drive
out, the cop at the gate looks glad to see it go. Then he waves
as a young actress and her massive grim-faced aunt edge
quickly past me in a damask Cadillac embroidered from
radiator cap to rear mudguard with mother-of-pearl.

It becomes a day for interesting cars. Stopping at a drugstore for cigarettes, I park behind a twenty-five-year-old
Rolls-Royce that I know very well. A landaulette, painted
silver and white, and the royal crest of the old Austro-
Hungarian empire engraved on the doors. A young chauffeur
sits at the wheel, chewing gum.

The drugstore is fairly empty, at the soda fountain a
group of girls sip chocolate malts and a Filipino workman
eats a hamburger. Everyone else is watching the Countess
Osterberg-Steblechi, who pays no attention but very slowly
revolves the paperbacked crime novels on their stands. It is
the fate of the Countess to be stared at, and one cannot be
surprised. She is like a balloon blown up into roughly human
shape and ready to burst. All swollen and sagging contours
except for her face; her beaky nose and sharp hooded eyes
remind you of a falcon. She has hair that looks like a wig
but is really her own dyed red, and wears a piece of garish
linen printed all over with flowers and cornucopias like old-
fashioned wallpaper.

Each time I see this great aristocratic wreck, I have the
impression she has *got inside* her shoes, her dress, her hat if

she wears one, by mistake. And she cannot get out. She is trapped, any movement could be fatal. She waddles danger-ously up to me now, a paperbacked novel in one hand, a crocodile leather bag in the other.

'Dear child, have you read *The Case of the Black-Eyed Blonde*?' I shake my head as she holds up the book in front of me. 'How strange, nobody has. I looked at the first page and nearly fainted with excitement. Are you coming to tea with me Sunday?'

'I'd love to.'

She wheezes with pleasure, but the strain contracts her face. Now it looks like the moon after an explosion, the features are blasted fragments. 'There may be a kind of jumble sale, I hope to raise a few hundred dollars.'

'For what?' I ask, though I know the answer.

'For myself, of course, dear child. I wish I were not so heartrendingly poor.' She scratches her nose with a jewelled and freckled finger. 'Are you sure you haven't read *The Case of the Black-Eyed Blonde*?'

'Absolutely.'

'Then I shall have to take it on trust. With an opening paragraph like that I think ... ' She breaks off vaguely, fumbling in her crocodile bag and giving the assistant a quarter.

The assistant says: 'Thirty-five cents, please.'

She takes an alarmed step backwards. 'You mean it's one of the expensive ones?'

'It's thirty-five cents.'

The Countess replaces the book in the Westerns rack. 'Much too expensive,' she says firmly, 'when no one knows if it's really good. I adore pulp literature but one must re-tain one's sense of values. Where is your selection of twenty-five-cent crime novels, please?'

She is the widow of a distinguished European banker.

It is only a few miles' drive to the ocean, but before reaching it I shall be nowhere. Hard to describe the impression of unreality, because it is intangible; almost supernatural; something in the air. (The air ... Last night on the weather telecast the commentator, mentioning electric storms near Palm Springs and heavy smog in Los Angeles, described the behaviour of the air as 'neurotic'. Of course. Like everything else the air must be imported and displaced, like the water driven along huge aqueducts from distant reservoirs, like the palm trees tilting above mortuary signs and laundromats along Sunset Boulevard.) Nothing belongs. Nothing belongs except the desert soil and the gruff eroded-looking mountains to the north. Because the earth is desert, its surface always has that terrible dusty brilliance. Sometimes it looks like the Riviera with a film of neglect over villas and gardens, a veil of fine invisible sand drawn across tropical colours. It is hard to be reminded of any single thing for long. The houses are real because they exist and people use them for eating and sleeping and making love, but they have no style of their own and look as if they've been imported from half a dozen different countries. They are imitation 'French Provincial' or 'new' Regency or Tudor or Spanish hacienda or Cape Cod, and except for a few crazy mansions seem to have sprung up overnight. The first settlers will be arriving tomorrow from parts unknown.

Los Angeles is not a city, but a series of suburban approaches to a city that never materializes. The noisy populous down-town section with its mixture of Americans and Mexicans, Negroes and Orientals, its glass and concrete new structures jostling fragile wooden slums, its heavy police force and ugly untidy look of sudden industrial growth, is a little like Casablanca. The older parts are exotic but tired, collapsing under the sleek thrust of commerce. There is a modest little Japanese quarter with movie houses, gift shops, *sukiyaki* signs, a steam bath and massage parlour and the Bank of Tokyo; a Chinatown pretty and synthetic as a planner's lifesize model; a Mexican quarter with a gaudy street market, sombreros and bullfighters' capes and scented candles always on display. There are oil derricks and power plants massed like geometrical forests, and a thin bitter smoke hangs in the air on a windless day.

No settlement can ever have grown more wastefully and swiftly. A century and a half ago pirates still raided this coast, were captured and hung in the village square, Indian slaves were dragging timber from the mountains to build first a jail and then a church. Invasion began with the Gold Rush, fishermen from the East and Scandinavia and Italy found the Pacific rich in salmon and tuna, even convicts arrived from Australia in stolen ships. Now Los Angeles is a welter of nearly five hundred square miles and four million people making aeroplanes and pumping oil, assembling automobiles and movies, processing food and petroleum, building quick frame-houses that you can see being drawn along the streets at night by a truck and placed on a vacant lot like scenery for a movie set.

Along the main boulevards, between the office blocks, plots of untouched land are still for sale. On one of the plots, not long ago, the skeleton of a prehistoric animal was excavated. In the palaeozoic past, before the land dried and crusted into desert, this was a quagmire under a hot sun, sloths and mastodons were trapped and dying there. Now the last victim has gone, the grave is cleared and the offices of a great insurance company can go up.

How to grasp something unfinished yet always remodelling itself, changing without a basis for change? So much visible impatience to be born, to grow, such wild tracts of space to be filled: difficult to settle in a comfortable unfinished desert. Because of the long confusing distances, the streets are empty of walking people, full of moving cars. Between where you are and where you are going to be is a no-man's-land. At night the neon signs glitter and the shop windows are lighted stages, but hardly anyone stops to look. A few people huddle at coffee stalls and hamburger bars. Those dark flat areas are parking lots, crammed solid.

I suppose that Europeans, accustomed to a world that changes more calmly and slowly, are not much interested any more in imitating its surface. It becomes more exciting to see appearances as a mask, a disguise or illusion that conceals an unexpected meaning. The theme of illusion and reality is very common in Europe. In America, illusion and reality are still often the same thing. The dream is the achievement, the achievement is the dream.

The ocean appears suddenly. You turn another hairpin bend and the land falls away and there is a long high view down Santa Monica Canyon to the pale Pacific waters. A clear day is not often. Sky and air are hazed now, diffusing the sun and dredging the ocean of its rightful blue. The Pacific is a sad blue-grey, and nearly always looks cold.

Each time I drive down here it feels like the end of the world. The geographical end. Shabby and uncared for, buildings lie around like nomads' tents in the desert. There is nowhere further to go, those pale waters stretch away to the blurred horizon and stretch away beyond it. There is no more land ever.

High lurching cliffs confront the ocean, and are just beginning to fall apart. Signs have been posted along the highway, DRIVE CAREFULLY and SLIDE AREA. Lumps of earth and stone fall down. The land is restless here, restless and sliding. Driving inland towards the mountains, it is the same: BEWARE OF ROCKS. The land is falling. Rocks fall down all over and the cliffs called Pacific Palisades are crumbling slowly down to the ocean. Who called them Palisades, I wonder? They cannot keep out the Pacific. There are mad eccentric houses above the Palisades, with turrets and castellations and tall Gothic windows, but no one wants to live in them any more in case the ground slides away.

It has slid again this afternoon. On one section of the highway a crowd has gathered. An ambulance stands by, winking red lights. A sheriff directs operations. From a great pile of mud and stones and sandy earth, the legs of old ladies are sticking out. Men with shovels are working to free the rest of their bodies. Objects are rescued first, a soiled table-cloth and a thermos flask and what looks like a jumbo sandwich, long as a baby eel. Then an air cushion and more long sandwiches, and a picnic basket, and at last the three old ladies themselves. They are all right. They look shaken and angry, which is to be expected. A few minutes ago they had been sitting on the Palisades, in a pleasant little hollow free from the wind. The cloth was spread for a picnic. Miss Natalie O'Gorman laid out sandwiches on a plastic dish, her sister Clara unscrewed the thermos flask to pour out coffee, and their friend Willa North decided to blow up her air cushion.

Absolutely silent at first, the ground beneath them disappeared. The slide meant for a moment that there was no ground at all, it ceased to exist, and then as it gained momentum and scudded away like clouds breaking up in a gale, there was a light rumbling sound. The three ladies, Natalie O'Gorman with a sandwich in her hand, her sister with the flask and Willa North with her mouth pressed to the air cushion, went with the land and were practically submerged by it at the side of the highway below.

Now they are brushing their dresses with distracted motions and shaking little stones out of their bosoms and little clods out of their hair. Everyone is saying it is a miracle.

Natalie O'Gorman would like to find her hat. Bones are felt and nothing is broken; they are scratched and bruised, that is all. 'We are all right,' they tell the crowd. 'Yes, we are quite all right.' Willa North says: 'I was taken completely by surprise!'

I drive on, past another SLIDE AREA sign. The beaches are still quite full. A group of tanned young men are wrestling and playing ball. Two girls watch them, eating hot dogs. An old Negro in a tattered blue suit walks by the edge of the ocean, a mongrel dog following him. Out to sea, someone is surfing. Stretching his arms, the muscular young lifeguard watches from his tower.

The southern end of Santa Monica, the ocean suburb, is not impeccable. Unlike the correct mechanized residential areas, Beverly Hills, Westwood, Glendale, it is rather slatternly and interesting. Little wooden houses, their green and blue and yellow paint fading, slant above narrow streets. There are bins overflowing with garbage and trash. People walk in the streets, hang about on corners or outside bars where a juke-box is always playing. There is a pier, due to be condemned soon, with all the usual sideshows: hot dog, hamburger and ice-cream stands, and a submarine contraption that takes you under water and shows you an old disgruntled whale. The beach has fine dull sand and the water smells faintly rancid.

It is only five o'clock but the bar called The Place is quite full. *Mackie Messer* comes from the juke-box. An old man in a panama hat and dark glasses dances slowly with his cane. At the bar a tall drunk woman finishes her whisky and lights a cigarette from the stub of the one she has just finished. She has once been beautiful, but now her face has something ruined about it, as if she's been waiting too long, in vain, for the telephone to ring. She sees me, waves, runs unsteadily over, pulls at my arm and speaks in a fierce urgent whisper.

'She's dying!'

'Who?'

'Hank, my sister Hank.'

'What happened?'

She makes vague distracted movements with her hands. 'He shot her, darling, that's all I know. It doesn't matter. It's too late!' She pulls at my arm again. 'I call and call the hospital and they won't let me speak to her, and the nurse says not to worry in a way that means it's no use.' Tears are streaming down her face now. 'Hank's dying, darling, dying!'

I offer to phone the hospital.

'No use! They'll lie, it's a conspiracy of lies.'

'Let me try, Zeena.' I go to the telephone and put in a coin. She follows, muttering, 'hopeless . . .'

'St Judith's.'

'I want some information about Miss Henrietta Nelson, please.'

A pause, a whispering, a clicking, and presently a new voice with a German accent comes on the line:

'St Judith's.'

'I want some information about Miss Henrietta Nelson.'

'Who are you?'

'A friend of Miss Nelson.'

Another pause. Zeena clutches my elbow. 'You know they're all nuns? *Nuns!*'

I can hear footsteps approaching, then going away. The line crackles for a moment.

'Are you still there?'

'Yes.'

'Miss Henrietta Nelson is dead.'

'What?'

'Miss Nelson died shortly after four o'clock this afternoon.' The voice is merciless, pedantic, never shifting its level. 'We did not inform her sister as we did not care to break such news on the telephone. We asked her to arrive here and see us immediately, but her reply was not comprehensible. We received the impression she was not ... sober. Last night we were obliged not to admit her to visit her sister as she arrived not ... sober. Excuse me, but are you a responsible person?'

I hang up. Zeena is no longer there. The old man still dances with his cane.

The barman says: 'She just wandered out the way she does.'

She is not in the street outside. I get in my car, drive alongside the beach, which is almost deserted now. The sand looks grey, a fine white mist is dredging colour out of everything as the hazy sun slips down.

A figure walks uncertainly by the water's edge.

'Zeena,' I say as I come up to her, 'I'm afraid it's bad news.'

She has a weary look, throws her cigarette into the sea. 'Was it the German, darling? She's the worst.'

'They say Hank is dead.'

Zeena is very pale. A wave breaks, runs along the sand and wets her feet, she doesn't mind.

When the sun cools and everyone leaves the beach, only messages remain. Often there are dozens of them, traced with a stick or a finger in the sand. Zeena is looking at one now. JIMMY LOVES ELLA. And a little further away, MY NAME IS GRIFFIN.

She smiles, mutters 'I'll see you later,' and walks away.

She walks past I'M MAD ABOUT BOB, JOHNNY WAITED HERE and OH BILL I WANT TO MAKE YOU and a dead gull.

All this will be washed away tomorrow.

Dusk falls as I drive home. The mountains look black and farther away. The road winds uphill and there is a point where you can see Los Angeles sprawling away in the distance. Lights are coming on there now. Looking down on the straight intersecting lines of pink and yellow and green is like finding a vast abstract painting laid out on the earth. It has nothing at all to do with living. It is a bright winking mirage in the desert; you are afraid to look away in case it has vanished when you look back.

A mauve searchlight sweeps monotonously across the sky like a great silent pendulum.

When I get back to my apartment the telephone is ringing. 'Will you come immediately please?' The German nun from the hospital sounds a little breathless, but dry as ever. 'Miss Zeena Nelson refuses to go home. The police have asked all their questions and we give her a sedative, but she lies down in the waiting-room and refuses to go home. Come please.'

Unlike her voice, Sister Hertha seems plump and friendly. She wears a capacious white robe and a silver crucifix on a chain round her waist. When I ask her to tell me what happened, she looks surprised and straightens her rimless glasses, which have been a little askew. 'You know nothing?'

'Nothing. Except, something about a shooting.'

'That is so.' Sister Hertha lowers her voice. 'Last night a young man ... ' A nun passes with a tray of tea, Sister Hertha smiles and gives a little bow. 'Good evening, Sister!' She turns back to me. 'A young man in a red jacket came home with Miss Henrietta Nelson last night. He ... eventually shot her through the head.' She fingers the crucifix at her stomach. 'A neighbour saw him leave, she saw his jacket but not his face. It appears Miss Nelson had many young friends. The police try to find if any of them wore a red jacket. Naturally.'

She leads me to the waiting-room, where Zeena lies back on a couch with her eyes closed. Sister Hertha coughs, and she looks up.

'Hello darling.'

'You still have no recollection of a young man in a red jacket?' asks the nun.

Zeena shakes her head. 'If he's been in The Place or any of the places, I must have seen him. But what does a person look like when he's crazy?'

Sister Hertha makes a sympathetic little noise with her teeth.

'Zeena, you mustn't stay here,' I tell her.

She gets up obediently. Sister Hertha gives an encouraging smile. 'I advise rest. A great deal of rest. Such situations are ...' She wrinkles her nose, partly because she is searching for a word, partly because she has just noticed a pile of cigarette stubs on the floor near Zeena's feet. 'They are most disturbing,' she says, rattling her crucifix a little.

Zeena decides she wants to go home. We drive in silence, towards a full moon low in the sky. I feel that Sister Hertha has found the right word. There is a case like this quite often in the newspapers: SEX FIEND SLAYS GIRL. Tomorrow it will make a row of headlines on the studio rack.

'Turn the radio on, darling.' A moment later we are listening to Brahms. Zeena twists the knob, then drowses as somebody sings *Your Cheatin' Heart*.

Two months ago I passed a second-hand furniture store on the street along which we are now driving. There was an elegant little coffee table in the window. I went inside, found Zeena and Hank sitting on a broken-down antique couch with the stuffing split out, drinking canned beer.

Probably I was the first customer they'd had for hours. The place was vague and untidy, like somewhere after an earthquake. 'This is really catching on,' Zeena said, trying to interest me in a heavy Victorian commode they'd sponged over with gold and white paint. I bought the coffee table. After that, I saw Zeena and Hank occasionally: in bars or on the beach. Once, coming out of an all-night movie theatre. This is how everybody met them. This is how I am with Zeena today, by accident.

She lives in Venice, near the furniture store. A mouldering unfinished little town along the coast beyond Santa Monica, it began fifty years ago as an imitation of the Italian city. Moonstruck, an industrialist from the Middle West decided to create a romantic resort on the dreary tidal flats. He built some florid villas, a copy of St Mark's Square, a network of bridges, canals, lagoons, colonnades. The aged Sarah Bernhardt was imported to play *La Dame aux Camélias* on what is now a tawdry, neglected amusement pier. Hardly anyone went to see her. Hardly anyone hired a gondola for a trip along the mosquito-ridden flats. Then oil was struck, machinery converged upon the lagoons. A few bridges still remain, spanning dried up canals, with pumps and derricks stretching away beyond them. Drugstores, banks, service stations have settled in the empty spaces between colonnades, and the villas are apartment houses with rooms always vacant.

As we pass St Mark's Square, I notice a group of young motor cyclists dressed in black, with tight belts and slanted caps, leaning against the colonnades. Pigeons cluster nearby, then disperse as the cyclists set off with a roar, speeding along the empty boulevard, past a neon sign announcing BEER, past the Bridge of Sighs and the derricks in silhouette.

The noise rouses Zeena. She blinks, looks out of the window and recognizes landmarks: a closed-up hotel with broken windows, a plot of waste land with an abandoned moonlit sign, BOATS FOR SALE. She murmurs: 'Why, I'm almost home!'

Nukuhiva!

MARK CUSDEN and I went to the same public school in England and without disliking each other never became friends. I used to think he had no friends or enemies, he seemed on principle to avoid any binding relationship. He was a very handsome boy, perfect and idealized as a piece of Greek sculpture, and unlike many schoolboys he looked clean but not freshly scrubbed. He managed to be elegant and athletic at the same time, and I envied him that. With boys like myself who were rather sophisticated but bad at sports, and spent most of their time with books and going to the movies without permission, he was sympathetic yet a little mocking. With the 'others' he was exactly the same. There was something amiable and remote and challenging in his manner which said: 'I can get away with anything.' He usually could. Once I found myself sitting next to him in a cinema showing *Camille* with Greta Garbo when the whole school should have been watching a cricket match. I could never understand how I was found out and Mark wasn't.

He was much sought after, and I felt this influenced his choice of a role in life. Many people wanted him but he refused to want anybody. The world in which others lived was not really important to Mark, and the world in which *he* lived was none of our business. It was rather like what politicians call 'peaceful coexistence'.

The only thing for which I ever heard Mark express a real enthusiasm was painting. He used to buy books of reproductions and study them, on Sundays he often went off into the countryside with a sketch-book. He never showed his work to anyone. The 'others' might have distrusted him for this if he couldn't also amuse them by drawing caricatures and impress them by his skill at rugger.

One day he came up to me with a book of Van Gogh's letters in his hand. There was a sentence in it he liked very much and quoted with a wry elation: *When Tersteeg or my brother says to me, 'What is that, grass or coal?' I answer, 'Glad to hear you cannot see what it is.'*

During his second year at school Mark was discovered in bed with a younger boy. It was about four o'clock in the afternoon and they should both have been at the gym. Although Walsingham College had strong military traditions and was supposed to cling contentedly to established methods, like a sea-anemone to rock, a new headmaster called Loftus Jones had begun to make changes. He was the author of a pamphlet called *Commonsense about Sex* and he used to say the future belonged to Science. The incident goaded Loftus Jones to show how progressive he could be.

He realized at once that the younger boy had a weak character and was easily led. There was no question of expelling him. In a frank and friendly way he told the boy how he'd done exactly the same thing himself at the age of fourteen, and been whipped for it, which might have been dangerous to a less balanced person; then he sent him off with a pat on the shoulder to the school doctor, who explained the sexual act between men and women with the help of magic lantern slides, and taught him a lot of new words.

Loftus Jones was sterner but no less understanding with Mark. He was prepared to make no punishment and keep the episode from Mark's parents on condition he went to a psycho-analyst. Loftus Jones knew a very good one in the town. Mark said he was grateful for this attitude and would like to go to an analyst, but who would pay for it?

'Thought I had the old noodle there,' Mark said to me later, 'but he only smiled and said he'd put it on my bill as doctor's fees and I could tell my parents I had measles or something.' After that, he went off for consultations while we played football. I asked him what the analyst was like, and he said: 'Oh, just an old noodle.' At the end of a month he confessed he'd made up all his dreams and lied about his mother bringing strange men to the house. Loftus Jones abandoned the whole scheme.

The younger boy ran away from school. He was brought back and tried to hang himself. Loftus Jones expelled him.

During his third year at Walsingham College, Mark was discovered in bed with an Irish housemaid. It was ten o'clock on Sunday morning and he should have been in chapel. A simple affectionate girl of less than sixteen who could hardly write her own name, she cried as they led her away from Mark and over to Loftus Jones, who had read the second lesson that morning and received her in the vestry. He went straight to the point in the way that made him so remarkable, and asked if Mark had destroyed her virginity. She denied it, and cried all the more loudly. Loftus Jones decided to check up, he sent her to the public hospital and ordered an examination. The girl had told the truth, but he dismissed her regretfully and after telephoning her father arranged for her to be sent back to Ireland.

Mark was summoned for a talk which lasted over two hours. By now he had become a heroic figure and a small crowd of us gathered furtively outside Loftus Jones's house, waiting for one of them to come out. It was like the crowd outside 10 Downing Street when a Prime Minister is expected to resign. We hoped at least for someone to appear at a window and wave. It got very cold and as dusk fell we were preparing regretfully to go off to supper. Then the door opened, and Mark came out. We looked more furtive than ever, some of us tried to hide. Mark walked off in the opposite direction; I don't know whether he saw us or not.

That evening he was very cheerful and made jokes and did an imitation of Loftus Jones greeting parents on Speech Day, but he wouldn't speak of what had happened. We respected his silence and were very good about passing him more bread and butter and asking if he wanted another cup of tea.

The next morning I was late for chapel, and hurrying out across the yard I noticed Mark there, in shorts and an old sweater, sweeping up autumn leaves. He winked at me and I took this as a sign it was all right to ask questions.

'What happened, Cusden?'

He gave a funny nervous laugh. 'Lofty thinks I'm suffering from surplus energy. He's giving me a series of manual tasks to work it off.'

'Common sense about Sex,' I said.

'I tried to explain some people develop more quickly than others, but he wouldn't listen.' Frowning, Mark took a cigarette from his pocket. 'He's morbidly interested in details, you know, I almost had to draw him a picture. Think the old noodle's impotent?'

I said: 'Yes, but I'm late for chapel.'

His look pitied me. 'It doesn't matter whether you go to chapel or not. It's not the end of the world, and who cares if it is, anyway?'

'I know, but I always get found out.'

'Would you rather go and sing a stupid hymn or share this cigarette with me?'

He held it out. I took it and had a puff. I asked: 'What are you going to do when you've swept up all those leaves?'

'I'm supposed to dig a trench but I think I'll just go off somewhere and get drunk.'

I gave him back the cigarette and glanced nervously at the windows of the house. Mark smiled, took a puff and handed the cigarette back to me. He watched me as I smoked and there was a mysterious intense look in his eyes. They were very blue, like a noonday sky. I had the feeling he wanted something, but I didn't know what it was.

There was a long silence between us. We smoked, passing the cigarette back and forth, standing very close to each other. He blew rings into the cold air. Then I said I had to go.

'Don't let me keep you.' His voice was hard, he shrugged and returned to his sweeping.

I walked away feeling something had been lost. Once I looked round and saw him standing with his back to me, gazing at the drab chalky hills above the town, then at a break in the grey clouds where the sun was trying to come through. What had gone wrong? I was angry with myself at first, then with him. People who avoided getting involved had no right to involve others. Tears crept out of my eyes and I passed the red-brick Victorian chapel thinking it was the ugliest thing I had ever seen.

Two days before Christmas it is impossible to believe in Christmas, with a light summer haze in the air and blue unbroken sky over my head. Down at Santa Monica the beaches are still full, while artificial Christmas trees flank Hollywood Boulevard ten feet high, like white cardboard cut-outs. Icicles resist the sun, snow is paint, baby pines dyed pink, white and blue are ranged on vacant lots and look as if they're made of sugar. Coloured lights weave in and out of the hot dusty palms.

Waiting to buy a bottle of whisky at a liquor store, I listened to a man and his wife arguing with each other whether they wanted bourbon or vodka with a musical box attached. When you lifted it up the bourbon played *Away in a Manger*, the vodka *Oh Come All Ye Faithful*.

'I've been looking for *Good King Wenceslas* everywhere,' said an English voice behind me. 'Do you think it only comes with cream sherry?'

I turned and saw Mark Cusden.

Twelve years had passed but I knew him at once. He was more handsome than ever, lightly suntanned, though his skin had just begun to slacken in little tired pouches under the vivid blue gaze of his eyes. He was dressed in Californian style, blue jeans, white sweat shirt, black belt, suede boots, and his hair was cropped short.

He was carrying a key chain, playing with it, throwing it from one hand to the other. He laughed suddenly – 'a-ha-*ha*!' – in a nervous, rather vacant way which brought back to me a sharp clear image of the past. The air froze, the sky went grey, I saw him bent smiling over a clumsy broom, dead leaves fluttering and myself walking disconsolately away along a cold provincial street.

'I loathe Christmas,' he said. 'Always did.'

At the counter the man and his wife turned to look at us for a moment. She held up the bourbon, the carol tinkled. She frowned and said, 'I think I'll take the vodka,' but her husband put his arm round her shoulder and squeezed it hard. 'It's torture for you to make up your mind, honey, you'd better take both.' He exchanged winks with the assistant, creating a bond of male complicity in the art of handling women.

Mark nudged my elbow. 'What are you doing on Christmas Day?'

'Making rounds, as people do.'

His eyes flickered impatiently. 'I'm staying at home and pretending the whole thing doesn't exist. Would you like to come and see me or are you too much in demand?'

I said I could probably manage to fit him in, thinking he made me feel all over again that I had to choose between sharing a cigarette and going to chapel.

'Then come at four o'clock. If I'm not too drunk I'd like to tell you the story of my stupid unpromising life.'

He threw the key chain up in the air and caught it as he turned away. I noticed he drove off in a new Jaguar, scarlet and white.

East Hollywood is unfashionable. Sycamore trees seem planted along the streets especially to allow the shabby little houses to retire into their shade. Colours are more muted here and a faded canary yellow front door is almost shocking. It affronts the sober and careful daylight, sudden brightness or noise is like laughter in church. Even movement surprises, like two children playing with a hose on a front lawn.

I parked in front of 7128 Arcadia Drive, a house with muslin curtains screening the windows and an old swing chair on the porch. 7128½, where Mark lived, was the back part of the house reached through an adjoining patio. A blade of sunlight pointed at the Jaguar, disconcertingly sleek and new outside the broken patio gate.

From a window in the house a girl was watching me, wearing a striped dressing-gown. Wagner came rich and faint from a radio. She turned away when I looked up. At the end of the patio a door stood open, and I found Mark sitting on a low couch in a dark low-ceilinged room like a log cabin, walls of stained wood and a kind of ladder leading to the upper floor.

He stretched and yawned. 'Merry Christmas,' he said. He was wearing the same clothes; I don't think I ever saw him in any others, though they always looked clean; his eyes were still a little heavy from sleep. He walked over to a table on which stood several bottles, most of them empty, poured vodka and orange juice into a Japanese bamboo tumbler and handed it to me.

'Why do you hate Christmas so much?' I said.

'I've a very large and stupid middle-class family and they always have a very large and stupid middle-class Christmas.' He was pouring out a drink for himself. 'Funny hats and masses of food, but I always felt it was me they were eating.'

'Are your parents still alive?'

He nodded. 'All the members of my family live for ever.'

'What's your father?'

'Do you really want to know?' He made a little grimace. 'He's a lawyer. Plodding rather than bright, but you can get away with that in a country town. And my sister married an assistant bank manager, and my brother, who's my father's junior partner, just got engaged to a bishop's daughter. Everyone says that's rather a catch.'

The telephone rang. 'I know who that'll be.' The conversation was very guarded. 'Yes ... No ... A friend's with me now ... ' He glanced at me. 'No, I'll call you later.'

He lay back on the couch and gave his nervous laugh. 'It's a funny thing, I always rather liked you at school.'

'You never gave the impression you liked anyone very much.'

'I don't usually. I don't know why it is. I never get terribly interested in other people.' He seemed to be thinking it over. 'Too interested in myself, I suppose. Though I was sort of interested in painting once.'

'Not any more?'

'I don't know.' He frowned, looked thoughtful again. 'If you're not *really* good, nothing's worth it. I came here on a scholarship, you know – to the Colony.'

The Colony was created for artists and writers by a millionaire named Chandler Moyes. He owns an important petroleum company with subsidiaries and believes that most modern art and literature is decadent. He disapproves especially of abstract art and has written a pamphlet against it. He built the Colony to encourage young writers and painters to work along non-decadent lines on a very pleasant estate near the coast. They are well looked after, and allowed to stay a year. If their work is satisfactory they are granted a second year. A committee of distinguished older writers and artists judges the candidates, but is often resigning because Moyes finds some of their choices decadent and refuses to admit them.

'I painted some pictures especially to get admitted,' Mark said. 'I was very careful and dreary, and the old noodles let me in. Once I got inside I started doing a kind of wild expressionism. It leaked out and they asked me to leave. I destroyed all the pictures. That was about three months ago, now I can't think of anything to do and I'm completely broke.'

I remembered the Jaguar and said so. He made a gesture of irritation. 'That doesn't belong to me, a friend of mine just lets me use it.'

He got up suddenly. 'I want to show you something.' I thought perhaps he meant a picture he had saved, but he moved to the window, lifted the muslin curtain and stood looking out.

The girl in the striped dressing-gown was staring very intently at us from her window. She leaned her arms on the sill, I could see her better now; she had long blonde hair and her lips were tight with suppressed anger. Expressionless, Mark stared back. He let the curtain fall again, very slowly. She slammed her window shut, cutting off Wagner, and disappeared.

Going back to the couch, Mark stretched his legs. 'Her name is Elise.'

'That explains everything, I suppose?'

He told me she lived on the first floor of 7128, and had asked him if she could help when he moved in to 7128½. She said she wanted to be an actress and was making a little money as a photographer's model. Her family was in New York. One evening they went out to dinner together, then drove up into the hills and parked the car at a lonely spot overlooking the city's vast sloping map of lights. They lay on the ground in the warm night with the crickets singing, and afterwards Elise said she was in love with him. She moved into 7128½, but after a few weeks they quarrelled. 'I was disgusted with her. She revealed herself as a dependent sort of person and wanted me to accept responsibilities. You know how involving those people are?'

Elise moved back to the first floor of 7128. 'But she's still obsessed with me in this strange way. She watches to see who comes and goes.'

'I think one of you should move.'

'I don't see why I should, nor does she.'

'You mean you've discussed the matter?'

He nodded. 'She says she hates me.'

'What do you feel about her?'

He shrugged and went to pour out more drinks. 'She's quite a beautiful girl, isn't she, but ... You know, it reminds me of something. Do you believe in God?'

'No. Is there a connexion?'

'A very personal one.' With a wry little smile he handed me the bamboo tumbler. 'When I was a little kid I used to suck my thumb. My mother tried everything to stop it and smeared it with bitter aloes last thing at night. I washed it off and went on sucking my thumb in the dark. One night she found me sucking it and said, "Even if I hadn't caught you at it, God knows." I asked her how God could know. "Because God can see through that window," she told me, "even though the curtains are drawn across, God can see through that window and see you sucking your thumb in the dark." "What a bore for the old Noodle," I said, and she called for my father. Later I lay awake thinking about God. Ever since that moment I've hated Him.'

He looked very directly at me. 'So when I'm in a situation of that kind, you see, I like to sit it out.'

I didn't see Mark again for nearly six months. He asked me to telephone him and I did so, but there was a new tenant in the apartment and he said Mark had left no forwarding address.

The New Year brought rain. It rained for about two weeks, intense and monotonous, and then it became cold. I had saved a little money and actually started on my novel. It went slowly. One day, a story in the newspapers about another landslide on the coast made me drive down to the beach. The ocean was a dead chilly grey, the sand looked like mud. Part of the highway was blocked off, where a sheer jagged bluff had crumbled. A new sign said, WATCH FOR ROCKS.

I went into a restaurant called Good Sam and ordered hot rum. Good Sam fronted the ocean and had a terrace where one could sit in summer and eat excellent seafood. Empty crates lay about it now and a screech of gulls passed overhead. Inside, the atmosphere was partly nautical: a ship's wheel and an anchor chain on the wall, some stuffed barracuda in glass cases, a porthole window. Opposite the ocean was a wall entirely of glass, tinted blue. In summer it used to make the Pacific look bluer than it really was, and the beach glowed with a faint spectral green.

Now this window blackened the world. The coastline here is untidy anyhow, with long stretches of nothing, scrubland waiting for houses to be built, a motel solitary in the desert of its own parking lot, a hamburger stall, a wooden cabin

shaped like a loaf of bread with a neon sign, THE WHIRL-
POOL – COCKTAILS. With the colours shrivelled out, as
in a strip of old film, it looked more than ever like the end
of the world. I sipped rum and watched an old man walking
slowly by himself along the beach. It was the window, I
suppose, that made me think of Elise watching Mark in
7128½ Arcadia Drive. I drove back past The Place, which he
said he used to go to, but he wasn't there. It was strangely
empty, a tall man in dark glasses drank beer and leaned over
the juke-box, watching the record spin.

A few days after this it snowed. People looked stunned or
indignant. The fall only stayed on the ground for an hour
and disappeared, but the thin white flakes dripping untidily
from the sky were almost as strange as flying saucers.

Then of course summer began and the beaches filled. One
day in early June I went down to celebrate by lying in the
sun, and saw Mark coming out of the sea.

'I've been moving around a bit,' he said. His tone was
vague. 'Matter of fact, I had a stroke of luck during that
awful winter. I met that old Countess – you know, the last
of the Osterberg-Steblechis – and she'd just lost her chauffeur. She took me on. The only thing was, I discovered why
the chauffeur left. You have a terrible time getting any
money out of her.'

While he talked, he kept looking at one of the parking lots
above the beach. I noticed a scarlet and white Jaguar draw
up. A stout man in a flowered shirt got out.

'What are you doing now?' I asked.

'Nothing special.' His blue eyes glittered. 'But you can't
sit inside an old Rolls when the sun's out.'

At the time this didn't strike me as a particularly odd or
significant remark. In fact I was aware of an anti-climax in
our meeting. It may have been wounded pride because I had
looked in at The Place a few times over the last six months,

thinking Mark might be there, but I felt angry with him now for being so casual.

The stout man crossed the beach with a slightly mincing walk.

Mark clapped me on the shoulder. 'I'll see you again soon, I suppose.' But he didn't offer to give me his new address or telephone number, and I didn't ask him for it. 'Good-bye, now,' he said, very cheerful, and walked away.

It was easy to see Mark again because he was always on the beach.

He was always in the same place, always alone. Each time I saw him lying on a white towel in the sun, jeans and sweat shirt neatly folded by his side, his tan was deeper. Often he seemed to be asleep. Sometimes he propped himself up on one elbow and lazily watched people strolling along the shore. He knew many of them and waved, but never made the first move to start a conversation. A few came over and talked for a few minutes, the others simply waved back and strolled on. Towards one o'clock Mark took a swim, sunned himself dry, smoked a cigarette, then went over to the hot-dog stand or crossed the highway in his bathing trunks and entered one of the cafés. Ten minutes later he would be back again, motionless under the sun.

Once I noticed him stand up, stretch, yawn, examine his body, and lie down again very carefully in a different position.

I didn't always speak to him. I only stayed on the beach for a couple of hours and often he didn't move during that time. Yet I had the feeling he always knew when I was there. One day he sat up quite suddenly and called me as I walked past. He looked critically at my body and said: 'You'd get a better tan if you came down here more often.'

'I know. But I haven't the time.'

He lay back and closed his eyes. 'I don't understand how you can just come and go here as you please.'

'What on earth do you mean?'

'I mean, the sun's the only thing that matters.'

When I didn't answer he sat up again and looked gravely at me. 'Doesn't the sun *mean* anything to you?' He stood up, took my arm, and we began to walk together along the edge of the ocean. 'I've suddenly realized,' Mark said, 'I'm nearly thirty and I've spent all but a few months of my life in England. It was all a waste.' He picked up a flat pebble and shied it into the ocean, playing ducks and drakes. 'Everyone there's so pale. Almost grey. They go off to the south of France or somewhere for three weeks and look wonderfully tanned when they come back, but it doesn't last. A month later they're pale and grey again and it's another long winter.'

He made another pebble skip. 'The idea of a pale body disgusts me now, I couldn't touch one.'

'Well, there are plenty of brown ones here.'

'I'll tell you another thing,' he said. 'If your life is meaningless and you feel vaguely ashamed but you don't see a way out, you should lie in the sun. It makes you forget things. If you've had an operation and it's left a bad scar, the doctor usually advises you to lie in the sun. It helps the scar to heal. All through the winter when I was working I was terribly restless, and kept thinking about Elise. Now I'm doing nothing at all and I'm broke and I can't see any future, but it doesn't matter. I lie in the sun and don't think about Elise, about anything.'

'Did you speak to her again?'

'Only to say good-bye when I moved out.' He smiled. 'She's gone back to New York.' He shied another stone, then breathed deeply and bent down to touch his toes. 'Listen, I hate to ask you but could you lend me five dollars?'

I said yes.

'You'll probably never get it back. That's understood, isn't it?'

As he spoke, Mark looked up at the sun. His eyes could meet it without blinking.

A week later he was there, lying on the sand as if he had never moved. His body was very brown, the hairs on it had turned gold, his skin seemed to glow. The whites of his eyes shone like ivory.

He wanted me to come and see where he lived. As we walked, he liked to walk everywhere now in his bathing trunks, shoeless, he said: 'Things have been difficult and I haven't really been living anywhere lately.' We crossed the highway and turned into a street leading uphill. 'All that's changed now, for the first time I'm living the way I want to.'

The houses were clean and white with broad windows, terraces and verandas. Oleander and bamboo grasses sprouted in the gardens. We turned into a drive where the scarlet and white Jaguar was parked. Mark lifted up a doormat on the porch and took a key from under it. We went inside and stood in a bare unfurnished hall. The windows were uncurtained and a pool of sunlight glittered on the parquet floor.

Mark looked very proud. 'There's no furniture except a bed and a chair in the master bedroom. But there's an ice box in the kitchen and a washing machine in the garage.'

'Who owns this house?'

'A friend of mine. He's trying to sell it and letting me use it until he does.' I followed Mark into the living-room, which was large and high and painted white. A giant cactus stood in a tub. He looked at it and said: 'I have to water this.'

We went upstairs and he showed me the master bedroom. It had a double bed with a blue quilt and a white basket chair. French windows led to a veranda.

'Come out here.'

I stood beside him on the veranda. He pointed down at the pale ocean beach. People were bright anonymous points of colour there. The air was vaporous but not soft. Cars poured along the highway as if it were an assembly line.

'I'd like to buy this house,' Mark said. 'Let off some of the rooms, maybe. Zeena and Hank said they'd come in with me, and I expect you would too.'

'It sounds like a beautiful dream.'

He frowned. 'It could happen.'

'How?'

'I dare say this man who owns the house would take a very small sum as down payment, and let me pay in easy instalments.'

'What's a very small sum?'

'Well ... At the moment I think I could raise about sixty cents.' He laughed. 'The world's so damned unfair, isn't it?' Breathing deeply, he stretched out his arms. 'I made a calculation on the beach this morning. There's a hundred and sixty-eight days to November. Say even ten per cent are bad – but there shouldn't be any rain – that means a hundred and fifty-one days of sun.'

'And then?'

'I don't know. If I could raise the fare I'd go to Australia and catch another summer there.'

We were both silent. Then he asked me for a cigarette. Giving him one, I said: 'You've made up your mind to go on living this way? For life, I mean.'

He blew out the match. 'It's the only way. There isn't any other.'

'How do you manage for money?'

'Have to cadge a bit, I'm afraid. But I like the beach people, they're generous.'

Since he went to the beach every day, Mark had met about a hundred people. 'Some of them I just say Hello to and they say Hello back. But they all know about me. I think we recognize each other instinctively, not just because we're so tanned, but there's something *relaxed* about people like us. And when somebody looks at somebody and thinks he's seen him before, he *has* – either on the beach or at The Place – and that's all either of them needs to know.'

He lowered his voice. 'We believe in helping each other. Why, there are people who will give me a dollar or two without my even having to ask.'

I couldn't understand why Mark took money from people he met at The Place or on the beach when he had a friend who 'let him use' a car and a house. I presumed it was the same friend who loaned him both, the stout man I had seen in the flowered shirt. I decided to ask him about this, when he smiled and began to walk back into the bedroom.

'I know what you're thinking.' In the bathroom doorway he paused to examine his body in the wall mirror. 'You think people should work or do something or have money coming in. In a moment you'll say your pride wouldn't let you do what I do.'

'It wasn't that.'

'What was it?' he asked in a disinterested tone, still looking at his body.

'This friend of yours,' I said. 'He lends you a house and a car, but no money. Why?'

'Oh, I could get anything I want out of this man.' Mark still sounded remote. 'He's crazy about me. But I find that to have a lot of sex with somebody, they have to be really attractive. So I'd have to give more to get more, you see. It doesn't matter. Nothing's any good unless you're free.'

'Free for what?'

He looked surprised. 'To lie on the beach, for one thing.'

'There must be more to it than that,' I said. 'You never read a book or anything down there, you hardly even talk to people.'

He shook his head. 'It's not worth it. Gets in the way.'

'Of what?'

'Of . . .' He gave a long contented sigh and stretched out on the bed. 'Just being there, of course.'

'Then what do you think about all day?'

'Well, I told you about that calculation I made this morning. And the idea of going to Australia. And – don't sit on the edge of the chair like that,' he ordered rather sharply, 'you cast a shadow. Did you know you walked past me at a very crucial moment today?'

'You gave no sign of it.'

'It was a secret. But I was going to shoot you with my thumb.'

I stared at him.

'I'd been shooting everybody on the beach with my thumb.' Mark snapped it against his forefinger. 'You were about the last living person, you know. I wanted to see how it would feel to be the only one there this morning.' Then he dismissed the subject with another snap. 'I was feeling a bit lonely and depressed and it seemed to do the trick.'

It was late August and still getting hotter. I couldn't remember a day without sun and began to lose all sense of time. On every lawn the sprinklers played. It became almost impossible to park a car anywhere near the beach, except for one afternoon when an ocean breeze sprang up about three o'clock and brought a thick grey mist. It blotted out the sun, the light went dead, and cars made a traffic jam for eight miles into Hollywood and Beverly Hills. I had never seen a place empty so quickly and completely, life vanished as from a town in wartime that enemy soldiers have passed through.

Then time became real again when two weeks passed without Mark being on the beach. No one knew where he had gone. There was a different car outside the house on the hill.

One night in The Place I saw Zeena and Hank, sitting at a booth with a little portable radio on the table. 'A man I know slightly gave it to me,' Hank said. It had a Geiger counter attached. They planned to drive out to Arizona and search for uranium.

I asked if they'd seen Mark.

Zeena shrugged. 'He's all right, darling.'

'How do you know?'

'He'll come back,' Hank said.

They seemed not to care at all. Hank ordered another round of drinks. I said: 'I thought you were fond of Mark.' Zeena nodded emphatically. 'Oh, he's a nice boy.' 'One of my favourite people,' Hank said.

'You don't think anything might have happened?'

'Oh yes it might,' Hank agreed.

'Nobody's seen him at all, have they?' Zeena said vaguely. Hank shook her head. They pondered. 'I expect he went to New York,' Zeena said finally. Hank objected: 'He doesn't know anyone there.'

Mackie Messer started from the juke-box and the old man in the panama hat got up and danced with his cane.

'He loves that tune,' Hank said.

'Who is he?' Zeena asked.

An hour later we were all rather drunk. I looked accusingly at Zeena. 'Someone should do something about Mark!'

'I would but I feel so helpless,' Zeena said.

'It's amazing how nobody cares. He's sliding into an abyss before your eyes and you don't care!'

Hank patted my shoulder. 'I wouldn't go as far as that, darling.'

At two o'clock in the morning, when The Place closed, we decided to go up to the house on the hill. We were very tight and took a long time to find it. Then I saw the scarlet and white Jaguar parked in the driveway.

'He's back!' Zeena said.

I beat on the door. Nothing happened. Zeena and Hank suddenly joined hands and sang together, mimicking children's voices.

> Take a local
> Take an express.
> Don't get off
> Till you reach success.

Then they played hopscotch with imaginary squares on the porch. A window on the first floor of the house next door opened, and a woman shouted at us.

Zeena and Hank began to dance more wildly. Hank pretended to skip with a rope. They lisped up at the woman, hideous and shrill.

> Betty Boop
> Fell in the soup.
> When she came out
> She said, Boop-e-de-doop.

I beat on the door again. There was a long wait, then I heard footsteps approaching.

The stout man opened the door. He was wearing a red silk dressing-gown. Zeena and Hank danced up to him.

'Where's Mark?' I said.

He had a thin mouth, pursed with disapproval. 'You're drunk!' He started to close the door.

I put my foot in the doorway.

'Mark Cusden,' I said loudly. 'He was staying in this house.'

Zeena had been humming. She stopped, and stood in a menacing attitude. Her face swayed close to the stout man's. 'Have you murdered him?'

Hank shouted: 'You can see it in his eyes!'

The stout man was trembling with anger. 'Go away from here or I'll call the police.'

We looked at each other.

'Are you sure Mark Cusden isn't here?' I asked.

'Search the house darling,' Zeena cried.

'I'm warning you,' said the stout man. 'Take those drunken women away.'

They joined hands and danced in a circle round him, faster and faster. They sang:

> God made a river
> God made a lake
> But when God made you dear
> He made a big mistake.

'Come on,' I said, grabbing their arms and starting to push them down the drive. The stout man watched us for a moment, scratching his hip, then closed the door. Hank aimed a kick at the Jaguar. 'Why didn't you let him keep it?' she yelled.

'I hope Mark's all right darling, don't you?' Zeena said.

Next day I was waiting for a traffic signal to change on Sunset Boulevard. A car drew up alongside mine. Elise was at the wheel, tight-lipped. Beside her, resting his head on the back of the seat and staring up at the sky, sat Mark. The traffic signal changed and they moved on without having seen me.

'It's definitely over between us,' Mark said. Grains of sand sparkled on his dark shoulders; he brushed them away. 'I'll never let anything like that happen to me again.'

Elise returned to California two weeks ago and found him on the beach. 'We had a talk and I brought her back to the house. Next morning we were lying in bed and the owner came round and,' Mark hesitated, 'he said he'd sold the place and I'd have to get out at once. Of course he was furious about Elise. We went to a motel and she started unpacking at once. It made me angry. Well, it was such a domestic thing to do. I said I was going down to the beach. She got angry then and cried and insisted I look for a job.'

Farther along the beach, someone was playing bongo drums. People drifted towards him. Mark listened for a moment, digging his toes into the sand. 'I landed up as a barman,' he said. From the first moment, wearing a uniform and a collar and tie round his neck, it was like being in prison. Instead of the sun, there was dim concealed lighting and artificial coolness. He thought most of the customers looked pale and was frightened he would soon be the same.

At the motel one morning he took a shower, and as he stepped out of it, examined his body in the mirror. The tan was definitely not as deep.

'Elise was still in bed. I wanted to strangle her. I threw my barman's trousers at her instead.'

'Poor Elise,' I said. 'Did she ever know what hit her?'

'She yelled a bit but I just wouldn't speak to her. I put on my ordinary clothes and wrapped my shaving things in my beach towel and came down here.'

I asked where he was living now.

'They've given me a little room at the back of The Place. But not for long, because it's in the old part of the building and it's due to be pulled down.'

Towards the end of September there was a night when The Place was unusually crowded. Zeena was having a birthday party there, and had invited most of what Mark called 'the beach people'. They all looked happy, casual and mysterious. What did they do? The girls worked occasionally at modelling and walk-on parts in television shows, sometimes they disappeared for a month or two and one heard they were being waitresses at a restaurant in Hollywood or downtown. The boys were mostly small part actors and dancers, sometimes they worked in bars and filling stations or as lifeguards on the beach. There were a few struggling young writers and painters, and some more eccentric figures: a Turkish fortune-teller called Madame Shahrazad who had a booth on the pier and wore a satin cape embroidered with the symbols of the Tarot pack, an elderly midget who had once been the stand-in for a famous child actor, a tall handsome woman with bright red hair who practised black magic. Zeena said she could kill a dog simply by looking at it.

Voices battled with other voices, landslides of laughter and the juke-box that never stopped. People carried glasses above their heads as they made their way through the dancers. In one corner the midget stood on tiptoe, telephoning.

The bar was lit by three huge Japanese lanterns suspended from the ceiling. Cigarette smoke twined round them. They shivered from the noise and movement, the whole bar seemed to be vibrating. It was impossible to do anything except drink or dance. I was carried off almost at once by Madame Shahrazad, who waltzed me dizzily round while I stared fascinated by The Man With The Scythe on her cape. We passed Mark, dancing with Hank. He wore his usual jeans and sweat shirt, and his skin was much darker than anyone else's; under the misty oriental light it looked almost black. When the dance was over, Hank kissed him and wedged a dollar bill in his belt. He took off his shoes and danced barefoot with Zeena. As he passed me, he said: 'It feels wonderful, sawdust on the floor.'

At two o'clock the barman was frantically, uselessly

shouting 'I have to close!' He cried: 'Do you want me to lose my licence?' Someone started another record on the juke-box. Then Zeena and Hank took charge, and miraculously made people leave. I never understood how they did it, they only whispered and pushed gently and in five minutes The Place was almost empty.

The barman switched off the juke-box and silence came into the room like an unknown night visitor. It was the door opening of its own accord, the mysterious figure on the threshold. The lanterns were steady now and shone down on a floor covered with black sawdust and cigarette stubs, a few of them still smoking.

I said good night to Zeena and Hank, and went out to my car which was parked a few yards up the street. The air was cool and salty, a light wind blew from the ocean. In darkness the pier looked like a gigantic reptile asleep in the Pacific.

A voice called, 'Good night!'

It was Mark sitting on the kerb, his knees drawn up, resting his chin on his hands. He still had no shoes.

'Where are you going to sleep?' I asked. He gave a shrug.

'You mean you've got nowhere?'

'They've started pulling down my room, but Zeena says she can fix me up with something in a couple of days.'

'It's cold,' I said.

He stood up. 'I could sleep in your car, I suppose.'

'In my apartment, if you like. There's a spare room.'

He seemed to think this over. 'A guest like me is always a bit of a risk.' He laughed. 'So difficult to get rid of.'

'You're welcome to it.'

He shook his head. 'Walk with me to the beach.'

We crossed the highway and stood looking at the ocean. There was no moon. The Pacific was a soft, dark, murmuring expanse with occasional lights from cars along the highway catching the waves, blinking like stars and vanishing again. The wind was cold.

'Last night I slept under the pier.' There was something clumsy, schoolboyish in Mark's confession. He shifted his feet. 'Zeena says don't do it again, might be dangerous. She says there are pretty strange types sleeping under the pier, but I didn't see any. It smells bad, though.'

I was silent, and it made him angry. 'There's nothing worse than the judgement of silence !'

'It's not judgement,' I said. 'It's just a question mark, as it's always been with you.'

'Always?'

'Ever since I knew you at school.'

'Remember Lofty?' He jutted out his chin and squinted at me, accusing and headmasterly. 'It is no Good denying the fact that Sex is an Urge. I must put a very frank question to you, my dear Cusden. How many times a week do you – um – practise self-abuse? Sir, between sixty and seventy, sir, but less in summer. Cusden, I must confess your attitude interests and bewilders me. What is the point of it, Cusden? Eh? It does no good to *you* – no good to *me* – no good to the School ...'

A moment later he was quietly nostalgic. 'Wish I could have bought that house. Might have made all the difference.'

'That's ridiculous,' I told him. 'You know I don't judge you, and you wouldn't care if I did, but have you ever thought how far away from the real world you're going?'

'You think I'm a case?'

'We're all cases. You're more serious than some.'

'All I've ever wanted is independence.' His tone was obstinate. 'It was so easy at first. I mean, at school and at home they were all such noodles. And I could fool the lot. Then ...' He frowned, and stopped.

'Then?' I echoed.

He shifted his feet again. 'I don't know. When I wasn't at school any more – well, it seemed to me the world was still full of noodles, but they were bigger, and somehow I hadn't grown. It was a very peculiar feeling. There was nothing I could do.'

'Mark, who *are* the noodles?'

'Oh, you know who they are,' he said with a grin. 'Lofty. My family, and all the lawyers and bank managers and bishops and psycho-analysts. And the millionaire who runs the Colony, and the man who lent me that house. Of course, I've kept my independence in spite of them all. And yet . . . There's something missing now.' He glanced up at the sky. 'I feel a bit lost, except when I'm out in the sun. Then I'm warm through and through and it's like being on an island. I can glow and dream, and nothing touches me.'

'But when you're safe and warm on this island,' I said, 'is it enough just to stay there and do nothing?'

'If I *did* anything, I'd lose it all.'

His eyes clouded over, he was fidgeting now, I could see he was getting bored: regretting the moment of confidence, probably. He looked at me with an unwilling shock of recognition, like Crusoe meeting the first stranger on his island. 'I won't sleep in your car. I feel terribly awake.'

'Where are you going?'

'Give me a cigarette.' I did so. 'Zeena and Hank let me have a key to their furniture store. There's an old bed for sale in the back, and it's quite comfortable.'

'At least let me drive you there.'

'Thanks. That would be a help.'

I left him in Venice, at the corner of St Mark's Square. Everything was cool and dark and still. You could hear the sound of the ocean faintly.

At first I thought it must be the telephone and groped for

the receiver, but when I lifted it the bell went on ringing. As I went to the front door, I looked at my watch. Three a.m.

Mark came in immediately I opened the door. I hadn't seen him for two weeks. His eyes looked restless and frightened, and he started pacing up and down the room. 'I'm in a bit of a spot.'

'What is it?'

'I'm a Public Charge!'

I gave him a baffled sleepy look.

'In the eyes of the Government.' He was trembling. 'They're going to deport me.'

I jerked myself fully awake, lit a cigarette and handed the pack to Mark.

'I owe a chap fifty dollars and he's taking it to court and the whole thing's coming out. They're going to deport me.' He disappeared into the kitchen to mix himself a drink.

'If I let you have the fifty dollars, won't that make it all right?'

'It isn't any use, I gave him a dud cheque and he won't tear it up even if I raise the money.' Mark hesitated. 'You can guess who it is. He's very bitter, he's made up his mind to get me into trouble.'

The ice tray slithered out of his hands and hit the floor. Mark just looked on stupidly while I picked it up and made him a drink. As he took the glass he said thoughtfully: 'There's one thing you can do.'

'What?'

'Give me your car.'

I stared at him. 'It's too old, Mark, you won't get very far in it.'

'You always said the engine was a wonder.'

'Well yes, it is really. Where do you plan to go?'

'Mexico. It's easy to get across.'

'Do you have any money?'

'Zeena and Hank organized a collection. About two hundred dollars. I can live on that for months down there. Hank knows someone in Soconusco.'

'It's no good trying to persuade you to do anything else, is it?'

'You'd be a noodle if you did, and I'd despise you for ever!'

Defiance made him breathless. It was like a child saying he couldn't live another day without a bicycle. He finished his drink, looking at me above the rim of the glass. He waited for my answer with a dreadful impatient hope: was I going to be part of a blind adult world that couldn't understand?

'When you think what this means to me,' he said, 'I'm not asking for much. It's not much, but it's everything.'

This is the last image of Mark, eyes anxious and brilliant in a sunburnt face. He seems no older than on the day we shared that cigarette in the yard. Time is a layer of sun; I can strip it off and find a pale proud schoolboy looking for brightness in a dull English sky.

He flung his arms round me when I gave him the keys.

It is almost Christmas again, but this year the rain has come earlier. The days are cool and grey. I am working on another script, for which my novel has been put aside, and leading a dissatisfied uneventful life. Yesterday two police officers came to visit me. They wanted to know if I owned a 1947 Chevrolet with a battered front. Then could I explain how it had been abandoned nearly two thousand miles away in the small Mexican village of Soconusco?

This kind of efficiency is amazing. There were no papers in my old car. I couldn't help feeling it ought to have been more difficult to trace the owner, and tried to disguise my alarm as admiration.

The car must have been stolen, I said. The officers' attitude changed to weary dislike. How could I doubt such a thing; wasn't there a day when I came to get my car and found it missing? I said yes, but I didn't care much about the car anyway. It was very old and would fetch twenty dollars at most, so I had decided not to report the theft.

They left after refusing a drink. As I opened the door for them, I saw the Chevrolet standing outside. I think I started as if I'd seen a ghost.

What really astonished me is that it survived the journey.

Hank has had a letter from her friend in Soconusco, who liked Mark very much. He stayed nearly three months in the village, lived mainly on the beach and ate raw fish. Then he left for Guatemala, where Hank's friend said he would find friends.

The day before Christmas a card arrives from San Salvador. It is just signed 'Mark'. Zeena and Hank receive one too. We are not sure exactly where this place is, and consult Zeena's atlas, which is a genuine antique she bought in a junk shop years ago. It was printed in Edinburgh in 1897 and dedicated to Queen Victoria with her gracious permission.

'I see.' Zeena runs her finger along the Caribbean. 'I wonder if he's making for Peru; I've got a friend in Caracas.'

'But that's in Venezuela.'

'Is it darling?'

When summer comes, there is nobody at all near Mark's old place on the beach. A little desert of emptiness and silence that people seem instinctively to avoid.

And now Zeena has had a postcard from Nukuhiva. We consult the atlas again. Nukuhiva is a very small island in the middle of the Pacific, a few hundred miles north-east of

Tahiti. The atlas says it is French, but that was in 1897. 'These things change don't they?' Zeena says.

Mark writes: *This is a perfect little island though I'm not sure I want to stay. The trouble is, it's impossible for me to leave.* We wonder what this means. He doesn't explain how he got there, but says he has been greatly helped by a man who sends his love to Hank. *He tells me you met in The Place about four years ago.*

Of course Mark hasn't heard about Hank's death. Zeena goes mistily through a long list of encounters at The Place but cannot decide who the man from Nukuhiva is.

'I suppose he'll turn up one day,' she says finally. 'Or we'll turn up *there*. The important thing is, Mark's got what he wanted. And why should he ever want to leave a place like Nukuhiva?'

'We don't know what it's like.'

We consult the picture on the card: ocean, beach, coconut palms and some flat white houses.

Zeena laughs. 'Anyway we put him there, all of us. We're an Escaping Club!'

We go to The Place and celebrate with a round of drinks. The old man in the panama hat drowses on a chair, cane across his knees.

'It's a very long way away,' I say.

Zeena doesn't answer. She has fallen into a trance of happiness, and puts an arm round my shoulder. 'NUKUHIVA!' She yells the name like a battle cry. 'Isn't it marvellous to think you have friends all over the world?'

The End of the Line

COUNTESS MARGUERITE OSTERBERG - STEBLECHI
lives in a big grey patrician house in the Hollywood hills.
Steep and narrow roads twist through these hills, where
living was fashionable in the twenties. Valentino and Nazi-
mova built homes here. Stateliness hangs in the air. Most of
the houses are large, but you have the impression half their
rooms are closed now, furniture draped with old sheets and
blinds pulled down.

A flight of stone steps leads up to the heavy oak door of
the Countess's house, and two old yucca trees put out thin
white blossoms each year. The fine spacious living-room with
fake panelling has an open fireplace at one end, two 'French
Provincial' arches at the other, and its windows open out to
a high-walled patio. It seems odd there is no door from the
living-room to the patio, but this is because the patio was
added later. It was the first of a series of miscalculations.
The man who added the patio liked to sunbathe in the nude
and ordered a high wall so he shouldn't be overlooked, but
the wall is so high the patio gets only an hour or two of sun
each day in summer, and none in winter. The sun never gets
through to the living-room at all.

A door in the patio wall leads to a neglected garden, the
ground slopes down to a swimming pool shaped like a half
moon. There are usually a few hundred eucalyptus leaves
floating on the water, and a faint sour-sweet perfume haunts
the air. A chipped stone cupid with a broken arrow presides
over the deep end.

Portraits painted by the Countess thirty and forty
years ago hang everywhere in the house. Jean Cocteau,

Mistinguette, Somerset Maugham and Queen Marie of Rumania are side by side as you go upstairs. The Countess herself looks down at different ages from different walls. In the 1900s she is delicate and unreal, everything white except her long coppery hair: a soft slender figure in a white dress, white parasol in one hand and white hat in the other, behind her a mountain peak covered in snow. The last portrait is in 1933, when she is rather sternly middle-aged, still handsome but putting on weight against a background of the Grand Canal in Venice.

The Countess has been blind and fairly deaf for more than a year. Through a strange error for which she cannot be held responsible, she believes her house is in the Arab quarter of Marrakech. She is convinced she came to Morocco after an extensive European tour more than a year ago, and liked it so much she decided to settle there. And when she sits out in the patio she can hear strange flutes and drums, Arab cries from the seething market-place called Djema el Fnaa. These sounds are weak and blurred as they reach her failing ears, but she finds that distance increases their allure. Sometimes, she says, they seem to be beckoning.

She will tell you she is the only European in the Medina who can bear the terrible hot season from June to September when a fiery wind blows from the desert and the sky turns blood red. It seems no worse than California at the height of summer. Every Thursday night she eats couscous.

Except for her two unmarried nieces, myself and Mark Cusden, who first introduced me to her, everyone in Hollywood who knows the Countess also believes she is in North Africa. They send greetings at Christmas and occasionally remark how they miss her Sunday teas. They wonder how she fared during the recent political disturbances, and some feel she would be safer in Tangier.

For a long time I couldn't see any way out of the situation. I felt I should have done. I used to think that if a story about the Countess appeared in print, something was bound to happen. The nieces would receive a visit from the police, most likely. But that would have made a rather feeble ending and solved very little. I decided to wait and see if life itself couldn't provide something better; after all, it had already provided so much. In a way this was an immoral decision, though now it is all over I can't see that any harm has been done, or that much has been lost. The nieces have certainly gained. They have changed their names and are among the richest women in Florida.

It is a strange thought, too, that if I hadn't decided to do nothing, quite a few people whom none of us has ever met might have died in Budapest during the uprising against the Soviets, or at least still be in prison there.

The Countess arrived in America in December 1939. Before this she spent five years of widowhood in a Venetian palace, last of several great houses bought by her husband.

Count Gabriele was the only son of two noble families. An Osterberg of Budapest married a Steblechi of Rome and they made their home on the vast Osterberg estates near Cracow. Their son Gabriele showed signs of financial genius at school in Lucerne, and by the time he was twenty-five it was clear he would turn the bank founded by his grandfather into a great international corporation.

Spanish and Belgian blood excellent on both sides flowed in Marguerite's veins. Like Gabriele she was sent to school in Switzerland. She fell into his arms while ski-ing at St Moritz in 1901.

Their life together was cosmopolitan from the start. The Countess once showed me her collection of cuttings from *Vogue*, the *Tatler*, *Harpers* and so on, with photographs of

herself and the Count together in their various beautiful
homes all over the world. They were always elegant, smiling, arm-in-arm, and the captions praised their dinner parties, their clothes, their antiques and their patronage of the
arts. After the marriage they went to live on the Osterberg
estates, but Gabriele travelled a great deal, opening new
branches in new capitals. They sat out the first world war in
Geneva. The Austro-Hungarian Empire fell and the estates
became part of a new country called Poland. This involved
years of litigation, never brought to a head. They moved to
Paris. Marguerite loved the arts, she bought some early
Picassos and Matisses, commissioned a ballet from Diaghilev
and gave a masked ball for the young Cocteau. One of the
guests was Gertrude Stein, who later wrote *Portrait of Marguerite Osterberg-Steblechi at the Villa Tricorne.*

The Countess began painting, but her style was much
more conservative than her subjects. The portraits now in
her Hollywood home are surprisingly flat and literal. Soon
after she arrived in Hollywood a small gallery held an exhi-
bition of her work, which was enthusiastically reviewed by
Elsa Maxwell.

In 1926 they moved to London and took a beautiful
Georgian house in Curzon Street. Marguerite gave dinner
parties reported in the society columns, but hated the climate.
Unfortunately she arrived in the year of the General Strike
and near Notting Hill Gate a group of workmen threw potatoes at her Daimler.

They left to visit New York, then bought a castle in Prov-
ence. After three years Count Gabriele remarked that the
Riviera had somehow lost its charm, and in Venice they
found a vacant palazzo which they cleared of damp and neglect, hung with pictures, furnished with antique pieces collected all over Europe, and warmed with acres of carpets.
Only Gabriele didn't live to enjoy it long. He had taken up

flying as a hobby and piloted his own plane. On New Year's Day 1934 it crashed over the Dalmatian coast.

The Count's death was reported in newspapers all over the world. Most of them added in smaller type the fact that a passenger was killed with him, describing her simply as Mrs Thelma Brighouse of Canterbury, England. Recently I wrote to Carlotta, eldest of Marguerite's two nieces, and asked what she could tell me about this. She replied from Florida in her dry, factual and peculiar English:

This is ancient history and Pia and I is not very good at it. 23 years has passed now and memory is not so sharp. Will you have guessed that Mrs Brighouse was last of a very long line? Naturally we cannot remember all names of ladies favoured by the attention of our late Uncle the Count, and send you only an incomplete list representing our best efforts.

The list contained fourteen names, of Spanish, French, Italian, American, English, and Rumanian women. In some cases Carlotta added a date in brackets. She went on:

We can be sure these ladies caused poor Marguerite much pain. She *never* favoured no one else and all rumours to contrary is disgusting. She was devoted to the Count, though Pia agrees *he* would not have minded.

After Gabriele's death the Countess continued to live alone at the palazzo with six servants and a personal maid. She was fifty now and a little stout. Gabriele's death seemed to hasten a physical decay. She grew bloated; her hair greyed and her eyes dulled; she began to wear the hideous flowered prints I knew so well in California. She gave up painting and shuffled round her sixteen beautiful and opulent rooms in a pair of frayed old mules. When Gabriele was alive there were always guests at the palazzo, rich or titled

or brilliant. Now people still came to stay, but they were
mediocre and grasping. Servants sometimes reported the loss
of ornaments or silverware.

Dictators were growing powerful in Europe now, but the
Countess seldom read a newspaper. She preferred to start
writing her memoirs and leafed endlessly through photographs of the old life in half a dozen different countries. If
she heard predictions of war, she shook her head wisely or
gave a faint wheeze of laughter. On 3 September 1939 she
sent Hitler a telegram: PLEASE MAKE EVERY EFFORT
AVOID WAR STOP AM CONVINCED YOU DO NOT WISH
BRING DISASTER ON CIVILIZED WORLD – MARGUERITE
OSTERBERG-STEBLECHI.

By the time it arrived, Warsaw was burning. Two weeks
later the Cracow estates had been overrun.

The bank's funds in Germany, Austria, and Czechoslo-
vakia had already been confiscated by the Nazis, and Marguerite felt poverty dreadfully near. She decided to leave
the palazzo, but couldn't sell it. She dismissed her servants
and managed to dispose of her Picassos and Matisses, most
of her furniture and carpets. As she watched all the beautiful things being taken away on a steamer, she fainted. Afterwards she told her doctor it was a most extraordinary feeling. The ground had seemed to open up under her feet, and
she had a vision of all Europe falling down the crack.

She travelled to America with her jewels and the portraits
she had painted; about a hundred knick-knacks; a bedroom
suite and a few pieces of furniture she particularly liked;
only two trunks of clothes but eleven of letters, newspaper
cuttings and photograph albums.

Water lapped at a shuttered palace until the end of the
war. When they opened it up in 1946, they found it full of
dead cats. Today it is a hotel. Wealthy tourists sit in a dining-room where the famous long table used to be laid with

crested silver and china bearing the two crowned eagles of
the Austro-Hungarian Empire. An oil painting of Count
Gabriele Osterberg-Steblechi, suffocated with varnish, hangs
in a shadowy part of the hall.

Alone in California, Marguerite sat out the second world
war. Her banks fell in country after country, but like the
Cracow estates seemed too far away to worry about. She
took up her memoirs, abandoned them again. Memory was
failing. Was it the Queen of the Belgians or the Grand
Duchess of Luxembourg who had entertained her to tea at
La Panne when the news of Jutland arrived? Or was she
confusing this with a picnic lunch on the shores of Lake
Geneva when reports of the armistice came through and she
danced with the Count of Klausenburg? The old life that
had always seemed so vivid and certain began to elude her.
She went to the movies and read a great many mystery
stories.

Although she had lost a good deal of money, people said
the Countess was still 'worth' between two and three million dollars. But in her own eyes she was threatened with
ruin. Money was the only thing left for her to preserve. In
one of her albums is a photograph taken during a dinner
party given by herself and Gabriele in 1907. The guests included international royalty and society figures. By the time
Marguerite reached California, everyone at that table at
the Ritz in Paris, except herself, was dead. 'If the rest of my
money goes,' she said once, 'I am finished. I am like Warsaw.
Razed to the ground, dear child.' So she scoured remote
second-hand stores to furnish her new home, and would
bring back an old rocking chair, a dressing-table with a
cracked mirror, as if it were a priceless bargain. Apart from
the furniture she had brought with her, and occasionally
hired to film companies for historical reproductions – she
once went without her own bed for a month – there

was nothing in the house that didn't look worn or makeshift.

Remains of her Venetian period were concentrated in the hall and living-room. Here nothing matched but everything was graceful and distinguished. Any vacant space was filled with Dresden figurines, little Indian buddhas, Lowestoft China, lacquered boxes from Japan, all kinds of glass and silver. Down in the cellars were crates and trunks that had never been opened. She couldn't remember what was in them, and grew tired of unpacking.

The Countess didn't lack new acquaintances. Snobs took her up very quickly and pumped her for anecdotes of royalty. At one dinner party in her honour she exposed the host as a false Papal Knight. The Sunday afternoon teas at which there was nothing to eat and the tea was made in bags were an attempt, I suppose, to create a *salon*. Decorators came to bargain for her antiques – she was always willing to sell anything – and she could hold expatriates spellbound with a fairly rambling account of the first performance of *The Rite of Spring*.

A popular rumour at one time was that she had secretly married her houseboy to get American nationality. Another was that she had bought a burlesque house in downtown Los Angeles. I know she always drove eight miles to buy food at a market in the San Fernando Valley because prices were a few cents lower there. And Mark Cusden assured me, the first time he brought me to see her, that she was wearing a linen dress he had helped her choose from a rack marked 'Factory Rejects' at the Hollywood Bargain Centre.

I didn't want to kiss her hand. It was a limp speckled claw ringed with emerald, topaz, and garnet. I touched a knuckle with my lips, and it seemed to satisfy her. 'You look like a dear child to me,' she said.

'As it's not Sunday,' Mark suggested, 'why don't you

bring out something more interesting than tea?' He had wanted to avoid a Sunday reception for our first meeting and show me the Countess in private.

'The most interesting thing in this house is already brought out!' The Countess jabbed herself in the stomach and winked a hawkish eye. 'However, I will confess the icebox holds its charms.'

'A bottle of Dubonnet?'

She chuckled. 'He knows all my little secrets. Fetch it, sweet one.'

Breathing deeply, she wedged herself into a chair as Mark went to the kitchen. Behind her, on the wall, hung her first self-portrait. I went to look at it.

'It's charming, isn't it?' the Countess said. 'A very exact likeness, as a matter of fact.'

Eyes looked out softly from a pale fragile face. I glanced at the ancient hulk in the chair and said: 'You were a great beauty.'

The chair trembled under her wheeze. 'So what do you expect me to do about it? Sit here and remember it?'

Mark returned with the Dubonnet and three glasses on a tarnished silver tray. The Countess got up, walked very slowly to another chair and seated herself in it. 'It's my birthday,' she said.

We congratulated her. She waved a hand. 'It's a melancholy occasion, really. More like a funeral. But I've been wondering how old I am.'

'Do you know when you were born, Marguerite?' asked Mark, pouring the Dubonnet.

She nodded. 'Eighteen seventy-eight. But it's too much to count.'

'You're seventy-nine,' I said.

She gave a chuckle. 'You bring me good news. I thought I was eighty.' She raised her glass to herself. '*Bonne fête!*' she said, then got up again and moved to another chair. 'I've been doing this all afternoon. I have a great many chairs. I move about from one to the other. It's a depressing way to spend one's birthday, but I can't think of anything else to do.'

'You're looking well,' Mark said.

She patted her hair. 'Yes, I think so. I'm glad you didn't see me yesterday. Yesterday was bad; I thought I mightn't get through it.'

'What happened?' I asked.

'Nothing, dear child. That's exactly it. It was one of those days without pain, without pleasure. Hour after hour of appalling nothingness.' She licked her lips. 'I finally cheered myself up by eating six éclairs. It's not a very healthy diet, éclairs and Dubonnet, but sometimes one is driven to extremes. I shall try and eat nothing except boiled eggs tomorrow.'

With a sudden convulsive movement she got up and directed herself towards the kitchen.

'Where are you going now?' Mark asked.

'Surprise, surprise!' She propped herself against the purple velvet couch for a moment. 'Don't help me. I usually get there in the end.'

Finally she disappeared into the kitchen. After what seemed a very long time, she came back with a large coffee éclair on a cracked antique plate. She handed it to Mark. 'Divide this into three, sweet one.'

Mark did so.

'*Bonne fête!*' the Countess wished herself again, swallowing her piece at one go.

'You only brought one napkin,' Mark said.

'It's enough for the three of us. Divide it also!' She watched sharply while he tore it into strips, then turned to me. 'Who do you know in England?' She muttered a few names under her breath, and ended clearly: 'Sir Harry Lauder.'

'He's dead,' I told her.

'I painted him.' She took a pair of spectacles from a mother-of-pearl case hanging on a chain round her neck, and perched them on the end of her nose. 'But I can't remember where I put him.' Looking up suddenly at Mark, she went on: 'You can't stay long, my lawyer's coming about the Cracow estates.'

I asked if there were any chance of getting them back.

'Getting them back?' She laughed until she gasped. 'They don't *exist*, dear child. During the war they were a concentration camp, now they're a collective farm.'

Mark yawned and switched on the little portable radio which stood beside an Indian buddha on a satinwood table.

'The first time it happened, Gabriele didn't worry because he said Poland would never last. I suppose if we wait ...' The lids drooped over Marguerite's eyes. 'But isn't there so little left of Europe now?'

'You'd find it very changed.'

She scratched her nose and let her hand drop slackly to her lap. Everything about her became vague and slow, like clockwork running down.

'Dear child, have you ever stayed at the Hotel d'Altri Tempi in Venice?'

'Much too expensive,' I said.

'It was ours.' She gave a sigh. 'Before everything stopped.'

Just One of Those Things came from the radio. The Countess made curious rhythmic sounds in her throat, I supposed she was humming. 'Sinatra is still the best,' she said quietly. She looked at Mark. 'We loved Sinatra, didn't we?' She hummed again. 'I would like to go back to Europe, you know. Only I'm too tired.'

Then she yawned and fell asleep with the spectacles still on the end of her nose. We thought it better not to wake her.

As we went out through the hall, I noticed another portrait of the Countess. She must have painted it in the twenties. Slightly askew, it hung next to Nijinsky. I straightened it, sending up a thick cloud of dust.

I first met the nieces at a Sunday tea about two months later. In fact they weren't nieces at all, but the daughters of some remote Steblechi connexion whose mother had died and left them penniless in Naples. 'Really it is impossible to decide what they are,' the Countess said, 'but we agree they shall be considered nieces.' Anyway, apart from Marguerite herself, they were the last surviving Steblechis. The Osterberg line had come to an end with Gabriele's death.

The nieces were both in their early forties, tall and bony in black silk dresses and long low-heeled shoes shaped like gondolas. They had sallow Latin complexions and faint moustaches, sharp chins and long anxious necks. As I came into the room I heard Carlotta say:

'Tea in bags is horrible and must be stopped.'

Pia, who was the younger, made a knowing grimace. Then both assumed ghastly hypocritical smiles as the Countess brought me over. 'These are my poor dear girls, they miss their mother.'

They watched the Countess move slowly away, then Carlotta seized my wrist. 'Everything is mad and ridiculous!'

'You should see my bedroom,' Pia hissed. 'Like a market.'

'There is eighteen dresses with flowers in her cupboards.'

'There is nothing but old pictures and chairs that fall down.'

'On Sundays there is tea in bags.' The tea bags seemed to obsess Carlotta. She glanced round the room. 'Either these people is worth nothing, or is worth more than tea in bags.'

'There should be cookies,' I suggested.

The nieces considered this, then Pia asked: 'How much is cookies?'

'We ask because expenses is terrible here,' Carlotta explained. 'Aunt Marguerite thinks she is clever to drive eight miles to a market with lower prices. But she is not clever, because that big old car does only seven miles to the gallon.'

'Typical false economy,' said Pia.

I was wondering how naturally mean they were, or whether the Countess had already convinced them of her poverty, when Carlotta asked: 'You think Aunt Marguerite is nearer two or three million dollars?'

In what I hoped was a discouraging tone, I said I didn't know. Its only effect was to make Carlotta ask another question. 'You think she got a good price for that old palazzo?'

'Why don't you ask her?'

They muttered to each other in Italian, then Carlotta answered: 'You think we want to create a bad impression?'

Two weeks later they put a stop to the Sunday afternoons. They announced the Countess was unwell and had been ordered to rest completely for a while, but we knew it was really because they had decided we were all worth nothing.

Then I met Carlotta in a supermarket. She was buying yesterday's bread at reduced prices, and told me the Countess had gone blind. I asked if nothing could be done, and Carlotta shook her head. 'Even if operations was not doubtful, Aunt Marguerite is too old for them.' She went on to tell me that they'd dismissed the houseboy. 'Nothing has been dusted for years, and he never waters the garden, so everything is dirty or dead.'

She advised me not to go and see the Countess, but I decided to pay a call. I couldn't tell Mark about it, for this was one of the periods when he disappeared and no one could find him.

'Two minutes is all,' Carlotta announced, admitting me reluctantly. She seemed to include time in her stringent economies. The Countess lay on the purple couch in the living-room, nibbling a banana. She wore a bright flowered print and a lot of jewellery. The red dye was beginning to grow out of her hair.

'Dear child,' she said when Carlotta told her loudly who had come. 'I am in the dark.'

She raised her face and gave me a blind unblinking look. I noticed Pia on a canvas swing-seat in the patio, taking sun. She wore an old-fashioned black bathing suit, nodded rather curtly and didn't come in.

The Countess appeared in good spirits but her responses were alternately vague and sharp. She was also growing deaf. Once she couldn't remember who I was, a moment later she stretched out a hand and closed her fingers over the little buddha on the satinwood table by her side.

'Do you like this little treasure?'

'Yes,' I said.

'You can have it for three dollars.'

Carlotta watched disapprovingly while I paid for it. 'Such robbery,' she said and forced her lips into a smile. Without a word, I put the buddha in her hand. 'Excuse me please,' she said and went out to the patio, presumably to tell Pia.

The Countess asked me to light a cigarette for her. She smoked thin brown Havanas. She took a puff, then sniffed the smoke as it curled away from her nose. 'I cannot taste much,' she said. 'It takes away the pleasure of tobacco. However, I can smell a little.' Then she ran her hand along my arm, up to my shoulder. 'Dear child, you will have to be my mirror. My mirror that speaks. Tell me, mirror, is the dye running out of my hair?'

'Yes, a little.'

'I knew it!' She gave a grunt of satisfaction. 'Carlotta and Pia lied to me, as usual. You know, I am sad when I cannot see my beautiful antiques, I miss them very much. But I am not so sad,' she began to shake with laughter, 'when I cannot see my nieces. It helps, if you will pardon the expression, to look on the brighter side of things. . . . '

Carlotta returned and said it was time for me to leave.

'You must come again soon,' the Countess said, 'and I'll show you my memoirs. Did you know I'd started them again?'

'They will never be finished!' Carlotta hissed at me as I left. 'We have to sit for an hour each morning while she dictates ridiculous nonsense. She gets all the names and dates wrong, no one can make anything of it.'

Opening the front door, she saw my battered Chevrolet parked on the opposite side of the street.

'Your car?' I nodded. 'Will you please tell me how much it cost?' 'Seventy dollars,' I said. 'You spend much money on it since?' 'No,' I said. 'You spoil the front yourself?' 'No,' I said, 'that's the way I bought it.'

Carlotta became almost friendly. 'Most economical.' We shook hands. She held out her left hand, which had been hidden behind her back. The little buddha lay in it.

'Pia and I discussed this matter. We decided,' she gave a little sigh, 'what is paid for, *belongs*.'

I thanked her gravely. She stood at the top of the steps, plucking a flower from the yucca tree and sniffing it as she watched me drive off. I thought that the Countess had gone as far away as any human being can without actually dying. Cut off from seeing, soon without sounds to hear, and confused by her memories, she seemed scarcely more part of the world than the little buddha in my pocket.

Not long after this, Carlotta telephoned.

'Good-bye! We have to take Aunt Marguerite round the world.'

'What on earth for?'

'It cannot be stopped. She is bored and refuses to go on with her memoirs. She wants a last look round.'

'But she can't see.'

'This is unnecessary. She can hear a little. She will know all the places and wants just to be in them again.'

'I think you should dissuade her.'

'Impossible. There is trunks and bags already in the hall. She packs all those dresses herself.'

'What did the doctor say?'

'She has the strongest heart of any old lady he ever listened to.'

'Then I suppose there's nothing you can do.'

'Such expenses is bad for *my* heart!'

'You'll have to make the best of it, Carlotta. After all, you complain you never get out of the house. When do you leave?'

'Tomorrow . . .' A long thin sigh. 'We take a train to New York and then a Greek boat to France. It saves a little.'

For a while I hardly thought of the Countess again, except to hope for a postcard from time to time; but I knew Carlotta and Pia would be too mean to send any.

One afternoon I was buying records at a store on Hollywood Boulevard. A woman wearing a black silk dress and funereal hat with thick veiling hurried out through the swing doors. I followed her into the street, and glimpsed a pair of gondola-shaped shoes as she disappeared into a cab and it drove quickly away.

It must have been Carlotta. Nobody else dressed that way, except Pia. Then was the Countess back already? I telephoned the house that evening and a recorded voice informed me that I had reached a disconnected number.

Still convinced I had seen Carlotta, I drove up to the house next day. It looked neglected and aloof, shutters drawn across the windows, tall weeds sprouting in crevices on the stone steps and one of the yucca trees dying. But as I stood looking at it, I heard an extraordinary sound. I couldn't believe it, and listened again. No doubt of it, loud bursts of flamenco music were coming from somewhere.

From the house next door? No, the music faded when I went over there. Tracing the sound of mandolins and castanets and a gipsy voice, I went past the yucca trees, up the stone steps to the shuttered windows. I rang the doorbell. Waiting, I noticed that a little peephole had been cut in the door. The music seemed very loud now and underneath it I thought I detected the rattle of a train.

Nobody answered the bell. I was about to ring again, when I saw a pair of eyes on the other side of the peephole. They met close and level with mine in a fixed alarming stare. It was a fantastic moment, as if two dreams had collided. At last the eyes went away, the door opened a few inches and Carlotta peered furiously round the crack. When I moved a step closer she gave a piercing scream and slammed the door in my face.

I could see her watching me again through the peephole, glassily. This wouldn't do at all. I moved off towards my car with a deliberate saunter, got in and ran the engine for a minute. Then I walked round to the back of the house and inspected the patio wall for footholds. Luckily there were flying buttresses too and I managed to scale it.

Carlotta was not expecting an attack from this quarter. Staying close to the wall, I moved up to the windows without being seen. Venetian blinds had been added now, but they were half open. Bars of shadow lay across the living-room.

A space had been cleared in the centre of the room, and was occupied by part of a railway carriage. There was a seat with a luggage rack above it, a window on one side and sliding glass doors on the other, opening directly to the fireplace. In a sable coat and a pink straw hat topped with artificial fruit, the Countess was settled on the window seat. Sightless eyes were raised to her own patio; but in her mind, I suppose, she saw strange distances. There must have been a mechanical device under the seat, because it rocked slightly.

With ungainly flamenco movements, Pia circled the carriage. She clicked a pair of castanets, stretched her long neck and flapped her arms like a hungry distracted bird. From the couch Carlotta clapped her hands and shouted an occasional '*Olé!*' Three record-players stood side by side on a long table against the wall, issuing music and the sounds of a train. The performance continued for about two minutes, Pia grew breathless and rolled her eyes in supplication at her sister, who took no notice but clapped her hands and shouted in sharp implacable rhythm. Sometimes the Countess smiled and nodded, beating time with her foot. Then the sound of the train slowed down.

Carlotta stopped the flamenco music. She put a record on the third player and filled the room with trains whistling and steaming out of a station, crowds of people bustling and muttering, carriage doors being opened and heavy trolleys passing. Pia threw away her castanets with relief, leaned over the Countess and pulled her to her feet. Each taking an arm, the sisters led the old woman out of the room.

After a moment, Carlotta came back. She silenced the last

record player. I tapped on the window. She looked across at me, stiff with fright at first; then she shrugged. She let me in through the dining-room door. I noticed a wind machine standing in the corner.

'Where's Marguerite?' I asked.

Rather wearily she pointed down the cellar stairs. 'She'll be back in a minute.' From below I heard faint sounds of an engine whirring. A horn blew, a door slammed.

'Excuse me a moment,' Carlotta said.

I followed her. Pia was helping the Countess up the stairs from the cellar. She gave me a nervous glance and said loudly in her aunt's ear: 'Only eleven more!' The Countess appeared suddenly dazed, and asked: 'More what?' 'Steps,' said Pia. 'Where to?' 'The hotel.' 'Oh,' said the Countess, 'then what time is it?'

They had reached the top, and '*Buenos días, Señora!*' came in a deep bass voice which I realized had been assumed by Carlotta. The Countess seemed happy and vivacious now. 'Pia, is our luggage all right?' she asked as they led her along the hall. 'Tell Carlotta to count it, last time I was in Madrid . . .' She broke off again, dazed. 'I can't remember when it was.'

'Nineteen ten, you told us yesterday,' Pia said.

'No, it wasn't. It was nineteen nine. Anyway, the porter lost a hat-box.'

'Señora, I regret to announce the elevator is temporarily not working,' said Carlotta in her deep Spanish voice.

A shadow of irritation darkened her aunt's face. 'Pia, you have a genius for finding hotels with broken elevators.'

'Only seventeen stairs to the first floor,' Pia said cheerfully.

On the way up, the Countess asked again: 'What time is it? Is it night?'

'No, it's day.'

They took her to her own bedroom and sat her in an arm-chair. 'You'd better rest,' Carlotta advised. 'It's been a long journey.'

'Is the window open?'

'Yes,' said Pia, closing it.

The Countess frowned. 'Why did you tell me I lost a hat-box in Madrid?'

'It was *you* who told *me*.'

'Impossible. Anyway, it was in Amsterdam. In nineteen six. We must look for it.' She scratched her nose. 'Is it Sunday?'

'Yes.'

'Then there's a band concert in the Retiro.' The Countess started to get out of her chair.

'Band concerts is on Saturdays now,' Carlotta said quickly, pushing her down.

'Are you sure?'

'I saw a notice in the hall.' Her niece's voice was firm. 'It said, all band concerts on Saturdays until further notice.'

The Countess sighed. 'Everything's changing. Ring for tea.'

'Wouldn't you rather sleep first?'

'No.'

With a look of exasperation, Pia left the room.

'It's not worth waiting another six days for a band con-cert. Careless girls.' The Countess sounded peevish. 'We'll leave tomorrow.'

'So soon? Where do you wish to go?' Carlotta asked brokenly.

'Rome. No, Rome may be too cold.'

'In July?'

'Is it July?' With a look of alarm the Countess stroked her sables. 'But I'm wearing my sables, in July in Madrid one should swelter in sables!'

'Exceptionally cool summer, everyone is talking about it here!'

After a pause the Countess asked: 'Is there something on my head?'

'Your hat.'

'Take it off, please.' As Carlotta did so, the Countess added: 'We go to Venice, see about the tickets.' An uncertain look came over her face. 'Where am I now?'

'How tired you get after long journeys, you really should sleep. You're in Madrid,' Carlotta said with a touch of impatience.

Her aunt smiled. 'I haven't been in Madrid since –'

'Nineteen nine!'

'Much longer ago than that. What a bad memory you have, Carlotta. In nineteen nine I was near Cracow.'

'Shouldn't you take off your coat?'

'Not in an exceptionally cool summer,' said the Countess and yawned. 'Tell them to hurry with the tea.'

I followed Carlotta downstairs. She sank exhausted to the living-room couch. As Pia passed through the hall with a tea-tray, she called: 'We leave for Venice in the morning!'

'Doesn't she like it here?' Pia asked.

'It was my fault.' Carlotta sighed. 'For telling lies about band concerts. But we had no music.'

'Couldn't we find out there is special concerts on Mondays and get records tomorrow?'

'Cheaper to go to Venice.'

Pia took the tray upstairs.

I watched Carlotta. She lay back on the purple couch and stared at the ceiling. Presently she said: 'Gipsy flamenco music on Spanish trains is possible?'

'In the third class, anyway,' I agreed.

She pointed to the railway carriage. 'This is all we got. Long journeys is impossible, we cannot describe landscapes and stations for ever. Today we said a gipsy is on the train and passengers ask her to dance.' Carlotta tapped my wrist. 'This kind of thing is very good because it excites her, then she is tired out and now she sleeps a little.'

'Fraud? Oh, that is not a word I should use,' Carlotta was saying a few minutes later, when Pia came back with the news that their aunt was asleep. 'What we are doing is economy.'

'The cost of living rises all over the world,' Pia remarked. 'Extravagances must be stopped.'

'Old ladies of seventy-nine must not start travelling everywhere when they cannot even see where they are going!'

When the Countess decided to revisit Europe, her nieces had been appalled. It would cost a fortune, and they couldn't bear to think of their aunt's remaining millions shrinking away. After all, she had no one else to whom to leave them. 'Have we no rights?' Carlotta said. 'Are we to return to the slums of Naples?' What they had been allowed to see of California had begun to please them, especially the boom in real estate; already they were making plans to buy apartment houses and rent them out when the Countess died. They tried everything to dissuade their aunt from the trip, until she threatened to cut them out of her will. Two days before they were due to leave, they sat complaining as usual and Carlotta said again:

'She is blind and does not hear well. She will hardly know where she is!'

And in the silence that followed, these words held a new meaning. Next morning Carlotta and Pia got up early. They had a list of what they needed, and by lunchtime had ordered everything, from guide-books to wind machines, electric fires for heat and fans for cold. When the time for departure came, they settled the Countess in the Rolls and Carlotta drove it very slowly down the hill, along Hollywood Boulevard, then turned round and arrived back at the house. For the next three days the Countess sat and slept in the railway carriage in the living-room, under the impression she was in a Pullman bound for New York.

The ship to Europe had a state-room rigged up in the dining-room and a record of ocean sounds, the surge of waves and the cry of gulls, played incessantly under her berth. An occasional walk in the patio with the wind machine gently blowing served as a stroll on deck. The Countess could take the sun there too, on the swing-seat carefully adjusted to suggest a steady rolling movement. As she lost all sense of time on long journeys, they cut down the tedium of an Atlantic crossing to two days.

'We had three weeks in London,' Carlotta said, 'a month in Paris, a few days on the Riviera and now we arrive in Madrid.' The Countess had stood in her patio running her finger along a wall that she believed was part of her house in Curzon Street. She had attended Mass at Notre-Dame, the living-room sprayed with incense and Pia tinkling a bell in her ear. She had been to the Opéra-Comique, sitting between her nieces in a box overlooking a beautiful sideboard she had brought with her from the palazzo. She had gambled at Monte Carlo, with Carlotta and Pia taking it in turns to be croupier, and making sure she didn't lose too much.

The only thing that distressed the Countess was that everyone she knew was dead.

'We have to be firm about this,' Carlotta said. 'Impersonating old barons or princesses is really too difficult.'

'And most of them is dead anyway,' Pia added.

After a moment, I burst out laughing. The nieces stared at me, reproachful and unamused. I laughed more wildly, and they looked a little frightened. Finally, wiping the tears from my eyes, I managed to say: 'I'd like to talk to Marguerite.'

'He is still joking,' Carlotta said disapprovingly to Pia.

I shook my head. 'And I'll tell you how it's going to be done. The day after tomorrow, I shall be on holiday in Venice.'

The Countess had never cared about her garden. You opened the door from the patio and looked down a steep slope overgrown with shrubs and long dry grass. There were no flowers, only laurel bushes, banks of yellowing ivy and tall slanting eucalyptus trees that dripped their leaves. A path with cracked crazy paving led to the swimming pool at the end of the slope.

This morning, rubbish was burning in the incinerator and a twist of smoke sidled towards the pool. Sunlight made the leafy water gleam, and played on the bright artificial fruit of the Countess's hat. She was sitting among cushions in a rowing boat, moored off the deep end. She trailed her fingers absently in the water, and a gondolier's song came from the distance.

Carlotta and Pia were side by side in deck chairs, near the stone cupid, as I arrived. 'Aunt Marguerite!' exclaimed Carlotta, pulling the boat a little nearer the edge with a rope. 'How extraordinary, here is someone we know!'

The Countess looked up at me with her blind eyes and extended a hand to be kissed. 'Dear child,' she said vaguely.

'Such a coincidence!' Carlotta insisted. She seemed nervous about it. 'He was coming out of the hotel –'

'I haven't the courage to go in,' the Countess said. 'I am trying to find it, but I haven't got it.'

'You know the Altri Tempi was Aunt Marguerite's palazzo before they converted it?' Pia said.

'I thought I had the courage.' The Countess spoke in a low voice. 'But then I asked the gondolier to tie us up and let me sit and ... and think about it.' In a whisper she asked: 'Is it completely changed?'

'I'm afraid so.'

'But Gabriele's portrait is still in the hall,' Carlotta said.

The Countess smiled faintly. 'And the chandeliers in the dining-room?'

'Still there!' said Pia loudly.

The Countess trailed her hand in the water again and asked Carlotta for a piece of chocolate. 'You stayed here when you were children,' she said. 'Don't you remember the day your mother brought you?' I noticed a tear welling in Carlotta's left eye. 'There was piccata for dinner,' the Countess continued with one of her surprisingly exact flashes of memory.

'Very good piccata.' Pia sniffed. 'But we wasn't children, Aunt Marguerite. I was nearly twenty.'

A heavy truck rumbled down the hill. Carlotta wiped her eye and looked up sharply to see whether its sound might disconcert the Countess, but she was deep in memory. 'I thought I sold the chandeliers,' she said at last. 'But perhaps ... When you have lived in so many great houses, it grows confusing. Is the portrait in good condition?'

'Yes,' I said. 'They take good care of it.'

'I made a stipulation in the contract, you know. People haven't much respect nowadays.' She frowned. 'Is this a good hat?'

'It suits you.'

'Sometimes it feels good, sometimes it feels like a mistake. But when there are no more mirrors, what does it matter?' She turned her blind sharp old face to the sky. 'Everything I knew is gone. It's all stone walls and flattering voices. Did you know it's easier to believe voices when you can't see faces?' Her head drooped, she was growing tired. 'Gabriele,' she murmured. 'I could see Gabriele's face, and I could never believe his voice.' A sigh that seemed to come from the bottom of a deep dry well. 'What a pity, such a handsome face!'

'Are you all right, Aunt Marguerite?' asked Carlotta.

She shook her head irritably. 'Those girls are idiots,' she whispered. 'Give them ten million and their world will be no more beautiful. Their values are all wrong. I knew this when they told me the dye wasn't coming out of my hair. It would have cost so little and looked so much better to dye it again, but they didn't mind looking at it, day after day, running out!'

She brooded. A sad wheeze escaped her. Then she said rather loudly: 'It sinks...'

'What sinks, Aunt Marguerite?' the nieces asked in chorus.

'Venice... Idiots!' she muttered at them, then turned to me. 'Year after year it is slowly drowning, sinking into the water. And one day...' She turned back to Carlotta and Pia. 'Take me home. Slowly.'

Carlotta loosened the rope. The boat drifted towards the centre of the pool.

'Too fast!' The Countess clutched her hat. 'Where are you, Carlotta? Where are you, Pia?'

'We're here,' they said, Carlotta holding on to the rope so the boat shouldn't drift too far.

'Facts is facts,' said Carlotta. 'You have seen her in her own swimming pool and she thinks it's the Grand Canal. She misses nothing. Would it make her more happy to be really in Venice?'

'If she really went to Europe, it might be fatal,' said Pia. 'This way she travels so comfortably.'

'Maybe so.' I glanced from one to the other. 'But what's your profit?'

Carlotta made a little clicking sound of disapproval. 'I have no time to count such things, I work my fingers to the bone.'

'Cooking is worst,' said Pia. 'We have to learn dishes of every country.'

'Making money out of blind old women was never our object.' Carlotta's tone was almost self-righteous. 'We only wish to stop Aunt Marguerite wasting her fortune.'

'And invest in real estate for the future,' added Pia.

'All the same,' I said, 'It's a fraud. A confidence trick. You're just helping yourselves to the old woman's money.'

Carlotta's eyes grew suddenly fierce. 'What is this money? Osterberg money!' She stood up, and began pacing the room. 'Money made by the genius of our late Uncle the Count! Most of it gone because of wars and countries changing hands – and the rest will go too, if we leave it to Aunt Marguerite! She has no values for this kind of thing. Pia and I is only poor girls from the slums of Naples, but we have business flair. Aunt Marguerite is past, we is future. We think it is time for Osterberg money to grow again, not shrink. That is our purpose!'

She sat down, rather flushed, in the railway carriage. I had never seen her so passionate before. She seemed to have gained a new dimension, I almost respected her.

Before I could answer, she had an afterthought. 'You think Pia and I is funny girls. People tell us the sense of humour is not our strong point, but we find nothing funny. We are *serious*.'

'If I could think of anything to do, I'd do it,' I said. 'But I can't. I suppose I'll just have to be an accomplice after the fact.'

'What is that?' Pia asked.

A bell rang upstairs and Carlotta frowned. 'Aunt Marguerite has woken, she wants to go over to the Lido tonight. But it's too difficult. Pia, we'll have to make another storm.'

Pia went into the dining-room and beat the thunder sheet.

'Not loud enough! Take it upstairs and beat it outside her door. And try a little wind.' Carlotta watched her sister hoist the contraption over her shoulders, then turned to me with a complacent joyless smile. 'Aunt Marguerite will never go out in weather like this!'

In Vienna, said Carlotta, the Countess wept a great deal and grew very confused. Sitting in her sunless patio which she imagined was a terrace at the Belvedere, she listened to records of old waltzes and conjured up the Danube at her feet. Once she was convinced they would be late for a parade in honour of the Emperor Franz Josef's birthday, another time she wouldn't leave the café and sipped weak coffee for five hours. When Carlotta complained, she said: 'The Count of Klausenburg promised to come by.'

They were supposed to go on to St Moritz, but the Countess changed her mind. 'I begin to hate my memories,' she said. 'It's time to go somewhere where I haven't any.'

'We are in Marrakech and cannot get out!' Carlotta announced over the telephone about three weeks later. 'It is a horrible blow.'

'You mean she wants to stay there?'

'She is infatuated with the East, it becomes a new lease of life!' Carlotta's voice trembled. 'She has taken a house in the native quarter and drinks mint tea. She likes the sounds of the market place and listens to ridiculous flutes and drums all day.'

'At least it means less work if she stays in one place.'

'But not this place, listening to horrible music! Are we to be stuck in an Arab city for the rest of her life?'

It seemed nothing would move the Countess. Carlotta and Pia warned her about the hot season, announced it had come, closed all the windows and filled her room with electric fires. 'It's not as bad as I expected,' the Countess said. Carlotta would add another fire. 'Makes me a little sleepy,' the Countess said.

They told her the climate was unreliable and arranged a terrific storm one night. Pia banged the thunder sheet for hours and turned the wind machine on her aunt as directly as she dared. They slammed and rattled windows and claimed the house next door had been struck by lightning. 'Ask them if there is anything we can do,' the Countess said.

They read her reports of terrorism from the newspapers. Machine-gun fire rang through the house one morning and Carlotta said all the windows had been boken. 'Mend them,' ordered the Countess. 'And don't forget to sweep up carefully.'

Desperate, they switched off the record-players and said all the musicians in the market place had gone away. 'Nomads I suppose,' the Countess said. 'But there'll be others.'

There was nothing they could do but agree, and start the record-players again next day. The Countess lay on her purple couch and listened and fell asleep. After six months she was still charmed by the sounds, but physically weaker. On many days she never got out of bed. She started her memoirs again, dictated an anecdote or two to Pia. 'It's all going further and further away,' she said once. There was regret and satisfaction in her voice. 'I can hardly remember California now.'

I saw her once in her Marrakech period. Carlotta and Pia had cleared all the furniture out of her bedroom and made it completely Moroccan. The Countess reclined on a mattress

on the floor, covered by a sheepskin rug. She was asleep; I
didn't want to wake her. Her hair was white as the sheepskin now, her skin very lined and mottled, yet she gave an
impression of calm and strength. Beside her was a low table
with a silver pot of mint tea on a tray. Flutes and drums
were gently piped through a loudspeaker.

'We think Morocco must be quite agreeable,' Pia said. 'In
fact, Carlotta and I would like to go there ourselves.'

Just before he left California, Mark and I discussed the
situation and tried to find a way of resolving it. It seemed a
pity to try and bring the Countess home; we were only
frightened she might somehow find out the deception and
never recover from the shock. Mark had an idea that Carlotta and Pia should be kidnapped. He would impersonate
the American Consul and inform the Countess that lust-
ful sheikhs had carried off her nieces. Under the circum-
stances she would have to agree to go home.

'But who will look after her then?' I asked.

'We'll have Carlotta and Pia rescued, naturally.'

'I think she'd suspect it. Besides, you and I would have to
spend eight days in that house pretending it's a boat.'

'Couldn't they rush up the gangway, just as it's leaving?'

'It won't do.'

After a silence, Mark said: 'Odd to think I used to dance
with her.'

'To Sinatra?'

He nodded, then asked me for a cigarette. His usual
gesture for closing a subject.

And later that night the telephone rang.

'We are back!' Carlotta's voice shivered with elation.
'Since an hour we are back in California, thank God!'

'How on earth did it happen?'

One could never have predicted the reason. The Countess

received letters from time to time, mainly circulars, which she imagined had been forwarded from California. Most of them didn't interest her, unless they contained offers of free samples, which she applied for on principle. A few days after the October rising in Budapest, there was a letter inviting her to a Victims of Oppression Dinner in Hollywood. The idea of the dinner was to raise funds for refugees from Hungary, and a telegram had already been sent to the State Department urging relaxation of the laws of immigrants. In view of the late Count Osterberg-Steblechi's connexion with Hungary, the letter suggested, wouldn't the Countess like to lend her support?

When the news of the rising came through, there was a good deal of activity in Hollywood. An émigré Hungarian producer joined with an émigré Hungarian composer to write a nostalgic song about Budapest, which they had both left over twenty years ago. It was played quite often on the radio. A Hungarian actress who had once appeared in a film with the Marx Brothers presided at a Help Hungary Cocktail. Somebody announced a film to be called *Beast of Budapest*. The Countess, too, was stirred. She ordered Carlotta to cable her lawyer to watch for news of the Cracow estates, ignoring reminders that they were in Poland, and sent Pia to buy tickets for the earliest possible plane.

'We think to attend this dinner is ridiculous,' Carlotta said, 'but it brings her home. We think if we say no more about it, she will forget.'

She didn't, however, and was determined to go. Carlotta asked me to accompany them, and on the night of the dinner I went round to the house to pick them up. They were still dressing the Countess, who stood erect in the centre of her bedroom in a rich blue velvet evening gown that she hadn't worn since the days of Venice. The nieces were worried it would be too heavy for her, and she finally allowed them to cut off the train. Pia was on her knees now, stitching the hem. Carlotta had opened the jewel box, the entire contents of which Marguerite had decided to wear. Rigid as an effigy in her magnificent blue velvet, she directed the diamond tiara to be placed on her head with its newly dyed hair; had three bracelets slipped on her arms, one above the elbow; seven rings on her fingers; five strings of pearls, and a sapphire clasp at her waist.

When I asked if she'd had a good journey, the Countess only gave a short disinterested nod. She seemed strangely indifferent to all of that now. 'I have returned just in time,' she said, then grimaced. 'The Sleeping Beauty has been awakened by a strange Prince!'

It took her a long time to walk downstairs. She wouldn't use a stick.

We drove out in the Rolls. Sitting very upright, occasionally patting her tiara, she talked about the revolution. Although it had failed by now, she was not discouraged. 'They are stirring, everywhere they are stirring. They want us back and we mustn't abandon them.' But a little later she asked anxiously: 'Have they asked the Count of Klausenburg tonight?'

About thirty people came to dinner, held in the banqueting hall of a restaurant near Hollywood Boulevard. The hall was plain and gloomy, walls of chipped sky blue with lifesize palms painted on them. The floor was bare, we sat at a long table in the centre and there was no other furniture except for a grand piano at one end. All the guests except the Countess and her party were originally immigrants from Hungary who had come to America thirty or more years ago. The organizer owned a canning factory downtown. Most of the others were business people, an oil producer, a hotel owner, a raw cotton dealer who had come up from the San Joaquin Valley. There was also a once famous playwright, now almost eighty and ending his days at a beach house in Malibu, and an old actress who ran a dramatic school.

Everyone wore tuxedos, and the actress had a red rose pinned to her low-cut black evening dress. Glowing with jewels and bright velvet, flanked by her tall nieces, the Countess made a striking entrance but was unaware of it. Advancing down the room with slow difficult steps, the sapphire clasp glittering in the centre of her enormous stomach, she looked like an exotic potentate arriving for some secret ritual. The organizer introduced himself and made a little speech to the others at table, saying how honoured they were by her presence. We guided her to a chair next to the old playwright, who burst into tears. He had been a week-end guest at Cracow before the first world war. 'Are you Ferenc Molnar?' the Countess asked. 'No, he is dead. But I knew him well.' 'Did you know the Count of Klausenburg?' 'Slightly,' said the old playwright. 'Is he coming tonight?'

The main dish was goulash and we drank imperial Tokay. Conversation was sporadic and uneasy at first, then suddenly everyone began talking about profits, new installations, and taking a trip to Hawaii. It grew very hot, this was an old room without air-conditioning, and with only one fan. After dessert the organizer stood up, mopped his forehead with a paper napkin and proposed toasts: to the liberty of free peoples everywhere, to the spirit of Budapest, to the United States of America. Then came speeches. The factory owner told of his arrival in New York just as the Depression started. Hard days and broken hopes, but he won through. 'This is a wonderful country, and I am proud to be a citizen of it. But I can never forget the land of my birth. Today,' he said, 'I am shedding tears for it.' It was true.

'Bravo!' the Countess exclaimed as he sat down. 'They

are stirring,' she repeated, her blind eyes fixed on the painted palms. 'They want us back, they are begging us to return.'

I realized that in her mind everyone at the table was part of a vanished aristocratic world. Somehow she believed this dinner was dedicated to its rebirth.

The old playwright spoke of Budapest at the turn of the century. 'Those were golden days, those days before nineteen fourteen.' He evoked the memory of his friend Molnar and told some whimsical stories about the neighbours in the little street where he used to live. 'The Danube,' he said, 'is the most beautiful river in the world. And it is most beautiful, and most blue, at Budapest. Alas, our river is no longer blue. Our beautiful river is stained with red. . . . '

Guttural and hierarchic, the actress spoke of Hungary's contribution to the theatre. In 1912 she played in Ibsen's *Ghosts*, later she had a theatre named after her. She described her country first under the jackboot, then the hammer and sickle. When the Russians occupied Hungary, they changed the name of her theatre. 'But in secret they still call it *my* theatre,' she finished proudly. 'I know. I have information.'

'I have never heard of this woman,' the Countess said. 'Is she famous?'

A malicious expression came over the playwright's face and he whispered something to her in Hungarian.

At the end of the speeches, came a long silence. We all seemed to be staring at the blue wall and the palms. The air felt heavy and stale. The Countess was still napping when the organizer took a cheque book from his pocket, laid it solemnly on the table, and asked us all to be generous.

For the first time, Carlotta and Pia stopped looking bored. Carlotta nudged her aunt. 'How much is it to be?' she asked in a nervous whisper.

The Countess awoke with a start. 'We mustn't abandon them,' she said. 'They are stirring.'

'Twenty dollars?' Pia suggested in a hoarse undertone.

'Idiot girls! What do you know of life as it really was?' The Countess sighed. 'I should give them everything I have!'

For a moment I thought the nieces were going to faint.

'A cheque has no poetry, no passion,' the Countess said. 'My gift must be symbolic.'

Slowly, her hands began to caress her jewels. They stroked her rings and bracelets, then groped up to her head. They removed the tiara. Wheezing, she laid it on the table. 'Cartier valued it at a hundred thousand, in nineteen twenty-eight, I think.'

A spot of colour tinged each cheek. She didn't know who she was giving it to, or what she was giving it for; it was a blessing on the old world that, too late for her, was struggling to come back. Her blind eyes stared at the ceiling while staid business faces gazed at her from each side of the table. Then the playwright took her hand and kissed it. 'When you see a thing like this, you feel all is not yet lost.'

The others clapped. Then the cheques were collected and the total announced: over thirty thousand dollars, plus the tiara. They thanked the Countess again, but she had fallen asleep. A final toast was drunk, Carlotta woke up her aunt, and we straggled out into Hollywood Boulevard and the parking lot where all the cars were massed. *Wrap Your Troubles in Dreams* was coming from a radio at a hamburger stand. Groups of adolescents wandered by in the warm airless evening, boys in jeans and sweat shirts, girls in vividly-coloured shirts and tight pants. A few turned to stare at the Countess, as Pia and Carlotta helped her into the crested Rolls. A little further up the street, crowds were leaving a theatre after a première. Lights tinted the night sky a harsh yellowy pink.

Now the only thing left is to bury her. The Countess died

in her sleep a few hours after the dinner. The nieces didn't find out till morning, when they went into her bedroom to wake her. The radio was still playing and Marguerite sat tightly wedged in a chair, a half-eaten peach in her hand. Carlotta supposed she had sat up to listen for news reports from Hungary.

Pia has saved a brochure pushed under the front door of the house some weeks ago, and now she brings it out. It is called the Boomtower Pictorial. Boomtower Mortuaries offer funerals at six different price ranges, from $52 to $282, they are rapidly expanding and have built two new Chapels this year to serve, as the Pictorial says, 'the community's ever-increasing needs'. Carlotta is interested in their scheme for buying coffins on the instalment plan.

After long arguments they decide on a $92 funeral.

On the morning of the funeral, Mrs Leota Sperling from Boomtower Mortuaries calls to advise on costume and make-up. She is a cheerful lady with tight brown curls and a brisk manner. She has a husband and two children, and when the time comes for each one to pass on, she is happy to think it will be 'through Boomtower'. She thinks it would be nice to bury the Countess in her blue velvet, which is so much more dignified than the flowered prints in the wardrobe. She will rouge the old lady's lips, rub some colour into her cheeks, and touch up her hair.

Carlotta asks her opinion of the $92 funeral and is delighted when Mrs Sperling says in her view it's the best value of them all. She puts it this way: 'Not drab, but not ostentatious either. We at the Mortuaries never encourage extravagance at a time of emotional stress.'

A black Boomtower Cadillac takes the body to the Chapel. Carlotta and Pia and I follow in the Rolls. The sun beats down on slow lines of traffic, and we are all perspiring slightly. The outside of the Chapel is calm and secular, it looks like a residential hotel. In a sense, I suppose, it is. An awning stretches above the entrance with BOOMTOWER in slanting letters across the fringe. On one side of the Chapel is a laundromat, on the other a restaurant.

Inside, it is cool. Attendants lay the Countess in an air-conditioned Slumber Room. It looks like any living-room in a comfortable Californian house, with a corpse on the couch.

There are armchairs with restful patterns, soothing lights and flower paintings on the wall. Music comes from a concealed loudspeaker like sweet religious scent. This is our last communion. Standing by the Countess with her painted cheeks and splendid gown, I can only think there is something horribly fitting about this final pretence of many pretences. The last journey is the only real one, yet more fantastic than any the Countess imagined.

It is time to begin the service. Through the Chapel windows we can see a patio garden brilliant with flowers. A fountain plays and sparkles in the sun. It is all so beautiful, we hardly notice when a panel in the wall slides away and the coffin disappears down a chute. The panel slides back and the music is still coming from all sides, reverent and soft.

In a minute the Countess will be burning.

Everything seems illusion; all troubles have been finally wrapped in dreams. Carlotta and Pia bring out their handkerchiefs. Each will soon have a million dollars in the bank, and later much more out of real estate in Florida. As we go out, Carlotta suddenly looks very white. She leans on Pia's arm and holds the handkerchief to her mouth. A moment later she is all right again, turns to me and says quietly :

'We heard this morning the tiara fetched ninety thousand. I wonder how many refugees that will bring in?'

'It was a birthday present,' Pia remarks in a reflective tone. 'From Gabriele.'

I watch them drive off in the imperial Rolls, and think of them back in that living-room in the hills.

The earliest portrait of Marguerite is still hanging there, the girl in a white dress in Switzerland more than fifty years ago. I believe it was painted a few days before she fell into Count Osterberg-Steblechi's arms.

The Closed Set

ON a hot winter's day an open truck containing a papier-mâché woman about fourteen feet high drove up Hollywood Boulevard and stopped outside one of the largest movie theatres. The woman had orange hair and wore a taut black evening dress with its skirt slashed between the thighs. One leg thrust contemptuously forward in a spangled stocking. I watched four workmen carry her out of the truck and fix her to the façade of the theatre, hoisting her into position on pulleys. Later, one of them climbed a ladder to paste a long sticker below her high-heeled shoes. It said, I HATE YOU HANNAH KINGDOM.

Slogans had been going up elsewhere for a week. All over the city you drove past black billboards with I HATE YOU HANNAH KINGDOM blocked out in massive gold type. In one of the newspapers, a lady columnist wrote:

Last night I saw Julie Forbes's new picture, *The Crime of Hannah Kingdom*. You'll be seeing it soon if you know what's good for you. It's a lulu. Julie should land another Oscar for this one. I told her so at the party after the showing, and she said: 'Yes, I feel I've done justice to a great character.' Coming from Julie that means a lot, because she's a perfectionist. . . .

I looked forward to seeing the film, I always enjoy watching Julie Forbes on the screen. Who can forget those emotional boxing matches in which the characters give, take and parry great bruising blows of love and rage and hate? I refer of course to the later, more heavyweight works. Julie Forbes belongs to that group of star actresses in their late forties who retain a hold on the public by dramatically changing their style every five or ten years. Just when it seems impossible for them to continue any longer, when fashion threatens to leave them hopelessly behind, they undergo some mysterious process of renewal and come back more powerful than ever. It is like the secret rejuvenation course run by a specialist in Beverly Hills. For two thousand dollars you may spend ten days in her secluded mansion. You are blindfolded most of the time, and it is said that people who emerge are not always recognized by their closest friends.

The Julie Forbes of 1927 who made her first appearance in *Look Out, Sister!* was a chorus girl with a jaunty grin and busily tapping feet. In 1933 she surprised everyone as the simple country heroine of *Life Is Like That*, shy and innocent and wronged. A few years later she wore extravagant clothes with a kind of melancholy sophistication, and smoked cigarettes through a long holder, in comedies about the idle rich. Then came an uncertain period, beginning soon after the outbreak of the second world war. She played a famous woman doctor who went blind, and a member of the Norwegian resistance. There were rumours that she was finished. She married a businessman from San Francisco and announced her retirement. They had a son, a divorce, and suddenly a 'new' Julie Forbes appeared once more. Mature but unravaged, she presented a ruthless schemer in *For Pity's Sake*, a woman who didn't care how many lives she destroyed in her quest for . . . what? She stole other women's husbands, became rich and feared and famous, drove her enemies to drunkenness or suicide, yet she never seemed happy. It led to even greater triumphs. For *The Big Angel* she won an Oscar.

Less than a month after the ceremonies, the same story appeared under enormous front page headlines in all the newspapers. Into Julie Forbes's swimming pool, drained of water because it was being cleaned, a man had fallen; cracked his skull; died immediately. It was three o'clock in the morning. When the police arrived they found the actress, her eleven-year-old son Timmy, her private secretary Mrs Lynch and her agent Canning Wallace, all waiting stiff and tallow-faced in the living-room. Two questions were asked at once: who was the man, and how did he fall into the pool? Miss Forbes became hysterical and couldn't answer either of them. The agent and the private secretary spoke up. The stranger was a friend of Miss Forbes, they'd had dinner together that night, he'd driven her home. He was very drunk, and when Miss Forbes asked him to leave, he refused. He wanted to go for a swim in the pool. Miss Forbes pointed out this was impossible, because the pool was empty. The stranger became very angry and insisted that Miss Forbes make arrangements to have it filled immediately. There was a quarrel by the edge. The stranger lost his balance and fell in.

The only person who could corroborate or deny this story was Timmy. The boy had been asleep and didn't wake up until he heard his mother cry out, after the man fell in the pool. The police asked him what Miss Forbes did after that. He said that she calmed down and drank a glass of brandy. This made Timmy feel thirsty, and he went to the refrigerator for some milk. When he came back, his mother was telephoning Mrs Lynch. Mrs Lynch said she was going to telephone Mr Wallace. A few minutes later, both came over to the house. Why didn't Miss Forbes call the police sooner? She was too upset, mightn't you be? said Mrs Lynch. Her shock and grief were almost uncontrollable, said Canning Wallace.

It turned out that the stranger had once been a barman at a club in Beverly Hills. Timmy said he first came to the house about a year ago. He didn't think his mother saw him very often. He drank too much, and even hit her once.

The actress had given him money to start his own bar, but it didn't catch on. At the inquest, the stranger's mother appeared. She was a dressmaker in Pasadena. While Julie Forbes repeated her story, she made a disturbance and was hustled out of court. Later she told reporters that her son never drank, but the police discovered she hadn't seen him for nearly two years.

The verdict was accidental death. No harm was done to Julie Forbes's career, and *The Big Angel* drew larger crowds than ever. She paid for the stranger's funeral, but didn't go to it.

There are some fine homes in the hills which separate Hollywood from the San Fernando Valley, and they give an illusion of country living. Near the highest point I glimpsed a wide commanding view north and south, across the valley shielded by gritty mountains from the dry Mojave desert, across the city sloping down to the Pacific in an envelope of dusk. Tall trees were silhouetted against the sky, and a blue jay flew above the driveway marked PRIVATE which led off the canyon road. This driveway passed a swimming pool with an adobe guest house overlooking it, and wound through a eucalyptus grove to a mansion built round three sides of a courtyard, like a Spanish mission. In the centre a fountain played, and at the far end marble steps led up to a front door inlaid with blue and white tiles.

A butler in tails opened the door and said in a near-English accent: 'Miss Forbes would like you to wait in the living-room.' I followed him through a bare rectangular hall without windows, only soft concealed lighting on oyster-pink walls. No furniture, except for a scarlet and white chess set standing on a table, foot-high pieces arranged as if a game were in progress but would somehow never be finished.

The L-shaped living-room bore no traces of living. Everything about it was an abstraction of comfort and elegance. The walls were white except for a strip of filigreed black and gold wallpaper above the pseudo-antique fireplace, at right angles to which stood two long low black couches. Pressed flowers lay under the glass tops of white marble coffee tables. A plaster-cast pink and blue angel floated above the grand piano, suspended on a gold wire from the ceiling. There were cigarettes in little glass bowls and book matches in gold leaf covers, each one with a facsimile signature, *Julie Forbes*. The only painting was of Julie Forbes, a pastel blur about five feet tall in a frame overlaid with black velvet.

The butler asked if I'd like a drink and I ordered Scotch. As he left the room, I went to look at the painting more closely. Almost at once a voice said:

'What do you think of it?'

I turned and saw a stocky, rather bull-necked woman, thick white hair brushed back smooth and straight from her forehead, standing by the window. She must have come in from the garden.

'I painted it,' she said before I could answer, and held out a blunt hand which enclosed mine in a naturally powerful grip. 'I'm Mrs Lynch. You didn't come with Mr Harriston?'

'No, but he should be along any moment.'

Mrs Lynch gave a little nod and smoothed the starched cuffs of her blouse. 'I understand you've already worked with Mr Harriston?' She cleared her throat loudly. It was the first move in an interview, not conversation.

'Yes, on a picture that's just finished. He thought he'd like me to be on this one, if he does it.'

'If?' Frowning, Mrs Lynch sat down on one of the couches. 'I think you'll find that everything's set.'

'I don't know,' I said. 'All Cliff told me was that Miss Forbes had a story she wanted him to do.'

He had told me a little more, but not much. Yesterday on the telephone: 'Can you have dinner with Julie Forbes tomorrow night?' I said I didn't know her. 'She wants me to direct a picture for her.' 'Are you serious?' 'I'm broke.' 'Where do I come in, exactly?' 'Maybe on the script.' 'Does she have one already?' 'I'm afraid so.'

Naturally I said nothing of this to Mrs Lynch. I had already decided she was a sinister bodyguard-figure, and relations with her should be strictly formal. I went over to the french windows and admired the view.

'It's the best in the canyon,' she said as the butler came in with my drink. She ordered vodka on the rocks with a beer chaser, then asked if I'd ever met Miss Forbes. I shook my head. 'In my opinion, she is one of the truly outstanding personalities of our time.' Mrs Lynch made a deep clearing sound in her throat again. 'And with all of that, so – so . . .' She searched for a word. 'So lovely. Why don't you sit down?'

She patted the cushion beside her. I sat on the opposite couch.

'It should be a great chance for you, working with Miss Forbes. She's a perfectionist, you know. Sometimes I think she'll wear herself out. But she's got more energy than a man.' There was an undertone of contempt in the last word. 'Have you seen *The Crime of Hannah Kingdom*?'

'Not yet,' I said.

'It's great.' She spoke in a flat businesslike voice. 'Simply great. No other word will do. She gets under the skin of things, you know. Sometimes it's . . . uncanny.'

'Have you been with Miss Forbes for long?' I asked.

'Since *For Pity's Sake*. That's nine years. She's more than an employer to me, she's a friend.'

'You live here?' I was pumping Mrs Lynch now, and trying to appear casual.

She nodded. 'Miss Forbes offered me a suite after – after the accident. She didn't want to live alone.'

'I thought she had a son?'

'Timmy's only thirteen. That's not quite the same thing, is it?' Smoothing her hospital nurse's cuffs again, she looked up sharply at me. I realized she had given this information very deliberately, to establish her position. Now her tone changed. Regaining the offensive, she became almost inquisitorial. 'In your opinion, is Mr Harriston truly interested in this project?'

Her methods were less subtle than mine, and probably more effective. For a moment I was taken aback. 'I'm sure he is. Otherwise he wouldn't be coming here to talk about it.'

Mrs Lynch appeared not to have heard this. She regarded her shoes, which were heavy black brogues. 'He's a very talented director, don't you agree?'

'Very.'

'At the studio they say, "he's good but you have to watch him."' She gave a rather bleak smile. 'Miss Forbes told me that.'

'They watch him too much, that's the trouble. He doesn't often get a chance to do what he wants.'

'I didn't mean that.' Mrs Lynch became brusquely matter-of-fact. 'He once socked a producer in the jaw.'

I laughed. 'A friend of yours?'

'I don't know the man in question.' Her mouth tightened with disapproval. 'But it was dislocated.'

'And he couldn't speak for a week.' I nodded. 'It probably saved the picture.'

I met her small, pitiless eyes. 'He was drunk when he did it.'

'I know nothing about that,' I said.

'I'm sure you must.' It was a statement, not an opinion. 'I understand you're one of his closest friends. We also have a report from the producer of his last picture. They used to find bottles of Scotch in his desk. Of course –'

She broke off as the butler came back with her drink. 'Would you like another?' she asked me.

'Please. I drink too – or don't you have a report on me?'

She took this quite seriously. 'That would hardly be necessary.'

'If Miss Forbes is so doubtful about Cliff,' I said when the butler left the room, 'why does she want to work with him?'

'But she has no doubts at all! How could I have given you that impression?' Mrs Lynch leaned forward and patted my knee. 'All this is just routine. As a matter of fact, she agrees with you entirely. "All that man needs is a good picture, and I'm going to give it to him." I quote her very words.'

The front door bell rang.

'That must be Mr Harriston.' Mrs Lynch swallowed her chaser. 'I hope you'll regard this as a friendly private talk.'

'I'm sure we both will.'

A sound of voices came from the hall. Mrs Lynch stood up smartly, as if going on parade. 'Miss Forbes has opened the door herself, I think.'

A moment later she came into the room. The first thing I noticed was her dress: deep, flaring crimson. Like everything else about her it had a bright perfect glitter. The diamond choker round her neck. The silver sandals with jewelled toes. From the smooth legendary face, beautiful luminous cat's eyes stared out. Cut short, her blonde hair gleamed. Her skin was golden, her figure trim and pliant as a young girl's. She had been created a moment ago. There was no childhood, no past, nothing. I thought of a joke about the mortuaries in California; they supply human ashes to cannibals in the South Seas, who make them flesh by adding water. Instant people, like instant coffee. Julie Forbes, I decided, was an instant person. That must be her secret. Every few years she was reduced to ashes, then reconstituted in a new form. Different. Shining. Instant.

'So lovely,' breathed Mrs Lynch. 'So very lovely.'

Julie acknowledged this by raising her hand. A tender smile cracked Mrs Lynch's face, she became like a loyal subject rewarded by her sovereign after waiting below the palace balcony for hours.

Behind Julie walked a tiny black Pekinese puppy, and then Cliff with his handsome leonine head, tall, broad-shouldered, almost lumbering. She scooped up the Pekinese in her arms and held it out to us. 'This is Chen, I just bought her today. Did you know there are only six bitches of the original strain left in the world?'

Cliff didn't answer. He let Mrs Lynch wring his hand and sprawled into a chair. Massiveness made all his moods seem heroic. When he glanced round the room, it shrank to a wretched little cage. He gave me a wink, which Mrs Lynch noticed.

'We hear your last picture is just wonderful,' she said.

'It's just lousy.' Cliff gave the wry discontented smile that so often crept over his face, and at other times haunted it.

'That's not at all what they say at the studio,' said Mrs Lynch.

'Cliff's an artist!' There was a slight throb in Julie's voice. She sat on the end of the couch, near his chair. 'He has tremendously high standards. I understand that so well.'

'Nobody works harder than Julie,' said Mrs Lynch.

The butler came back. 'Get Timmy,' ordered Julie, then turned to Cliff. 'I want you to meet my son. He's a wonderful kid.'

'How old is he?' Cliff asked.

'Thirteen.' She smiled. 'Age is one thing I never lie about.

I'm forty-nine.' Hands stroked her neat, perfect hips. 'I was nineteen when I made my first picture, *Look Out, Sister!* You know we ran it at the studio the other night?'

'How did it look?'

'Great.' She gave a flicker of surprise. 'A lot of those early musicals were great. Have you seen *Hannah* yet?'

Cliff nodded.

'Well?' She was fingering her choker.

'You ought to be ashamed of yourself.'

Her face showed no reaction. 'Go on.'

'It's your usual shoddy work-out of the glamorous life-wrecker who gets it all her own way till the last reel.' Cliff lay back in the chair, closed his eyes for a moment. 'I didn't find it interesting at all.'

Mrs Lynch gasped, but Julie only picked a black puppy hair from the sleeve of her dress. 'What kind of movies interest you, Cliff?'

'Something with a bit of truth.'

She considered this, frowning slightly. 'Of course you're an artist. A very fine artist in my opinion. Frankly I don't get all this talk about truth, but then I left school in Atlantic City when I was fourteen, and that's all the formal education I had.'

'It's not a question of education.' Cliff sighed. 'If you have any idea of truth, it comes from the kind of human being you are.'

'Well, I'm a doll. Just a doll.' She found another puppy hair. 'And speaking as a human being, I believe *Hannah* has truth. Women like that exist, all over this country.'

'But you admire them, Julie. That's why your picture hasn't any truth. That's why it's repulsive.'

'Now that's a very strong word,' said Mrs Lynch.

With a rustle of silk, Julie got up and stood by the mantel-piece, looking down at us. 'You think I admire Hannah?

You must have slept through that picture. Have you forgotten the things my daughter says to me when she accuses me of snatching her boy-friend away? And what about the fire, when I lose the only man I ever really cared about – and all my property?'

'You feel sorry for her then,' Cliff said. 'You go noble. You make it like a crucifixion.'

'Don't talk that way, Cliff.' Her voice was soft and low. 'I *understand* her, don't you see? That woman has the driving force inside every woman – she wants to be loved. But she's rejected. That turns her bad. Poisons her. She gets jealous of other people who find love, and she wants to destroy *them*. The beautiful original drive in every woman is twisted in Hannah Kingdom by bitterness. It makes her hate. And it makes her very lonely.' Her eyes glistened. 'It's lonely to hate. And it's even lonelier to be hated. I believe –'

A tall, rather pale boy in a grey suit came into the room.

'Timmy!' she said. 'I want you to meet some lovely new friends of mine.'

The boy walked slowly towards us. He looked unfriendly and intelligent. The only point of resemblance to Julie lay in the eyes, dark and lustrous. He shook hands and said very formally: 'Hello, sir. Hello, sir.'

'Tell us what you've been doing today,' his mother said. 'It's vacation time,' she added, looking sharply at him. 'You can sit down, Timmy.'

He perched stiffly on the edge of a chair and pressed his lips together.

'Did you ride, Timmy?'

'Yes, I rode.'

'We have our own stables here,' Julie said. 'Timmy loves riding. What else did you do, Timmy?'

He glanced furtively at us, then stared at the floor.

'You must be able to give an account of your day, Timmy.

These friends of mine are extremely interested in what you've been doing.'

'So is your mother, in case you've forgotten,' Mrs Lynch said in a hard tone.

He didn't look at either of them. The tension was automatic; from the moment Timmy entered the room the three of them had seemed caught up in it. After a pause he said: 'I read a book.'

'What book?'

'*The Scarlet Letter,*' he answered in a mechanical tone, then looked as if he wished he hadn't.

'Did you finish it?'

'No.'

'How long did you read it for?'

'Couple of hours, I guess.'

'That's not very long. There's still most of the afternoon to account for. Did you swim?'

'Yes.'

'Can you turn somersaults in the water better now?'

'I'm improving.'

'That's good, Timmy.' His mother frowned. 'They made a movie of *The Scarlet Letter*, didn't they? What's it about?'

He looked at the floor again.

'Tell us what it's about,' said Mrs Lynch.

Timmy drummed his fingers on his knees. 'It's by Nathaniel Hawthorne. It's about a girl in New England.'

'Go on.' Julie's voice sounded remorseless, almost vengeful. Mrs Lynch shook out a cuff. 'Your mother wants to hear about the book, Timmy.'

'The girl gets into trouble.' He shifted in his chair. 'A priest helps her.'

'What kind of trouble does the girl get into?'

He hesitated. 'Steals money.'

'Why?'

'Um – she's poor and her child's starving.'

Julie gave us an anxious smile. 'You think Timmy should be reading books like that?'

'It's a classic,' I said.

'So's *Peyton Place*.' She looked grim. 'Timmy, I'd like to see that book you're reading.'

He didn't answer this, but got up. 'Nice to have met you, sir. Very pleased to have met you, sir.'

He started to leave the room. Watching him go, Julie called as he reached the door: 'I'll be up later!' He nodded over his shoulder and disappeared into the hall.

After a silence, Julie leaned towards us. 'What should I do with a kid that lies?'

Nobody answered.

'I know all about *The Scarlet Letter*: I saw the movie.'

'So did I,' said Mrs Lynch.

'That girl gets laid by a priest. Timmy shouldn't be reading stories like that and he shouldn't be lying about it. Don't you agree, Cliff?'

'He was embarrassed because we were here. What are you after that kid for, Julie?'

'I thought you believed in truth?' She didn't give him time to answer. 'I've done a lot for Timmy. I've wanted him to have a lot of things I didn't have, like formal education. But I don't like him using education to try and make a fool out of me.'

I said: 'I think I read *The Scarlet Letter* when I was thirteen.'

'But I want to protect Timmy.' She looked steadily at me. 'I don't let him see my movies.'

'None of them?'

'I don't think it's right for Timmy to – to see me doing some of the things I do in my movies.' Her voice trembled.

'Kids are very imaginative. He might confuse me with the characters I play.'

The butler announced dinner. Julie led us round the corner of the L, through an interior tropical garden with dwarf palms and cacti and a floodlit fountain. At the far end, a door led into the dining-room. We sat on tall high-backed chairs at a long antique table. A circle had been cut in the centre, underneath the glass that covered it a single water lily floated.

Mysteriously the butler had arrived before us through another door, and stood waiting with a napkin over his arm. We ate off thick silver platters, with the *hors-d'œuvre* we drank champagne and with the Beef Stroganoff claret out of blue crystal goblets. Julie beat a small Chinese gong to recall the butler as each course was finished. When we reached dessert, a tray of pears in flaming brandy, she got up. 'Excuse me, I must go and see Timmy.' Cliff and I were left alone with Mrs Lynch, who slowly crunched a pear, then beamed with satisfaction.

She said: 'It's really great to spend an evening just shooting the breeze.'

Cliff gave her a fairly hostile look. 'Why doesn't Julie like her son?'

'She adores that boy,' Mrs Lynch answered promptly, with no sign of surprise. 'If she seems a little strict, it's only because she's so anxious for Timmy to grow up fine and honest.'

From upstairs, we heard a door slam. I thought Julie shouted something.

'She believes the general trend of modern education is over-permissive,' Mrs Lynch continued. 'And how can you say she's wrong, with delinquency flooding our country? We must get back to the old-fashioned methods. In my opinion they're our only hope. Did you take the book away from him?' she asked as Julie returned to the room.

Julie nodded. She sat in her chair at the head of the table and said immediately: 'You know, in June nineteen twenty-seven a train stopped at down-town L.A., and out stepped a girl called Julia Katzander. She'd had her first bit in a Broadway show which folded after two months, but there was a talent scout in the audience one night and he got her a movie contract. There wasn't anyone from the studio to meet her at the station, and she didn't know a soul in the whole mad town. When she called the studio, no one had ever heard of her. She told them she had a contract, and they'd be paying her a hundred dollars a week from now on, so they'd better take some interest. Then she took a room in a hostel, and for three months just sat there drawing her pay cheque and telling the talent scout she wasn't going to let him lay her. Whenever she called the studio, they'd say not to worry and she'd be hearing from them soon. You know, that was a pretty hard time for a nineteen-year-old sales-man's daughter from Atlantic City.'

'You weren't so green,' Cliff said. 'You were a hatcheck girl in Chicago when you were sixteen, or is that just publicity?'

'Certainly not. All my publicity is true and I check it before it goes out. Furthermore, when I was seventeen I had my first pair of fishnet tights and toured the Middle West in a vaudeville show.'

She tapped the gong. Light caught a cluster of diamonds on her choker. 'I've kept those tights,' she said, 'and I'll tell you something. I *can still get into them.* Anyway, one day in September the studio sent for me and took a lot of leg pictures, and a producer liked them and Julia Katzander became Julie Forbes.'

'The rest is history,' said Mrs Lynch.

'What else did you do in those three months while you sat around and waited?' I asked.

'That's a sixty-four dollar question. I made a mistake, boy. I got married.' Mrs Lynch guffawed. 'He was a pianist in some bar on the Strip, and we thought we were terribly in love. Kid stuff, you know. His name was Jeff Storm, he's a famous bandleader now.' She glanced at Cliff. 'How many times have you been married?'

'Three,' he said.

She put a hand on his arm. 'We're even. If I ever marry again, it's got to be for real. Not that I regret anything – I've always got a kick out of marriage somehow, whether it's just plain old Experience or little Timmy – but after a time the whole business starts to sicken you. Do you still believe in marriage, Cliff?'

He shrugged. 'I don't believe in women.'

Her hand slid down to his wrist and held it for a moment. 'We're even again. I don't believe in men.'

After dinner, there was a good deal more conversation of this kind. If anyone ever organized a talking marathon, like the dancing and eating marathons, I am sure Julie would win it. She not only loves talking, but has an alert photographic memory that supplies her with plenty to talk about. Mainly about herself, for there is no single event of her life that she has forgotten. If she leaves something out, it is because she doesn't want to tell you. She has an extraordinary talent for remembering facts like the plots of movies and books, even the names of their characters, just as she learns the name of every technician on her set the first day of shooting, and never forgets any of them. Cliff didn't talk much, but drank steadily and listened with a kind of ironic inattention. Behind anything he said was always an implied contempt for Julie's films and Julie's talent. She responded like a piece of highly tensile steel, you could stretch it indefinitely and yet it still held brightly together. I began to wonder just how far you could bend this delicate steel.

Mrs Lynch sat like an umpire at a tennis match, eyes switching from Julie to Cliff and back again, occasionally calling out the score with a laugh or a jocular protest. About every twenty minutes the butler silently appeared and put another drink in our hands.

It must have been three o'clock when Julie suddenly lifted the sleeping Chen from her basket and settled her on her knees. Fondling the little black head, she began to talk about her next film. 'It's time I did something new. Of course when you're a big success in Hollywood, everyone wants you to go on doing the thing that made you a success. But I've always believed in looking ahead. If you don't there comes a moment – bingo! – when Joe Public looks you in the face and says Stop Boring The Hell Out Of Me. And you're on your way out. So last week I had lunch with J.B.,' she referred to the head of the studio, 'and I told him I'd bought a fabulous story for myself and I'd like to bring it to the studio and produce it. J.B.'s crazy about the idea naturally.'

'So you're going to be an actor-manager.' Cliff slumped in his chair. 'That's a mistake, stars should never produce themselves.'

'It's only making official something that's been unofficial for years.' She watched him for a moment, eyes glittering and soft. 'Cliff, would you like to do this picture with me?' He didn't answer. 'You're a great director, Cliff. And I need you for this one.'

'What's the story?' he asked, very casual.

'You can tell it in two words.' In a low important voice, she articulated them clearly : 'Lydia Thompson.'

He looked at her with weary disgust. 'Another woman with a twisted driving force?'

'No, Cliff. Oh no.' She paused. 'Lydia Thompson is absolutely *not* Hannah Kingdom.'

She got up, walked over to the fireplace and stood with her back to it, stretching out her arms to rest them on the mantel. 'I take it you've never heard of Lydia Thompson?' She glanced at each of us in turn. We shook our heads. 'Strange,' she said. 'Lydia Thompson was a very great woman. She brought burlesque to America.'

'And vice versa,' said Mrs Lynch.

Julie nodded. 'A hundred years ago, this woman pioneered a troupe of strippers from coast to coast. At one time,' she gave me a reproachful smile, 'the act was known as Lydia Thompson and her British Blondes.'

'No, really?' I said.

'It's authenticated. Some of the first strippers were British girls from nice Victorian families.'

'That starts to be interesting.' Cliff sat up. 'A lot of strippers are very respectable girls who get shocked by the morals of the theatre. I've met some.'

'I'll bet you have, but the important character in this story is Lydia Thompson, and not her Blondes.'

Mrs Lynch cleared her throat. 'You know why Julie wants to play Lydia Thompson? To pay off a debt of gratitude.' I had the impression she'd been preparing this speech. 'Lydia created the great vaudeville tradition out of which Julie came herself. One pioneer wants to salute another.'

'Are you handling publicity?' Cliff asked.

If she was aware of his irony, she didn't show it. 'I handle a good deal of Julie's personal publicity. And there's another thing. Julie will sing and dance again, and show off one of the greatest figures in the country.'

Cliff yawned and stood up. 'I'm tired, Julie. We'll talk tomorrow.'

'Good idea,' Julie said, with no trace of surprise or disappointment. 'Sleep on it and call me in the morning.'

As we went into the hall, she smiled. 'I want to show you something I designed myself.' Standing by the wall, she pressed a button. Part of the wall slid away, revealing a closet behind it. A light went on automatically.

The closet was like a small room. It contained an armchair and a low table inlaid with mother-of-pearl. In the chair sat a dressmaker's dummy, without limbs or head. Hung on it was a starched evening dress shirt and a bow-tie. A white silk top hat and a pair of dancing shoes stood in a glass case on the table. Against the back wall was pinned a pair of fishnet tights.

'Memories,' she said quietly. 'Don't touch them please. They're my costume from the chorus line in nineteen twenty-seven.'

She pressed the button again, the panel slid back. When she pressed another, a second panel opened in the centre of the wall. This time the closet had a black ceiling with silver paper stars. A gold statuette glittered on the top of a broken marble column.

'My Oscar.' She looked gravely at us and closed the panel.

'What's behind the third one?' Cliff asked. 'Your husbands?'

She laughed. 'I like your sense of humour, I really do. In fact, you're one of the most interesting men I've ever met.'

'Have you ever thought of this?' Mrs Lynch said to me in an undertone. 'It takes just a few seconds to get from the first closet to the second. Just a few seconds. But it took Julie twenty-five years. She always wanted an Oscar. She worked and waited, waited and worked. Every year she'd see it go to someone else. But she never gave up.' Her voice sank even lower. 'And when *The Big Angel* came along, Julie *knew*.

She said to me, This Is It. And It Was. She can be so patient, you know – provided she gets what she wants in the end.'

I nodded and smiled at Mrs Lynch, but felt myself shiver.

Outside, it was cool and crickets were singing everywhere. 'Well, good night,' I said to Cliff.

There was a stubborn, hopeful yet disconsolate look on his face. 'Let's meet back at my place,' he said. He walked slowly towards his car, shoulders sagging with tiredness.

I followed him, driving through the courtyard where the fountain still played, past the swimming pool with a streak of moonlight on the water, out of the gateway where the PRIVATE sign glimmered in phosphorescent letters. Below the twisting canyon road ranged the city, lights endlessly blinking.

Cliff rented a second-floor apartment in an eccentric Hollywood block built during the twenties in the style of a Chinese temple. It had a black tower shaped like a pyramid, and the patio was planted with pagoda trees. Now, one window framed a solitary square of light. When I came in, Cliff was lying half-asleep on the couch. On the wall behind him hung a Paul Klee.

Before he opened his eyes and said anything, I knew he'd decided to make the film with Julie. He'd want me to be the voice of his conscience, to protest. Then he could say: 'It's the last time. It's got to be. One more bad picture and I'll die ...' We usually had this conversation in the small hours, sitting in a kind of electric disorder: Cliff on the couch with the Klee, the Kirchner, the Derain and the Ben Shahn looking down on him, myself in a chair, the books spilling over from their shelves on to tables and floor, the cigarettes and the Scotch, the unread scripts lying around everywhere. Finally a gleam of dawn appeared low in the sky, and I went home.

When Cliff first came to Hollywood after working as an actor and a director in the New York theatre, he made a very honest realistic film about the everyday life of a young couple living in Brooklyn. It was a setting he knew well, since he grew up in it. The film was praised, but failed to show a profit. He made more films, not so interesting but commercially successful. He had three quick marriages, with a night-club singer, a fashion model, and an Italian girl studying anthropology at the University of Southern California. By the night-club singer, he had a son. After the divorce she went to live in New York, taking the child with her. Cliff hadn't seen either of them for twelve years. 'Somehow the time just slipped by. I'd like to know my son – but what do I say to him?'

When I first met Cliff in Europe, he was planning to leave Hollywood for ever; but the film he hoped to make in Italy didn't materialize, and he went back. He had an affair with an actress, made another film and bought the Derain. A year later I met him again in California. He seemed full of contradictions. He disliked the company of women but had a morose sexual appetite. He talked about the next film he was going to make, which would give him a chance to return to his favourite subject, young married life. (Later I saw the film; it had an unusual, subtle tenderness. No doubt of it, he could be a fine artist.) He mentioned that he had started going to a psycho-analyst, then changed his mind. I asked why. 'My only real problem,' he said, 'is Hollywood. If I can get out of this place, I'll be all right.' Yet I thought that, in spite of himself, Cliff had been in Hollywood long enough to become part of it. There was nowhere else he really knew. He wasn't resigned to making films in which he didn't believe, but went at them in a state of feverish anger. To many people in Hollywood, especially the young and struggling, he was generous. 'I feel responsible to them,' he used to say. The analyst had told him he was acting out guilt at neglecting his son.

In the end, with a taste for self-punishment that was sometimes theatrical, sometimes despairingly real, he always seemed to trap himself. To earn money, he had to make 'bad pictures'; as soon as he earned it, he spent it, and the struggle started over again.

'Of course, I'd rather have Monroe for this one.' He had opened his eyes, got up, and started for the kitchen to get a drink.

'Or a bit of truth?'

'Maybe I can give her that.'

One up to Julie, I thought. She has made Cliff see himself in a role, the director who will give her 'truth'. He had been an actor himself; a trace of the actor's egotism was showing through. 'She doesn't want truth,' I said. 'She wants to sing and dance. She wants to put across a new, salty Julie Forbes with a sense of humour.'

'If I thought there'd be nothing more in it than that, I'd walk out now.' He sounded indignant.

'Can you really think anything else?' The discussion was under way now. 'After years and years, you know how to look a straightforward commercial picture in the face.'

Frowning, he came out of the kitchen with a glass of Scotch. 'After years and years, I refuse ever to recognize that I'm making just another picture. I've an obligation to go beyond that.'

'Then don't work for Julie Forbes.'

'And don't be so smugly idealistic. I can't start out by telling myself this is going to be another bad picture. I have to say, I'll try and do something with it, against all the odds I'm going to make it real.'

'But why give yourself such odds?'

'I've a contract to work out.' Cliff lay down on the couch

again. 'The studio wants me to make a picture about a base-ball player who becomes a priest. I'll take Julie Forbes.'

'Well, if that's the only choice –'

'I don't know how it happens. Every time I make a pic-ture, I get eighty thousand dollars. I've never bought a house since I lived out here, but I'm always owing back taxes and payments to my son ...' He sighed. 'I guess the less satisfied you are in this place, the more you spend. I made two pictures just to be able to divorce my wives.'

'You haven't got a wife now.'

'I have to keep her divorced.'

The door from the bedroom opened and a girl came out, wearing a striped pyjama coat. She had a pretty, oval face, tousled fair hair and a sleepy smile.

'This is Tina,' said Cliff.

'Hello, nice to meet you,' I said.

'Hi.' She yawned. 'I'll make some coffee, would you like some coffee?'

Cliff watched her for a moment, then said : 'She's a very talented girl. You ought to hear her sing.' He closed his eyes again. When Tina came back with the coffee, he'd fallen asleep.

'Don't wake him,' she whispered. 'He's got to see his agent in about three hours, though he doesn't know it yet, Canning called while you were up at the palace.'

'What did he want?'

Tina shrugged. 'It was just another pitch for Julie Forbes. How important it is for Cliff to direct a really big star, and all that sort of thing. What's she *like*, anyway?'

'Oh,' I said. 'Well. In a word, she's ... dogged.'

'I get it.'

'Of course, Canning Wallace is Julie's agent, too,' I said. Through the window I could see dawn coming up.

At the studio, the wardrobe department is a line of separate huts. Outside each one hangs a sign with the title of a film in production. *Queen Burleycue*, said the most freshly-painted sign. *Producer, J. Forbes. Director, C. Harriston.*

In the main building they had given us offices. 292, Cliff. 294, Julie. 296, Carmen Lynch. I was back in 298, with the heavy faded curtains and the set designer's sketches on the wall. Cliff had offered me the job of rewriting the script with him and working as his assistant during the shooting; I said I was delighted to accept, being as broke as he in a more modest way. (And we hoped to work together, one day, on a film we really wanted to do.) Julie established Mrs Lynch as Assistant to the Producer, and would later import the hairdresser, make-up artist, costume supervisor and cameraman who had served on all her films during the last ten years. She redecorated her office, installing a television set and a small bar with an ice-box. In the ante-room, her secretary sat under a framed scroll on the wall, certifying that *The Crime of Hannah Kingdom* had been voted Picture of the Month by *Screentime* magazine.

The original script of *Queen Burleycue* was slightly better than either Cliff or I had expected. Of course it was dedicated to Julie, who appeared in almost every scene and performed a fantastic variety of musical numbers, from Lydia's famous *Sinbad the Sailor*, which outraged Chicago, to a *danse du ventre* in Dodge City. The main problem was that Lydia lived to the age of seventy-two and her last twenty years were unadventurous. To contract this stretch of time, the writer had used a very old device: as an old lady in London, Lydia tells the story of her life to a young girl who has just got a job in a burlesque troupe going to America. The reminiscences were mainly of the men she had loved, and who had loved her. A romance was invented with Willie

Edouin, the English comedian with whom Lydia went into partnership. He toured America with the Blondes and actually married one of them, called Ada. All the Blondes had respectable English names like Ada and Pauline. Lydia never really got over being rejected by Willie. She nobly concealed her love, was a bridesmaid at his wedding, toasted the happy pair, but afterwards she broke down and said she could never fall in love again. I did some research on Willie Edouin and found that he was ten years younger than Lydia, a grotesque little pantomimist whose greatest success was as Wishee-Washee in *Bluebeard*. It was decided to ignore this.

After Willie's marriage, Lydia thought only of her career. She swept the Blondes from triumph to triumph, and offers came in from all over the world. They toured India, where Lydia was seriously tempted by a maharajah. On the Australian tour, a young cattlehand fell desperately in love with her. She remained true to her secret sorrow and never married. At the end we came back to Lydia as an old lady, and discovered that the young girl was the daughter of Willie and Ada, both long since dead. ... In the intervals of all this, Lydia acted and sang with her troupe, and skirmished with the puritans. An elderly female dramatist denounced her in San Francisco. Lydia easily drew the crowds away from her play and closed it after two nights. In Chicago, the editor of the *Times* printed a headline, BAWDS AT THE OPERA HOUSE! Lydia waited in the street outside his office, then publicly thrashed him with a riding whip.

'There should be more comedy,' I said to Cliff. 'With English girls doing the hootchy-kootchy in the old West, there should be more comedy. And the old lady has to go.'

We went into Julie's office. She was sitting behind an enormous desk, looking at publicity photographs of herself. One of them showed her in tights and low-cut blouse, cracking a whip.

'How's that, Cliff?'

He glanced at it. 'Pretty good.'

'Really?' She looked at him very intently, lips parted. 'You really mean it?'

'Sure. You look great.'

She gave him a radiant smile. 'Thank you, Cliff. I thought we might use it for the posters.' She pressed a buzzer. A moment later, Mrs Lynch entered.

'The boys are coming up with some changes,' Julie said.

Mrs Lynch gave a nod and seated herself squarely on the couch. They listened to our suggestions. When we had finished, Julie tapped a pencil on the desk.

'Well, Carmen, what do you think?'

'I like the old lady.' Mrs Lynch cleared her throat. 'I think it's a good idea to start off the story with the audience not knowing this sweet old girl is a retired burlesque queen.'

'They'll know it anyway,' Cliff said impatiently. 'They'll know what the film's about.'

Still tapping the pencil, Julie considered this. Then she said: 'I was looking forward to playing the old lady. I've never played an old lady. But you're an artist, Cliff, and if you're against it, that's good enough for me.'

'I'm totally against it,' Cliff said, with a glance at Mrs Lynch. 'It was always a stupid idea.'

'Then how do we end the show?' She looked at her shoes. 'There's no ending any more.'

'With Lydia's farewell performance,' I suggested.

Julie frowned. 'What makes her give up?'

'She's getting too ...' I broke off. 'She decides to try something new,' I said. 'She breaks into the legitimate theatre.'

There was a silence.

'And we leave her on the brink of a great dramatic career.'

'Well, Carmen, what do you think?'

'It's not bad,' Mrs Lynch said. 'But I'd like to *see* you as a great dramatic actress. Suppose we end it, not with the farewell performance, but with the opening night of you in *Camille* or something?'

'I like that, Carmen. But not *Camille*. We'll make the situation in the play just like the situation in real life with Willie. And all the critics will say Lydia played it from the heart.' She glanced at her watch, got up. 'I'm late for a fitting.' In the doorway she turned back. 'Oh, Cliff! I've got a table at the Grove tonight, will you be my date?'

Julie's white Lincoln was parked outside the main building. As I went out, I saw Timmy sitting in the front seat. He waved to me.

'Hello,' I said. 'What are you doing here?'

'Carmen picked me up from school, but she had to come back because my mother's got an interview with some magazine, and she wanted Carmen to help her give out the stuff.'

'And then she's going out,' I said. 'To the Coconut Grove.'

'I know. I'll be having dinner with Carmen.'

'Mrs Lynch is almost like one of the family, isn't she?'

He smiled faintly. 'Crazy sort of family.' Then, with no change of expression: 'Have they told you about my running away yet?' I shook my head. 'They usually like to tell people about my running away, and that kind of thing. Anything *bad*.' Impassive, he gazed out of the windshield.

'Your mother said you were a wonderful kid.'

'Oh, sometimes she says that first.' His eyes flickered. 'But she'd better be careful.'

'What do you mean, Timmy?'

He turned to look at me. A flat, terrible hatred came into his voice. 'She'd better be careful, that's all.' I didn't know what to say, but then he smiled again and touched my arm. 'But you could be my friend if you wanted to.'

'I'd like to.'

'I can get away and we can talk somewhere.'

'All right.'

He stretched out his hand. 'Shake.'

We shook hands.

'I'll tell you about the last time I ran away. I went downtown and stayed there all night, just wandering around the streets. Then a cop picked me up and took me home. I wanted her to feel worried and think maybe I was dead, but she was just angry and told me how ungrateful I was. If she could just admit ...' He trembled slightly. 'Well, if she could only just admit ... you know, one day she took me to see a movie she'd made. It was the only time. In the middle of it she pulled my arm and yanked me out of the theatre, because there was a scene coming up she thought I shouldn't see.' He contorted his face into an impression of Julie anxious and unhappy. 'My Timmy must never see anything bad happen to me,' he said in a hard falsetto voice. 'He mustn't think I'm bad or I get killed.' A cold, thoughtful pause. 'But I know the kind of thing she does. I know who she takes to The Pool House. I can see her car come back at night from my bedroom window.'

He glanced into the driving mirror, and his eyes flickered. 'Carmen's coming. I'll call you.'

While Julie and Cliff were at the Coconut Grove that night, and Timmy was having dinner with Mrs Lynch at the long antique table, I went to see *The Crime of Hannah Kingdom*.

I thought Julie must have found it a satisfying farewell to the period she now considered over. Near the end of the story, Hannah remarked: 'I came from nothing and now I own this lousy town.' She meant that she owned the factory which employed most of its inhabitants. In the last reel her jealous daughter set fire to it, her lover was burned to death and Hannah walked through blackened ruins in a fur coat. Smoke enfolded her distant figure as the great chimney with KINGDOM painted on it crumbled and fell.

Coming out of the theatre into Hollywood Boulevard, I saw the usual groups of adolescents who stand on the sidewalks or sit on the bus company's benches in twos and threes, mysteriously waiting in the small hours. Tonight, with their eager but unfriendly eyes, several of them reminded me of Timmy. They chewed gum and put their thumbs over the hip pockets of their jeans, posture to challenge boredom and impatience. They stared long and hard at every car that passed, and didn't want to go home.

In the corridor outside my office next morning, I met Mrs Lynch. She nodded and walked past me, then turned back.

'Excuse me . . .'

She'd never said that before. I looked at her in surprise.

'There's something I should warn you about.'

We were at the door to my office. I unlocked it, and she followed me inside.

'Yes?'

'Timmy. I saw you talking to him in the car yesterday. He's a wonderful kid, you know, but he has his problems. One of them is telling the truth.' Noticing that the date on the leaf of my desk calendar was two weeks old, she gave a genial smile. 'You're a little behind the times, my boy.' But her eyes were still beady as she began to tear off fourteen leaves, very deliberately, one by one. 'If Timmy said anything about his mother, it probably wasn't true.'

'He only said one thing. He said it twice, as a matter of fact.' I paused. '*She'd better be careful.*'

I watched Mrs Lynch. As she tore each leaf from the calendar, she crumpled it into a little ball and dropped it in the wastebasket. After I spoke, her hand hesitated for a moment in mid-air, then threw away another ball of paper.

'Oh, is that all? I expect you guessed Timmy says that when he's feeling neglected. It means he'll try and run away again if he doesn't get more attention. He thinks his mother's the most lovely person in the world, but he's terribly jealous of all the time she has to give to other people.' Mrs Lynch tore off the last leaf. 'There. Now you're up to date.'

Every Sunday, twenty or thirty people came round to Cliff's apartment. They started arriving at about three o'clock and some of them stayed until the small hours. They were not celebrities, but mainly unknown young actors, writers, and musicians. They came to talk about life and art and the movies, sometimes to perform a work they'd written, and to play records: Bach, Beethoven, twelve-tone, jazz. Cliff lay back in a chair with a glass of Scotch in his hand and talked about Hollywood. He advised everyone to get out of it. Meanwhile, he would do what he could to help these young people get jobs. He was a combination of judge, unofficial agent and father-confessor to them all. Much of the advice he gave them was good, but when he talked about himself, the melancholy smile came over his face.

Some of the married couples brought their children. They played games and looked at television in the bedroom. When they grew tired, they would stretch out on the double bed, or on piles of cushions on the floor, and sleep right through Schoenberg and Count Basie. During the evening, Tina cooked spaghetti or chicken.

Cliff called it his 'Sundays'. After we'd been working on the script for nearly a month, he invited Julie to one of them. She arrived about five o'clock, with Timmy. Silence fell as they came into the room. She wore a dress of brilliant emerald taffeta. Among jeans and sweat shirts she sat on a couch, and somebody put a Beethoven quartet on the record-player. Ignoring the other children, who were younger than he, Timmy smiled faintly at me and then wandered out to the veranda. With his back to us all he sat in a wicker chair, looking down at the view of the city.

During the first movement of the quartet, Julie watched the people in the room. She was like a tiger waiting, with infinite patience, to spring. Reconnoitred Tina. Fastened her brilliant eyes on Cliff. Granted me a fixed gracious smile. At such moments she could be almost enigmatic. Coming here, I supposed, was all part of the 'new' Julie Forbes with her desire to change, to adapt herself. When she went to New York to watch classes at the Actors' Studio, declining to do an improvization but saying it was all fascinating, it must have been rather like this. You couldn't believe in Julie changing. She was immutable. Playing a new character was only like putting on a new set of clothes, hand-tailored and immaculately fitted; skirts grew longer and shorter as Julie moved from comedy to melodrama and back again.

When the second movement started, Tina went into the kitchen. Julie moved to sit on the arm of Cliff's chair. 'That's a very pretty little girl. Can she act?' Cliff nodded. 'Someone told me she can sing and dance, too.' Cliff nodded again. 'Maybe she could play one of the Blondes?'

Cliff sat up. 'I was going to talk to you about that.'

'I knew you were.' Her eyes glittered. 'She's too young for Ada, of course, but,' looking across at me, 'don't you think she's right for Pauline?'

'Yes,' I said, thinking this was really quite clever of her.

'Then let's have her up for a reading next week.'

Cliff shook his head. 'I never cast an actor from a reading.'

'Well, if you can convince me some other way –'

'Just talk to her. Get an idea of her personality. You can take my word on her talent.'

Smiling, she laid her hand on his arm. 'For what, boy?'

Cliff didn't answer, but closed his eyes. He said: 'This slow movement is the greatest part of the whole quartet. Just listen to it, Julie.'

'Yeah, it's beautiful. Is Beethoven your favourite?'

'One of them.'

'Mine, too.' She appeared to listen for a moment. 'But if you want her to play that part, Cliff, I think she ought to give a reading.'

He sighed. 'When they put you in *Look Out, Sister!*, was that on account of a reading?'

'No, but they'd seen me in New York.'

'Then we'll run a picture in which Tina does a bit.'

Julie got up from the arm of the chair. 'I swear he's the most darned obstinate guy in the whole world,' she said to me on her way back to the couch.

The third movement began. I noticed Timmy signalling to me from the veranda.

'Like me to tell you something?' he asked with a crooked smile. 'It's important.'

'Then go ahead, Timmy.'

He looked mysterious. 'There's a friend of yours mixed up in it.'

'Who?'

'Mr Harriston.' He paused. 'She's stuck on him.'

'I don't believe you,' I said automatically.

'It's true. She's real stuck on him, but she's not getting anywhere.' He sounded satisfied.

I glanced back into the room. Cliff was listening to the scherzo. Smoking a cigarette, Julie rested her head against the back of the couch.

'How do you know?' I said.

'I've seen things.'

'What?'

'Last week she invited him over to the pool. I hid in the guest-house and watched them all afternoon. She was always – always touching him, you know, and then she tried to play games in the water.'

'Is that all?'

'No. I heard her talking to Carmen. She said something about him holding out on her. And Carmen told her about the girl – you know, Tina. She hadn't heard about Tina.' He giggled. 'And she didn't like it.'

'Well, maybe,' I said, not sounding interested and knowing it was true. The first time Julie had asked Cliff to take her to a night-club, she said: 'I like to get to know my directors as human beings. That's tremendously important for people working together.' I had assumed that Julie was exercising her public charm and Cliff, with his need for eighty thousand dollars and his bitter conscience, was struggling to be charmed. But she asked him out too often. In the pictures of them both together, there was something too eager and submissive in the way Julie kept her hand on Cliff's arm or smiled up at him with her welcoming mouth. This afternoon, her pretence of interest in Tina must have been a deliberate public gesture, making it clear they were just two professionals, keeping their minds on work.

'It's nice of you to take such an interest in Timmy.'

Her voice startled me. She was standing at the entrance to the veranda.

'He's an interesting boy,' I said.

'Imaginative, too. Come along, Timmy, we're going home.'

On her way out, she said to Tina: 'We're going to run your picture tomorrow, dear.'

'I don't know how much it'll tell you,' Tina said. 'I'm only on the screen three minutes.'

'Well, Cliff believes in you. And I believe in Cliff.' Her hand rested on Timmy's shoulder. 'He's such a wonderful person. You can imagine how important this partnership is going to be for both of us.'

Tina's eyes flickered, then she smiled. 'Yes, that's just what Canning Wallace said.'

We saw Tina's film next afternoon. She played a brief scene and sang a light romantic duet with the leading man.

'She's good,' Julie said. 'Pretty good, Cliff.'

Mrs Lynch cleared her throat. 'Pretty good figure, too. Though maybe a little *modern*. You think she can carry off the costumes?'

'That's an interesting point. What do you think, Cliff?'

He looked at Mrs Lynch. 'Would you describe to me exactly how women's figures have changed since eighteen sixty-four?'

'They used to be fuller.' Mrs Lynch sounded rather nostalgic.

'Julie, you'll have to put on weight.'

She laughed. 'He's got you there, Carmen.'

'It's not just physical.' Mrs Lynch was unruffled. 'She's got a modern quality about her altogether.'

'Well, I'll talk it over with J.B.,' Julie said quickly. 'I'd like to use Tina, but between ourselves, *he's* got a candidate for Pauline. Some little chick he's discovered and is going to sign up.'

'When did he tell you this?' Cliff asked.

'About a week ago.'

'Why didn't you tell me?'

She looked surprised. 'I didn't think it was important. The girl's no good. And remember what you told me once, Cliff?'

She paused. 'A producer shouldn't bother the director with that kind of front-office battle. A producer should take it off the director's shoulders and leave him free to *create*.'

'You see how thoughtful she is,' said Mrs Lynch.

Julie nodded. 'I'll tell J.B., maybe we can find a spot for his chick somewhere else. And talking of J.B., he called me in just before we went over to look at Tina's picture. The studio wants us to start shooting a week earlier. I told him we could – subject to your approval, of course, Cliff. We can start with the location scenes in Missouri.'

'That's okay,' Cliff said.

'I fought another battle for you there. I told J.B. how important the location scenes were going to be, and I got you a couple of extra shooting days for them.'

'Fabulous,' said Mrs Lynch.

The script of *Queen Burleycue* lay on Julie's desk. She drummed her fingers on the red cover. 'I went through it very carefully last night,' she said. 'Carmen read Willie, and we tried out some of the scenes together. Everything's great, except for one scene – when I horsewhip that editor in Chicago.' She got up, began pacing the room in front of us. 'That moment is very important to me, Cliff, and I think we should give it a little more.'

'She's got a wonderful idea for this,' said Mrs Lynch.

Julie stopped pacing the room and stood directly in front of Cliff. 'I see this editor as more than a guy who hated sex. He hated it,' she paused, 'because he couldn't get it.'

Cliff stared at her. 'Why couldn't he get it?'

'He was ugly,' she answered at once. 'He was really attracted to Lydia, but he couldn't admit it to himself – maybe he'd been rejected before by a beautiful woman, he was frightened of rejection, so he twisted this attraction into hate.'

'It was his only way of getting even with a beautiful woman,' said Mrs Lynch.

There was a silence.

'In that case, he probably enjoyed being whipped by Lydia,' I suggested.

'No, that's perverted,' said Mrs Lynch.

'And'll never get past the censor.' Julie chuckled. 'It's a pity. But we can do it this way. We can show this editor, while I'm doing *Sinbad the Sailor*, never taking his eyes off me, trying to get a better look, licking his lips and all that kind of thing. So when he attacks me in the paper, we know he's a hypocrite.'

'Do we have to be so obvious?' Cliff asked.

'Well, it needs something. Let's have dinner tonight and talk it over.'

He shook his head. 'I'm busy tonight.'

Julie gave a little shrug of annoyance. 'This is important, Cliff.'

'We'll work something out.'

'But I want to talk about it.' There was a sharp edge on her voice. 'Can't you change your plans?'

'Can't we have a conference here tomorrow?'

'I'm busy tomorrow. I'm busy every day this week.' She softened. 'You know how it is, when you get near the shooting date.'

After a pause, Cliff said: 'All right.'

She smiled. 'Eight o'clock?' As Cliff nodded and started to go out of the room, she said suddenly: 'Oh, I almost forgot something!' Opening a drawer in her desk, she took out a record album. Her voice throbbed slightly. 'I wanted to thank you for yesterday afternoon, Cliff.'

She put the album in his hands. It was a complete set of Beethoven's symphonies.

Next morning I came to the studio about half an hour late. Cliff hadn't arrived, and Julie wasn't in her office. Cliff's secretary told me that Tina had telephoned to say he wasn't feeling well but would come in during the afternoon. At that moment, Mrs Lynch entered the office with an envelope in her hand. Her greeting to me was extremely cold. She gave the envelope to Cliff's secretary and went out again. It was marked, *memo from Julie Forbes*.

The secretary wondered if she should let Cliff know about this, but decided not. Tina had said he was sleeping and didn't want to be disturbed.

I went into my office, swivelled in my chair, and felt uneasy. Something wasn't right. The atmosphere was lifeless but menacing, as before a storm.

'Where's Miss Forbes?' I asked Julie's secretary.

'In conference with J.B. She'll be tied up most of the day.'

There was nothing for me to do. I read the papers, and wrote a letter. Towards lunchtime, Cliff's secretary received another envelope containing a memorandum. This time it was delivered by an office messenger boy. I wanted to open it, but Cliff's secretary wouldn't let me. However, she telephoned Cliff again and said when Tina answered: 'I thought Mr Harriston would like to know there are two memos from Miss Forbes waiting for him.' Tina repeated that he was sleeping, and she didn't want to disturb him.

Julie didn't appear in the commissary for lunch. Neither did Mrs Lynch. From my office window, I saw them both coming back together at about two o'clock. But Julie didn't go to her office. Her secretary said she'd gone back into conference with J.B.

Shortly afterwards, another memorandum arrived for Cliff.

By now I was fairly nervous, and went for a walk. I drank half a bottle of Coca-Cola, then went to the barber's shop and had my hair cut.

Walking back to my office, I stopped to buy another newspaper at the rack. The cop said:

'Did you see about Canning Wallace's son?'

I shook my head.

'It's in all the late editions. That crazy kid's in trouble again, crashed his car, some girl with him got hurt.'

'Oh,' I said.

'Mr Wallace gave that boy every advantage. Do you know Mr Wallace?'

'No,' I said.

'He's a fine man.' The cop yawned. 'They should give that boy the cat.'

Maybe, I thought, there was an augury in the stars of just how bad today was going to be. Back in my office, I turned to the horoscope page. Under my sign, it advised: *If you concentrate, you can improve your professional standing. P.M. good for romance.*

The door opened and Mrs Lynch came in. 'Here's the rewrite of that scene with the editor watching Lydia's act in Chicago.' She laid some sheets of paper on my desk.

I stared at her. 'What rewrite?'

'A rewrite the way Julie wants it.' Mrs Lynch sounded calmly matter-of-fact.

'Who wrote it?'

She backed towards the door. 'It was written this morning.'

'Does Cliff know about it?'

'There's a copy on his desk.' She went out, closing the door behind her .

I telephoned Cliff. He'd just left for the studio, Tina said. Waiting, I scanned the newspaper story on Canning Wallace's son. There was a photograph of him, dishevelled and weeping, between two police officers.

Ten minutes later Cliff came in, looking almost as

desperate as Wallace in the photograph. He held out the three memos with a trembling hand. The first said, Tina was unsuitable for the part of Pauline, and the young actress recommended by J.B. had been engaged for it. The second said, all location shooting on the film had been cancelled. The third said, 'You are requested to observe the official studio hours, which are from 9 a.m. to 5.30 p.m.' All were signed, *Julie Forbes.*

'Have you talked to her?' I said.

Cliff's face was grey. 'Not since last night. She's still with J.B.'

'What on earth's going on?'

Before he could answer, my telephone rang. 'Is Mr Harriston in your office?' It was Julie's secretary.

'Yes,' I said.

'Miss Forbes is back now. She'd like to see you both immediately.'

Cliff rushed into her office ahead of me. Towering over her, he slammed the memos on her desk. She was reading the new scene that Mrs Lynch had distributed, and didn't look up. 'Carmen, this is perfect.' Mrs Lynch gave a gratified nod from the couch.

'What does this mean?' Cliff's fist hit the desk again.

Julie looked up slowly, her face steely bright. 'Exactly what it says.'

For a moment I thought Cliff would hit her. He took a step nearer her, then seized the telephone.

'And J.B.'s with me all the way,' Julie said. As he put it down, she jerked her thumb towards the bar. 'Better get yourself a drink, boy.'

As Cliff did so, Julie exchanged a glance with Mrs Lynch, then leaned back in her chair. 'When I produce my own picture, Cliff, I have to take a very hard decision as a human being.' She lit a cigarette and blew smoke towards the ceiling. 'I have a little-girl-head, you see, which is my love-head, and I have a little-boy-head which is my money-head. I have to take off my little-girl-head now. I have to put it in a safe deposit box until the picture's over. And I have to put on my little-boy-head, which is always telling me to think about a certain important investment called Lydia Thompson.' She paused. 'My little-boy-head is very tough.'

'Both your heads are tough,' Cliff said from the bar.

'But you don't want me to put my little-girl-head back on, do you, Cliff?'

He shook his head almost convulsively. 'You just keep your mind on the picture, and tell me why your little-boy-head cancelled the locations.'

'We have to cut down on the budget.'

'Why didn't you consult me first?'

'I decided to take J.B.'s advice. You may be an artist, Cliff, but J.B.'s the businessman around here. Anyway people won't come to see this picture for Cliff Harriston's location work. They'll come to see *me*, and they'll see me on the back lot and they won't know the difference.'

Thunderous, Cliff advanced on her. 'I cannot make a picture under these conditions! I'm handed actors I've never even seen, the script is rewritten without consulting me –'

'You want to try and get out of it?' Julie cut in sharply. 'Then talk to J.B. and find out how much it'll cost you.' With a sudden sinuous movement she leaned forward in her chair, arching her back like a snake. 'And here's something else. Your last picture hasn't turned out so well. Everyone, J.B. included, thinks it's a dog. The studio's worried about you, Cliff. Now I hate to hear everyone talking this way, because I believe in you. Maybe I'm taking a risk, but I want to help you.' She gave a little smile. 'And believe me, you need my help.'

He didn't say anything, but swallowed his drink. The ice

rattled in the glass. Then Mrs Lynch stood up. 'Julie, we should have been in the music department twenty minutes ago, hearing your theme song!'

We were sitting in a bar, a long dark tunnel with booths and heavily shaded table lamps and I knew we were going to get drunk.

'Cliff,' I said, 'for God's sake tell me what happened last night.'

He looked very tired. Hands were clasped together in his lap, shoulders massively hunched. 'You know those hurricanes that usually come in from the Florida coast? The radio gives out a bulletin on them every hour – Hurricane Hannah is heading for Tennessee, Hurricane Hannah switches course, she's going to hit Kentucky....' He signalled to the waiter for another round of drinks. 'Sooner or later, I knew Julie was going to hit me. I thought I could steer her off, I took her seriously as an actress, tried to make her see where she was dishonest and phoney ... And she played along with it, you saw her do that.'

I nodded. 'But she was only playing.'

'Of course. Last night I tried to talk about the script, but she didn't want to. For six hours she explained she was lonely. She pitied herself, she pitied me, she cursed the whole wide world. We drank a lot. Around four in the morning she wanted to swim in the pool.'

'Storm warning,' I said.

The waiter brought our drinks. Cliff ordered another round. 'I told her I was going home. That did it. She begged, she shouted, she put her arms round me, she slapped me. I told her she had a compulsive desire to get her directors into the bedroom. I asked, was it power? – or vanity? – or what? She slapped me again. Then I made a crack about the pool probably being empty, anyway. She told me to get out.'

'Where was the palace eunuch all this time?' I asked.

'Carmen? Confined to quarters, I guess.'

'And Timmy probably watching from his bedroom window,' I said. 'It's like an oriental court, you know, with everybody spying on everybody else.'

'Make them all doubles now!' Cliff called to the waiter. 'When I was driving home,' he went on, 'I thought it was like Hannah Kingdom. I'd twisted her beautiful original drive.'

'The more it's twisted, the stronger it gets.'

He gave a long sigh. 'It'll ruin the picture.'

'Oh no,' I said. 'She'll give the picture everything it needs from her point of view, just as she's always done. All she wants to ruin is you.'

We drank in silence, then Cliff got up. 'I'm going to call Canning Wallace.'

'Well, he has his problems too.' Watching Cliff disappear down the tunnel, I thought: *P.M. good for getting drunk, and nothing else.* He was away for a long time. I had another Scotch, and began to feel euphoric. Down the tunnel, a Negro started to play silky blues on a piano I could hardly see.

'First of all, I got Canning's wife.' Cliff had come back. 'She was crying, and said what had they done to deserve it. Then I got Canning, who talked like Julie. I've got to make a success of this picture, I need it. Can't I play along? I told him to come right out and admit he was backing his more important client. He said I sounded drunk, and I hung up.'

'It feels like the whole town's falling down tonight,' I remarked in a strangely contented voice. 'Like Hannah Kingdom's blasted chimney.'

Outside the stage on the day we began shooting *Every Inch a Lady*, as the story of Lydia Thompson was now

called, a sign announced CLOSED SET. POSITIVELY NO
VISITORS. The studio doesn't often close a set; but sometimes a star or director insists he cannot work in the presence of strangers, sometimes the publicity department decides that a cloak of secrecy is the best way to arouse interest
in a new film. No reason was given for closing this set,
though a columnist wrote that when he asked for one, the
reply came in a word: *Personal.*

Shooting was scheduled for forty days. Eight weeks.
Nearly four hundred hours, when you counted the overtime.
In prospect the routine looked unbearable. In practice it had
a soothing, almost anaesthetizing effect. Partly this was due
to Julie. Regulated as time itself, she was a source of power,
energy, habitual purpose. When she entered the brightly-lit
set, it was as if somebody stepped up the current. From every
side the lights glared white-hot.

I had never watched her work before. Most of it was
galvanic concentration, for she had very little natural talent.
The imaginative stroke, the sudden passionate instinct, were
never hers. Acting was hard labour, like coal-mining or road-
mending. After thirty years, she still found it difficult to
remember lines. She went over and over them with Mrs
Lynch in a half-dark corner of the stage. Before each take
she looked tense and grim, paced up and down in front of the
camera, snapping her fingers with a sound as hard as castanets. When Cliff called 'Action!' it was like an electric
shock. In a second all tension disappeared; she was precise,
confident, and extraordinarily young.

When she fluffed a line in the middle of a take, she stopped
at once and cursed loudly. Then she paced up and down a
few steps, snapped her fingers and glittered into action once
more. Watching her, I found dialogue and movements became ritual abstractions, stripped of meaning. Sometimes the
machine worked perfectly, sometimes it stopped.

LYDIA [*after a pause*] : You're in love with Ada, aren't
   you? ...

WILLIE: How did you know?

LYDIA: The night they threw that party for us in New
   York, you didn't dance with anyone except Ada. Didn't
   look at anyone. When I spoke to you, you heard what I
   was saying –

'Damn !' Julie waves at the camera, as if rubbing out a line
of chalk on a blackboard. ' "You *hardly* heard what I was
saying." ' Cliff calls, 'Cut it !' Lights are switched off. Out
of the darkness surrounding the set, Mrs Lynch appears with
a script. ' "You *hardly* heard what I was saying ... " ' The
fingers snap. Her make-up man runs up with a powder puff
and mirror.

The lights come on again. 'Ready, Julie?' She scans herself
in the mirror, nods. 'It's a very difficult line,' Mrs Lynch
says. The cameraman glances at her. 'Be a good girl, Carmen, and take your shadow away.'

LYDIA [*after a pause*] : You're in love with Ada, aren't
   you? ...

Portable dressing-rooms stood at the side of the stage.
Cliff's and Julie's were next to each other, the door to
Cliff's was usually closed but Julie liked to keep her door
open. Waiting between scenes, she often played records.
You Make Me Feel so Young and *I Get a Kick Out of You*,
her favourite tunes, drifted across the murk of different sets
and photographic backings, up to the high scaffolding of
lights.

The technicians adored her. She knew all their names, of
course. 'Good morning, Chuck – how's your lovely wife?'
She told dirty jokes to the camera crew and sometimes
played poker with them. With Cliff, she was quietly

professional, listened intently to his suggestions, always thanked him. 'That's really very helpful.' 'I was worried about that, Cliff, but now you've set me straight.' The dramas occurred in her portable dressing-room, and then the phonograph was silent and the door closed. 'We have to do something about that scene, Julie. Every time I look at those new lines, I want to throw up.' She gives a regretful smile. 'J.B.'s approved them, you know.' 'I'll talk to him.' 'You can talk to him all you want, but if I tell him I want those lines to stay, they'll stay. . . .'

They stayed. Occasionally, signs of conflict came out into the open. One morning a note was pinned to the door of Cliff's dressing-room:

Dear Cliff, you should be more attentive to Wardrobe Dept. I asked you to okay Diane's new costume because I was too busy. But when we started shooting yesterday, we wasted nearly an hour because it was too bright in relation to mine. *This is important*. Please concentrate more on your work, like

JULIE FORBES

Two outsiders were admitted to the closed set. One day I saw a tall thin-faced man with cropped grey hair talking to Julie outside her dressing-room. He wore a dark suit with protruding white cuffs, white silk shirt, silk tie and diamond clasp, black suede shoes. Cliff came over and they shook hands. Standing between them, Julie linked an arm with each of theirs, and a stills man took a photograph. 'I hear J.B.'s crazy about the dailies,' the visitor said. Julie nodded. 'Everything's just great now.' He turned to Cliff. 'You happy too?' 'As a sandboy, Canning.'

About half-way through shooting, a rather stout middle-aged man in spectacles came to see Julie for the first time. After that, he came almost every day. Cliff and I were introduced to him, but we spoke very little. He was a vitamin manufacturer called Dave Roeling II. He had a nervous blink and a genial smile. Whenever he saw Cliff, he said, 'Hi, D. W. Griffith!' and laughed.

A columnist predicted that Julie would marry him.

A Monday morning. Outside the offices of the Chicago *Times*, a carriage draws up. Lydia opens the door, steps down to the sidewalk. She is draped in a long rich crimson cloak. You can just see the toes of her little yellow boots. She waits. Some passers-by recognize her. A crowd forms. Behind the crowd, another crowd: Cliff in a sweat shirt near the camera, the silent crew, Mrs Lynch and Dave Roeling II on the sidelines. The editor, plump and rather dandified, comes out into the street. Cliff makes a rapid signal, the camera moves forward. Throwing back her cloak, Lydia confronts him. She wears her theatre costume, tights, a middy blouse, high-heeled cross-laced yellow boots, and carries a long embroidered whip. The crowd gasps. The editor takes a step back, but she brings down the whip on his shoulders. He starts to run. Lydia follows, cracking him across the buttocks. He falls into the gutter. Suddenly whistles are blowing, a squad of police breaks through the crowd. They seize Lydia.

The cameraman shakes his head. 'When he fell in the gutter, we lost him. He has to fall at least two feet earlier.'

'Okay, give him another mark and let's go again.'

Two hours later, Cliff and I had gone off the lot for lunch and were sitting in a bar. He ordered another Scotch and said: 'I was going through some papers at home yesterday and I found a poem. Poem by Cliff Harriston aged fourteen, very lonely and Thomas Wolfey, not really any good but it had a sort of private reality.' The wry smile crept over his face. 'I wanted to find that reality again, and I tried to look back down a long long time. All I saw was a line that got thinner and thinner. I couldn't get back to fourteen, I could hardly get back further than the day I came to this place. When I tried, it didn't mean anything. Somehow, it . . . ' His eye narrowed, as if he were trying to read a sign from a great distance, then he shook his head. '*It wasn't as real as Julie Forbes.*'

He finished his drink, put down the glass with a thud on the table. The barman came over with a faint, hateful smile. 'Same again, Mr Harriston?'

Cliff nodded. 'I took off in the car, drove down to the ocean, then along the highway, turned into the mountains, said to myself all the way – *trees. Look, the ocean. Sky. They're still here, why aren't you?* It began to sound like a poem aged fourteen. I turned back, stopped at a bar, had a few drinks, then called up some friends and they came over for cards.' The barman brought his drink. 'I lost three hundred dollars.'

A few minutes before lunchtime next day, I passed Julie's dressing-room. She was sitting on the steps in tights and blouse and a pair of soft slippers instead of the boots, examining photographs of herself.

'Hello!' She seemed in a very good humour. 'You busy?'

'No,' I said. 'They're just doing a close-up of the editor getting thwacked.'

'Come inside for a moment.'

Dave Roeling II sat on the couch. He blinked nervously behind his spectacles, sweat pricked out his forehead. He had undone the top button of his shirt and a spotted red and white bow-tie hung down the front.

Pulling at one end of the bow-tie, Julie perched on his knee. 'Shall I tell him?'

'Why him?' asked Roeling.

She gave the tie another pull. Her eyes gleamed. 'I just want to tell somebody.'

'Well, I guess it's no secret.' He tried to pull the tie away. Julie held on to it. 'Dave's asked me to marry him. Do you think I should?'

'Oh, honey,' he protested.

'Do you want to?' I asked.

'Sure. I'm crazy about him.' She got the tie away and started twisting it round her fingers. 'And he's very rich.'

'Aren't *you*?' I said.

Roeling blinked. 'She's just making a joke of it, to disguise her real emotions. But I think,' he put his hand on her thigh, 'she ought to come right out and say she loves me.'

'Vitamin king, I love you.' Julie touched his cheek. 'Let me tie your tie.'

'I don't know what's gotten into her this morning,' Roeling said. 'She's as full of mischief as a child. People always ask me how I stand her temperament. I tell them it's not temperament, it's just her mask to the world. Hi, D. W. Griffith !' he said as Cliff came up.

Julie put her arms round Roeling's neck and began to knot his tie. 'Oh Cliff, I looked at those dailies again with J.B. this morning, and he agrees we need that extra close-up of me.' Her voice was briskly professional, like her hands with the tie. 'I told him you didn't think it was necessary, and he couldn't understand why. Hold still,' she said to Roeling. 'So let's shoot it tomorrow morning, shall we?'

Cliff nodded and turned to me. 'Let's get some lunch.'

'Why don't we all get some lunch together?' With a brilliant smile, she pulled Roeling to his feet, slipped one hand through his arm and one through Cliff's. 'Do you realize, Cliff, we've never had lunch together since the picture started? I think that's simply terrible.'

'Honey, you're not going over to the commissary like that?' Roeling pointed to her tights. 'I guess it might be distracting,' Julie said, and put on a long green robe. 'I don't know what's gotten into her this morning,' Roeling said.

We walked over to his Cadillac. Julie tightened her hand on Cliff's arm. 'Dave's asked me to marry him.'

Cliff looked straight ahead. 'It couldn't happen to two nicer people.'

'Thank you very much,' said Roeling.

She pulled Cliff with her into the back of the Cadillac. 'You look tired,' she told him, then chuckled. 'Maybe you need vitamins, boy.'

As we entered the commissary, a small old man came out through the swing doors. He had a tanned but emaciated face and pale callous eyes. 'Isn't she great?' He held Julie by the shoulders. 'I don't believe she's more than twenty-five.'

'I've got news for you, J.B. I'm twenty-six.' She kissed him on the forehead. 'I told Cliff you agreed about that close-up.'

The old man took a monogrammed handkerchief from his breast pocket and mopped his face with a delicate, fussy gesture. 'Julie's right,' he said to Cliff. 'Shoot it.'

'He'll shoot it in the morning,' Julie said.

'Fine.' J.B. folded the handkerchief and put it back in his pocket with the monogram showing. Then he tapped Cliff on the chest with his knuckles. 'Happy?'

'As a sandboy, J.B.'

On the last day of shooting, Julie gave a party. She'd sung and danced *Sinbad the Sailor* nineteen times all the way through, while the camera covered her from different angles. 'Well, that's it, boys!' Cliff said after the final shot. Julie doffed her sailor hat. 'Now let's everybody get drunk, I've ordered enough liquor to keep us here through next week.' She walked off the set, not at all breathless.

Lights were turned out. The stage of the Chicago Opera House went dark. A long, hollow silence broken only by the echo of footsteps as we picked our way across cables to the New York ballroom set, brilliant with chandeliers. Under powerful arcs from the gantry, circled by darkness, it looked like an island suddenly risen out of the sea. At one end, a flight of stairs swept down from nowhere. Footmen in period costume had been brought in to serve drinks from a buffet. I saw Roeling and Timmy standing together under a tall bay window; and Mrs Lynch toasting two of the Blondes, who wore tight-waisted dresses with flounced skirts, ostrich plumes waving above their heads.

Then, piped at full strength through a loudspeaker, came Julie's voice singing the theme tune:

> 'I'm every inch a Lady,
> I've got everything to prove it.
> The basis of my act is
> To show how true this fact is. . . .'

A footman came up to Cliff and myself with a tray of glasses.

'How do you think it's turned out?' Cliff asked. He looked grimy and exhausted.

'Like a Julie Forbes picture,' I said quietly.

He made a grimace. 'Is that all?'

'I'm afraid so.'

He nodded. 'Yeah, I'm afraid so.' He walked slowly away and stood looking out of a window, at a long perspective of darkness.

Julie hadn't come back. 'Where is she?' I asked Timmy as he came up to me, neat in a dark blue suit and his hair freshly brilliantined.

He shrugged. 'Who cares? I can go on drinking vodka as long as she doesn't come.'

'Vodka, is that vodka in your glass, Timmy?' Roeling had joined us. He blinked.

'I'm developing a taste for it,' Timmy said gravely.

'I don't know what your mother will say.'

'She won't say anything unless you tell her.'

'Well,' said Roeling in a genial voice, and blinked again. 'I guess I can keep your secret for you. You're a pretty bright kid, you know.' He clapped him on the shoulder.

Timmy looked coldly at him. 'It says in the paper there's a slump in vitamins. What's that going to mean for you?'

'Now Timmy.' Roeling began to clean his spectacles. 'Not everything you read in the papers is true.'

He moved away to join Mrs Lynch and the Blondes. As a footman passed us with a tray, Timmy took another vodka and tonic. He came closer to me, and gave a peculiar smile. 'Not everything you read in the papers is true,' he said.

'What do you mean by that?'

'I've told you. I've seen things.' He was pale with excitement.

'What things?'

'Oh ...' He swayed a little on his feet. His voice dropped to a whisper. 'Once I saw a man fall into an empty pool.'

'Timmy, you'd better not have any more vodka.'

'It's true!'

His eyes, slightly bloodshot, searched my face. With an insistent pleading movement, he stroked my arm. 'I swear it's true.'

I said: 'What happened when the man fell?'

Timmy didn't answer at once. Then: 'I guess he died.' He smiled again. 'She didn't push him, if that's what you're thinking. All the same ... ' He broke off. 'You'll never tell anyone, will you?'

'No.'

'Swear it.'

'I swear it.'

'All the same,' he said, looking thoughtful, 'she could have called a doctor. Nobody called a doctor.'

'I thought he died at once.'

'She could have called a doctor,' he repeated, 'instead of leaving him there. And he cried out. And he tried to get up. And she wouldn't take any notice.'

The loudspeaker stopped, leaving a well of silence. Then the murmur of voices began again.

'What about Carmen?' I said. 'And Canning? Did you ever say anything to them?'

'They said I'm a liar. They said I have fantasies.'

'And why are you telling me?'

He frowned. 'I don't know. I sort of feel you hate her as much as I do.'

'No, I don't,' I said. 'Really I don't. I used to think I did. But she's too – too extraordinary, if you know what I mean.'

'Well,' Timmy said. He gave me a long look. 'Don't feel sorry. You don't have to feel sorry for me. She knows what I saw, and . . . ' I saw he was smiling in the prematurely old, crooked way that chilled me. 'I can get anything I want for my birthday. Christmas, too. So it's – '

The studio lights flickered and dimmed. From the gantry, an arc swung round to the staircase. Ragtime, very quiet and strict, came through the loudspeaker. A girl walked down the stairs into the spotlight. She wore fishnet tights, man's evening shirt, bow-tie and white top hat.

When she came nearer, everyone realized it was Julie. There were gasps of admiration. For a moment, we were all in the twenties. Serious, unsmiling, she advanced to the centre of the ballroom. The columnists rushed forward, making a semicircle round her.

Then she winked. Pulled the hat down at a jaunty angle over her eyes. Hips swayed to the ragtime, feet tapped a few steps. A photographer's bulb flashed. She tipped her hat. The tap of her feet echoed across the darkened stage.

Applause. The ragtime stopped. She held out her arms. 'Nineteen twenty-seven,' she said. 'I wore this in nineteen twenty-seven.' She extended one leg, then the other. 'You'll notice it's still a perfect fit.'

J.B. pushed through the columnists and kissed her. He was trembling. 'Julie, I'm proud of you.'

'No one but you, Julie,' said Roeling.

'An experience I shall never forget,' said Mrs Lynch.

Julie laughed. 'So give the oldtimer a drink.' She glanced across the ballroom to Cliff, who was still standing by the window. Then she made a little speech. She thanked the crew and all the actors for being so wonderful to her. She thanked J.B. for his faith. 'And I want to say a special word about Cliff Harriston.' She paused. 'Working with Cliff has been one of the most stimulating experiences of my life. He's – well, you don't need me to tell you what Cliff Harriston is.'

'Why did you close the set?' a columnist asked.

'We both felt the need for terrific concentration. This picture was very hard for both of us.' Julie turned away quickly, went over to Timmy and ruffled his hair. 'Timmy darling, this is your mother. What do you think of her?'

'Oh, you're the greatest,' he said.

'Isn't that the truth?' Roeling agreed. 'Timmy, I'm glad you realize your mother is just about the most fabulous woman in the world.'

'I do, I do realize it.' He giggled. 'But I think I'm drunk.'

Julie took the glass from his hand and sniffed it. 'Dave, did you know the kid's been drinking vodka?'

Sweat broke out on Roeling's forehead. 'Guess it's more tonic than vodka.'

She took a sip. 'More vodka than tonic.'

'I'll get him home,' Mrs Lynch said, and took Timmy's arm. He followed her without a word.

Julie watched them leave, then tipped her hat to the back of her head and went over to Cliff. They were alone by the window.

'It's a very nice custom,' she said quietly, 'to give presents at the end of a picture. I mean, the way stars and directors usually do.'

He nodded. 'I usually give presents.'

'But not this time?'

'I've got a present for you,' Cliff said rather slowly. 'I give you this movie, Julie. I'd give you all your movies if I had them.'

'I think that's a very nice present.'

'You know what you can do with it.'

She smiled. 'I'm so glad you got me a present, because I got you one too.' Still holding Timmy's glass, she looked over her shoulder. Then she threw the vodka in Cliff's face and slapped him on the mouth with the back of her hand. The force of the blow nearly sent him through the window.

Straightening her hat, she walked away. As she reached the door a spotlight was trained on her and a voice called from the gantry:

'Hi, Julie!'

An electrician with a creased veteran's face and a cigar in his mouth was up there, holding the light. He gave a wide admiring grin, keeping the cigar between his teeth.

'Good luck, Julie. It's been a pleasure every moment.'

Her hat glittered. She put her hands on her hips. 'And God bless you, Louie!'

He waved and held the spotlight on her till the door closed.

The empty stage looked like an enormous grotto, dark and

deep under the ground. At the far end, outside Julie's dressing-room, one light was burning. My footsteps echoed monstrously.

'Who's there?'

As I reached the dressing-room steps, I saw that she had taken off her make-up. Her skin looked fresh and smooth, only a little pale. She was wrapped in the vivid green robe. Behind her, the dressmaker's dummy stood like a totem pole, hung with shirt and bow-tie, festooned with the sacred tights.

'What do you want?' She spoke through gritted teeth.

'Somewhere here,' I said, 'I left a book.'

'A book?'

'Yes. I was reading it between takes.'

'You'll never find it in all this dark.'

'I think I know where it is,' I said, and turned away.

Her voice called me back. 'Enjoy the party?'

I turned round. 'Very much. It was fun.'

'Yeah, it was fun. . . . ' She sat down on the steps, folded her arms and gazed at the vacant stage with an expression of disgust.

I started to turn away again, but she beckoned me to come closer with a quick, irritated gesture.

'Do you want something?' I asked.

'What should I want, boy?'

'I don't know. But you look . . . ' I broke off.

'What?'

'Is it the after-the-picture-blues?'

She gave a short bitter laugh. 'I never get them. And the picture's fine. Great. I pulled it through. It'll make a lot of money.' She lit a cigarette. 'I'll buy Timmy that yacht.'

'He wants a yacht?' Julie nodded. 'Isn't he too young to handle it?'

'He'll learn fast,' she said. 'Timmy's very advanced for

his age.' Smoke from her cigarette twisted towards the darkness. She watched it, then shrugged. 'Dave's waiting, but for some reason I feel like sitting here, in this barn. Sometimes I get a feeling. I feel ...'

A curious thing happened. It seemed to me that the light went out of her eyes. They became like empty lakes. 'I feel that I'm in the middle of a purposeless, hostile universe.'

Her voice rasped across the shadows, the rows of heavy lamps, the dark outlines of painted flats.

'Isn't that strange?' Her eyes grew bright again. She got up, yawned and stretched her arms.

'Well, maybe,' I said, 'maybe you *are*.'

I haven't seen Julie again. Nearly three months have passed and tonight is the première of *Every Inch a Lady*. As they say at the studio, 'the word's gone round it'll be the money-spinner of the year'. J.B. is said to be convinced. A record of Julie singing the theme tune is already on the list of best-sellers, and goes into the nation's juke-boxes next week.

Cliff told me he wasn't going to the première. He is working on a new story, and is very excited about it. 'This one's going to be really good.' It will be for a different studio, as J.B. didn't renew his contract. Cliff looks better now than at the end of shooting *Every Inch a Lady*, but I always find a deep and almost fearful tiredness in his face. When he talks, he often looks away from you; his eyes are gazing out of a window, through an open door. I suppose they see a thin line stretching away, growing thinner.

Timmy has telephoned once. Julie and Dave Roeling II had a honeymoon in Tahiti, then Roeling flew to Brazil to promote his vitamins. Next time, Julie plans to accompany him on a business tour. A columnist says she intends to take an active interest in her husband's work. Timmy says she still uses The Pool House. He expects his yacht in about a week.

Outside the theatre in Hollywood is a papiermâché figure that looks even bigger than the skeleton of the imperial mastodon unearthed near Wilshire Boulevard before the new insurance company building went up. It is Julie as Lydia Thompson. She brandishes a glittering whip.

The ceremonies won't begin for another two hours, but already a crowd is massing. Police prepare cordons. People eat popcorn or peanuts and chew gum while they wait. They don't say much. A quiet middle-aged woman remarks: 'She's still the greatest.' A man nods: 'And she'll be the last to go.' The crowd grows more dense and impatient as there comes a light surprising shower of rain and dusk falls.

Dreaming Emma

ABOUT six months ago, there was a morning when I woke
up in the small hours and couldn't get to sleep again. I read
for a little, then felt completely awake. It was no good trying
to sleep any more, so I decided to drive down to the ocean.
The moon lay round and full near the rim of a cool dark
sky. The city was nothing but empty streets, traffic lights
winking at empty intersections, but stranger than other
cities at this hour because there seemed more cars than
houses. In the starchy moonlight cars lined streets and drive-
ways, were stored in gleaming rows on the open-air lots.
Along the road winding down to the coast a man stepped
out of nowhere and signalled for a lift, but I didn't stop.

In the quiet suburban section of Santa Monica all the
lights were out except at a café which stays open throughout
the night. As I went in I saw two waitresses whispering
together near the cash desk, the chef in a tall white hat
sizzling hot-cakes at a long grill behind the counter. Above
him, in a glass case fixed at a slanting angle to the whole
length of the wall, stood tiers of artificial sliced melon and
ice-cream sundae. Music drifted weakly from a radio.

The café was almost empty. At the counter a young man
in overalls, probably a garage mechanic, sat alone with a
cigarette and a cup of coffee. At one booth an army major in
uniform but without his tie had his arm round a woman with
long disorganized black hair. She was carelessly made up,
a smudge of purplish lipstick above her mouth. Both looked
as if they had got out of bed rather quickly.

One of the waitresses served me coffee, then went back
to her whispered conversation at the cash desk. She was

reading aloud from a letter. 'He actually told you *that*?' I heard the other waitress say. The major and his companion, heads close together, ate scrambled eggs from the same plate.

Through the window I could see the last of the moon, slipping over the horizon. Tipped with red by a neon drugstore sign as it flashed on and off, a row of palm trees loomed in silhouette across the street. Then, from the dark line, a small thin silhouette detached itself. After hesitating at the pavement's edge, the figure crossed the street and came towards the café. She passed the newspaper stand outside the entrance, hesitated again, peered in through the glass doors, finally entered the café and sat down at a booth in one corner. I guessed she was about seventeen years old. She had cindery fair hair cut in a short fringe across her forehead, her face was very pretty, round and childlike with a smooth white skin. A cheap silver and coral ornament dangled absurdly from each ear.

She ordered a glass of milk. The waitress brought it over and said: 'It's a shame you have to wait so long for that bus, honey, but no one's driving into town. Keep off the streets, though – really!' The girl nodded. She glanced without interest at the major and the mechanic, with a brief flicker of curiosity at me, then took a mirror from her purse and stared at her own face.

Presently the mechanic paid his bill and left. Outside, a police car drove past slowly. The moon had gone. The woman with the major spilt egg on his shirt and let out a harsh giggle. The girl put out her tongue at her face in the mirror, then sipped her milk. I picked up a movie magazine that the mechanic had left on a stool, and a handsome face smiled from the cover. As I flicked through the pages I was aware of the girl in the corner looking wistfully at me, like an animal begging for food. I felt sure she was waiting for me to put the magazine down so she could read it herself.

'Here you are,' I said, going over and handing it to her. She looked at the cover with a quick little sigh of pleasure, and her ear-rings wobbled.

'Excuse me,' she said in a rather high-pitched cheeping voice, 'but can I ask you a question?'

'All right,' I said.

She gasped. 'How-do-I-get-in-the-movies?'

'There are several ways,' I began, and her bright little mouth hung expectantly open. 'But none of them's very easy.'

The mouth bunched up rather crossly. 'Oh, everyone says *that*!'

'You've asked a lot of people?'

'I guess so. But I only got here yesterday.' She took another sip of milk. 'I came by bus from Galena, Illinois.'

'Is that somewhere near Chicago?'

'Well, it's not too far I suppose, though I've never been to Chicago myself. I rode in the bus for three days.' She spoke with a mixture of pride and astonishment. 'They go all day and night, you know, I never thought I could stand it.'

'Do you know anyone here?'

The girl shook her head. 'I guess I'm terribly impulsive. Sunday morning they went to church, I said I had a stomach ache. I packed my case, left a note on the dining-room table and took off while they were singing the last hymn. I just couldn't stand Galena, Illinois one day more.'

'It's as awful as that?'

'Oh, it's dying,' she said. 'You can't have any idea. Fifty years ago they say it was quite a place, but what's the use of that? Now it's dying. Even the Mississippi looks like nothing at Galena. I used to say it hadn't the heart to flow.'

When I asked if she lived with her parents in Galena, she shook her head again. 'Oh they're dead,' she said. 'Killed in a bus crash when I was three years old. I went to live with my two old aunts. They own the Galena Riverside Commercial Hotel.'

'Well, living in a hotel must have relieved the boredom a bit.'

'You think so? The place was always closed. I mean, they'd have opened it if anyone wanted to stay there, but there hasn't been a guest at the Galena Riverside Commercial Hotel in over ten years. You can still see the last name in the register, though someone spilt coffee over it. *Willis B. Jernigan,*' she said, closing her eyes for a moment. '*Salesman. Sleepy Eye, Minnesota.* I've always remembered his name though I've forgotten what he looked like.'

'Why on earth didn't your aunts sell the place?'

She giggled. 'Who would buy it? Besides, it gives them something to complain about. They still switch on the Vacancy sign every night, you know, then start grumbling that business is bad. I guess they're pretty crazy. They certainly disapprove of everything. If you're enjoying yourself you must be doing something wrong, that's the way they live. They used to follow me down corridors and peep into the closed-up rooms to see if I was reading the kind of magazine I shouldn't. It was certainly depressing, I can tell you. And just wait till you hear a rather unusual detail.' She paused for breath, then spoke in a low voice. 'They slept in the same bed.'

'They're sisters, aren't they?'

She gave a little snort. 'Oh, it's depressing,' she said.

Through the window I could see dawn. It lightened the newspaper stand on the sidewalk. The latest headline – TEENAGE KILLER OF 9 CAPTURED! – stood out in a chilly mist.

'What are you looking at?' she asked, then saw the head-

line too. 'Oh, another murder, how dreadful. I simply hate
to read about people killing people, you know. Honestly.
One evening about six years ago,' she leaned across the table,
'I walked down to the drugstore in Galena and there was a
note on the door saying Back in Five Minutes. There was
somebody else waiting, a man just passing through, he had
his car. He was kind of angry because he only wanted a
toothbrush and I guess it was aggravating to wait so long
just to buy a thing like that. I told him, why not drive on to
the next town and buy a toothbrush there? He said no, now
he'd stopped he might as well wait. *Well* ... three days
later his picture was in the papers and he'd killed his wife!
That certainly gave me a feeling. I mean, he was so ordinary
and polite to me, and then he went off and did a thing like
that.'

She glanced out of the window again, and this time gave a
little shiver. The ear-rings wobbled. She turned her wide
gaping eyes on me, and I wondered if she didn't enjoy playing at not being grown up. When she gave that round,
surprised look, which was often, her eyes seemed rather
cunning, older than the rest of her face.

'What's your name?' I asked.

'Emma,' she said in a rather doubtful tone. 'Emma Slack.
I don't think it's right for the movies.'

'I'm not sure you shouldn't take a bus right back to
Galena.'

'Are you crazy? I've come here to get in the movies. I've
dreamed about it for years, sitting in that awful empty hotel.
And I've got two hundred dollars, you know.'

I didn't answer.

'And I'm pretty! Even people in Galena could see I'm
pretty.' She touched my arm. 'You're worried about me and
I certainly appreciate it. But I'd die if I had to go back to

Galena, to those crazy old women at the end of the world. And I don't understand,' she added, 'why you think I shouldn't *try* and get in the movies.'

'There's a lot of unemployed actors in this town.'

'Oh, I know you have to sit around a few weeks and it's discouraging maybe, but girls *do* get discovered! I've read the magazines, and you know something?' Her voice became a whisper. 'At Las Vegas a woman got on the bus and sat next to me and we got talking and she used to be a movie star! Way back, she said, before they talked, but a part still comes up now and then. Also, she owns a rooming house and that's where I'm staying now. Also, she told me I had to find an agent and she'll fix it.'

'Well, you've made some progress,' I said.

'I certainly consider I have.' She slanted her gaze at me now. 'Though I guess you'll think me a kind of idiot when I tell you what I did yesterday. I was just so excited at being in movieland – you know, *living* where it all happens – I took a taxi to one of the studios.'

'You mean you thought you'd get inside?'

She nodded. 'But the man at the gate said you had to have a pass. I had a crazy idea, you know, I thought if I could just *get inside*, someone might see me and think I was pretty, and. . .' She gasped suddenly. 'But if I knew someone working in a studio, I could get a pass, couldn't I? Then I could start walking around –'

'It doesn't happen like that. Really.'

'I've read about it.' She sounded obstinate. 'Also, there are girls who take jobs as waitresses and they bring coffee to a man who looks at them and says: How-would-you-like-to-get-in-the-movies? It's true,' she said.

'Emma, why is it so important for you to be in the movies?'

Her mouth dropped open with surprise. 'I don't know.

Well, there's nothing else. I loved the movies since – oh, since I can remember. I've always been to the movies all the time. And if you'd lived in Galena –'

'I lived in a sort of English Galena once.'

'Yes, I thought there was something about your accent,' she said. 'Matter of fact, I thought it was just terribly affected. But didn't you always love the movies?'

I nodded.

'And what are you doing out here now?'

'I'm a writer,' I said, then smiled. 'At present I'm looking for a job in the movies.'

'Ha ha,' she said.

At the cash desk, the two waitresses were still talking. 'This year I've promised myself a real vacation.' They discussed places, Miami Beach, Vancouver, Acapulco. 'But I just can't get over that darned letter,' one of them said.

Emma looked out of the window again, her face rapt, her eyes hungry. She wasn't seeing the palm trees or the drug-store sign or the street cleaner's truck that rumbled past, leaving a trail of water. She was having a secret ecstatic vision, perhaps of a floodlit embrace on an enormous screen or a thousand hands fluttering autograph books.

'What I really meant was,' I said, 'do you feel you'll be happy if you become a movie star?'

'Are you crazy?' Her face became almost reverent. 'It's a funny thing, I've always believed in myself. I always knew I had to do *something*. My aunts are very religious people, but the worst kind if you know what I mean. They never go to the movies. They were always making me pray and I guess I believed in God because they told me to. Well, I used to wonder how I could attract God's attention. Honestly.' She gave herself a little hug. 'I felt – well, such a nobody. How could God ever notice me unless I was somebody? That's what I felt.'

I watched her face, intent and serious, her hands embracing at the memory of a prayer. 'What did you want God to do?' I asked.

'I told you, I wanted Him to notice me.' Her voice was sharp and practical now. 'Everyone in Galena used to say how pretty I was, and I used to pray to God to let me stay that way till I was forty-five at least. If you're going to be in the movies, that's important.' She smiled. 'Of course, I was only a kid. Do I talk too much?'

'No, I like it.'

'I talk the way I feel. In Galena they say it drives them crazy.'

'Tell me about this woman you met on the bus,' I said.

'Louise Lind? She used to know Theda Bara and everybody, and she thinks I have a chance. She told me she had this rooming house right in the centre of everything. Well, it's just behind Hollywood Boulevard near that theatre with the footprints of the stars in the courtyard – and I guess that's the centre if there is one.'

'Then what are you doing down here?'

'A man on the bus – I talked to a lot of people on the bus – this man I talked to before I met Louise said there are some places that stay open all night. He told me to go into one of them and sit down. Movie people come into these places when they can't sleep, he said, you might get noticed. So I found a place on Hollywood Boulevard but I didn't like it – oh, you've no idea!' Her eyes grew very round. 'Lot's of wild-looking boys hanging around and they all *stare*,' she said. 'So I asked a girl behind the counter if there wasn't a place with more class, and she said they had a quieter branch down here. I took a bus, but then I found I couldn't get back till morning, so I've been wandering around and hoping I can get back while Louise is still asleep.'

'She wouldn't approve?'

Emma shook her head. 'Everything is very straight with Louise. She told me herself she doesn't approve of anything immoral. I suppose,' she went on immediately, 'if you haven't got a job yet, you couldn't help me get inside a studio?'

'It's not such a problem just to get inside,' I told her. 'The real problem starts after that.'

'What do you mean?'

'Seeing the right people. You can't just –'

'Once I'm inside I'll be all right. Can you take me to a studio tomorrow?'

She looked like a hungry puppy again, almost panting with eagerness. It was impossible not to throw her a scrap. 'All right,' I said.

She laughed delightedly. 'Tomorrow's today, if you know what I mean. You know, before I started talking to you I was getting depressed. I was getting a pretty low opinion of myself. I'd been hanging around for hours and nothing happened. I thought maybe this is the story of my life. People in Galena always said I was pretty, but no one ever seemed to *notice* me. The first time I got noticed in a kind of way,' she frowned slightly, 'was when I spent a week-end in Dubuque, Iowa. I must tell you about that some time. But would you say – you live here and you ought to know, and I'd appreciate your honest opinion like nothing else – would you say this is really a difficult place for a girl like me to *stand out at once*?'

'I would,' I said.

'You certainly are a discouraging person.'

'You asked for it.'

'Well, maybe you don't entirely realize you are talking to a person who'll do anything to get in the movies. I guess I should be grateful to you for trying to stop my ambition running away with me, but *honestly*,' she said, 'you know, for a girl like me – well, it ought to be possible to attract attention!'

We left the café at about seven o'clock. The sky was still grey with early-morning fog. Emma talked for most of the journey back, mainly about the time she was fourteen and took a train to Dubuque, Iowa. She liked this town, a few miles away on the other side of the Mississippi, much better than Galena. All Saturday she wandered round a fair, had her fortune told and was disappointed when the palmist saw a husband and four children taking up most of her future; then she went to two movies in the evening. It was too late to catch a train back that night. Various men in the street asked her to come home with them. She refused and spent the night in a cornfield. When she came back on Sunday, walked past the deserted waterfront, heard the organ playing in the church and saw the line of shuttered stores along Galena's main street, she cried because it seemed to her she lived in the most hopeless town in the world.

I left her outside Louise Lind's apartment house, a faded white stucco building in a Hollywood side street. It had a silly conch-shaped turret and a flight of blackened iron steps leading up the side of one wall to the upper storey. Under a bright green aluminium awning recently installed on the porch, an old man sat in a wheel-chair with a blanket across his knees. Emma asked me to pull up further along the street, she couldn't be seen coming home with a man. I promised to call for her at twelve o'clock, after she'd washed her hair and massaged her face with a new cream that a woman had recommended to her on the bus.

Driving home, I wondered if there was anything that any-one could do about her. Could the magazines come true, and Emma Slack (with a new name, of course) be made a star? In a way, I didn't care. With her appalling, cruel, perfect egocentricity, it was difficult to conceive images of Emma helpless, Emma lost: the little figure behind the palm trees, wandering down Hollywood Boulevard, turned away from the studio gate, listening breathlessly to a retired star's useless reminiscences – this had to be a game, a chosen role.

Nobody could be as naïvely heartbreaking as that. In a few weeks' time she might have to give up the part, with her savings gone she'd take a job as a waitress or store attendant, or go back to the aunts. And it would all be over ... In another way, I cared a little. There was a kind of fanaticism about Emma, and perhaps this made her really helpless. In a city full of dreamers, she clung with such fierceness to an obviously fragile dream. When I thought of that, she struck me as about the most impermanent person I could imagine in the world.

Outside the apartment house, when I drove back at noon, I saw her waiting. She stood on the edge of the pavement in a white cotton dress with a flounced skirt, white cotton gloves up to her elbows, a pink straw hat with a wide brim and scarlet wedge-heeled shoes. The old man was still in his wheel-chair on the porch. A young man in a thin blue sweater and tight black jeans hurried past him out of the house. He nodded to Emma, who gave him a shy cautious smile, then got into an old sports car and drove off with a roar.

She watched him for a moment, then came over to me. 'That's Grant,' she said. 'He wants to be an actor. I don't really know him.'

'Is Louise helping him too?'

'Well, yes, I think she is, but she says she doesn't like the type.' Emma got into my car and glanced at herself in the driving mirror. 'Louise says a certain amount of personal elegance is the thing, even when you're bluffing.'

'Then may I make a personal remark?'

She caught her breath. 'You mean there's something wrong with my outfit?'

'I feel you shouldn't wear that hat in the studio.'

'Why not?'

'Well . . . it'll shield your face too much.'

Emma looked at herself again, then sighed. 'I guess you're right.' Taking it off, she held the hat in her lap for a moment, stroked it vaguely, threw it on the back seat.

'As you're not wearing a hat,' I went on, 'I think you should take off those gloves.'

'What? You mean you don't like my gloves?'

'Very much, but they're too formal without the hat.'

'I just hope you know what you're talking about.' She began to draw them off slowly. 'You certainly are a discouraging person, I saved up for this outfit and it's supposed to be Californian.'

'People dress very casually here,' I said.

'Well, I'm beginning to feel casual all right. Do you like my shoes?'

'Did Louise see you come in?' I asked, ignoring this.

'No, she was sleeping.' She threw the gloves on the back seat. 'Louise liked me in the hat.'

As we drove through Beverly Hills, Emma glanced at the lines of neat secluded houses, leaned out of the window and sniffed. 'You can smell the money here,' she said. 'Like jasmine. Is this where the movie stars live?'

'Some.'

'I bet all those houses have pools in back.' She was smiling. 'I've read about all those houses, I feel I could go into one and I'd be completely at home. Oh, it's starting to get like a dream,' she said, 'when you've never been to a place before, but somewhere you *have*, and you *know*.' She looked at herself in the mirror again. 'If I wear dark glasses, would that be a mistake?'

'Yes,' I said.

'Are you sure? They might think I was somebody else.'

'But you don't want that.'

'If they mistake me for somebody famous, I do. Once I can attract attention, I'm . . . ' She broke off and clutched my arm. 'Is this it?' she asked in a low voice.

We were approaching the studio gates.

'It's bigger than the one I saw yesterday,' she said.

The cop gave me our pass, and we drove up the hill towards the main buildings, past the exterior set of a Western town with its railway station by the roadside and the train waiting.

'Well, here we are!' Emma whispered.

At first it was all she could say. When we passed a truck laden with scenery, a group of extras dressed as German soldiers, two men in space-suits, 'Well, here we are!' she breathed.

I parked the car and she looked at herself in the driving mirror again.

'Are you sure I'm not too casual?'

'You look fine, Emma.'

'It's important to strike the right note, isn't it?' She glanced wistfully at the hat and gloves on the back seat. 'What stars are there at this studio?' I named a few. 'Will they be having lunch?'

'Maybe, but don't count on it.'

'And don't ever raise my hopes, will you?' She sighed. 'I don't suppose you know any of them?'

'No,' I said firmly.

'Do you know anyone?'

'A director called Cliff Harriston.'

'A man who *makes* movies?' Her eyes grew round. 'I bet he's quite important; will you introduce me?'

'All right,' I said.

When we sat down to lunch in the commissary, I knew we were going to be unlucky. It was twelve-thirty, and not a single star. Cliff hadn't come in, either.

'There *must* be someone !' Emma's voice trembled slightly. 'Who are all these people eating lunch?'

'Technicians, secretaries, accountants,' I said. 'Small part actors, extras, hairdressers.'

'Well, why don't the important ones show themselves?'

'Either they're not working today or they're having lunch somewhere else, I suppose.'

'I certainly call that frustrating.'

'Hello,' I said as a tall grey-haired woman in dark spectacles with spangled frames came up to our table. 'Miss Dunaway,' I explained, introducing her to Emma, 'is Cliff Harriston's secretary.'

Miss Dunaway gave Emma a brisk dry nod.

'Where is everybody?' I asked her.

'You mean the glamour?' Miss Dunaway wrinkled her nose. 'Oh, there's an official lunch in the banquet room for two Generals from Washington. They've come to bless an army picture.' She moved away from Emma and lowered her voice. 'Mr Harriston's having lunch off the lot, but he wants you to know you'll be starting on the script in two weeks. They fixed it this morning.'

Emma gave a little cry. 'You've got a job?'

'It looks like it,' I said.

'I bring you luck, don't I? I really bring you luck.' To Miss Dunaway she said: 'I have intentions of becoming an actress.'

'Are you from New York?'

'No, Galena, Illinois.'

'Experience?' Miss Dunaway sounded bristling, capable.

'You mean, have I acted before?'

'Yes, I mean that.'

'I have no experience but I intend to learn,' Emma said. 'But I've only been here two days.'

'Well, I hope you're not expecting everything to happen at once.' Miss Dunaway's tone showed that she was relenting slightly. 'There's an awful lot of hopeful young ladies in this town.'

'Everything's happened at once since the moment I came,' Emma said. 'I really consider myself unusually lucky.'

Miss Dunaway shrugged. 'Then my words are wasted. It's always exciting to meet a future star,' she said. 'Our side of the business is so drab, they just chain us to our desks.'

Emma watched her go, then grimaced. 'They get like that when they've never had a man, don't they?'

'She's really quite nice.'

'She was laughing at me.'

'She didn't want to raise your hopes.'

'I'm beginning to realize nobody wants to do that.'

'Because they don't want you to get disappointed.'

'I know the type,' Emma said, still nettled. 'Never had a man; there's a whole crowd of them in Galena.' Then, for the first time since I'd met her, she lapsed into silence. She hardly answered when I spoke to her, but stared at the two men in space-suits, eating ice-cream at the next table.

'I suppose this has been a failure,' I said at last.

She shook her head. 'I hate that word, I just hate it. Besides, it's all in the mind. I believe you only fail if you *let* yourself.' She gave me an artful smile. 'For instance, you could save the day if you wanted to.'

'How?'

'Well, I've just got to see *something* now I'm here, or I'll die. So why don't you take me on a set?'

But it really was an unlucky day. Two of the companies were out on location, and for the science-fiction film they were shooting only special effects. We walked down to a back lot and watched the extras dressed as German soldiers marching through a French street. It was a complicated shot, because when they reached a certain point, somebody had to throw a grenade from a window. We left after the ninth unsuccessful take. Naturally Emma had pressed me to introduce her to the director, whom I didn't know. She took it very well. 'I'm having a good time, really I am,' she said as we left, 'so try and look as if you believe me.'

Behind us, the soldiers started to march again. 'I mean I've been inside a studio,' Emma whispered, making it feel like church. 'I haven't seen anything or met anybody, but I've been inside.'

The grenade exploded again in the distance. Silence followed, then somebody shouted, 'No good – cut!' and a whistle blew. We turned a corner and found ourselves outside the Last Chance Saloon. The door swayed gently back and forth.

'And three days ago,' Emma went on, shaking dust from her scarlet wedge-heeled shoes, 'it was just another Sunday morning in Galena!'

I took her home and wished her luck. From the front door of Louise Lind's apartment house, she turned to wave with the hand carrying her straw hat and cotton gloves. I waved back. She was ridiculous and touching and improbable, and all things considered I didn't really want to see her again. But she was difficult to refuse. Three days later she telephoned me – I hadn't given her my number, but she'd checked with Information in all the possible areas of the city.

'I'm going to throw myself on your mercy – honestly!' Her voice was breaking with excitement. 'I've got an appointment with that agent Louise knows, and Grant – you know, the actor who lives here too – was going to drive me over there, but he's working today. And Louise doesn't drive at all. Well, I could take a cab but it'll cost me six dollars. Money just melts away in this town and my two hundred's melting fast. You can't imagine. So will you drive me to this agent? It may be the most important day of my life.'

It was two o'clock when I arrived at the apartment house. A garbage can stood at the foot of the iron steps leading up the side of one wall. Emptying trash from a pail into this can was a woman in pale green evening dress, red velvet cloak over her shoulders. She looked up and saw me, with the pail still in her hand called loudly: 'You come for Emma?' I said yes. 'Excuse me, I've been working this morning,' she said and replaced the lid on the can. As I came nearer I could see she was about fifty-five and plumpening, with metallic blonde hair restored and rinsed a faint blue. Her face was surprisingly unlined. She had a full rouged mouth but not much chin, sharp grey eyes with obviously false lashes.

'I work in the movies, just now I'm with Magnagram.' She bent down to pull off a gold-painted shoe, held it up and looked at it, wrinkled her nose and put it on again. 'Drat that heel. Name's Louise Lind.'

She watched closely for my reaction to this. 'I heard about you from Emma,' I said. It was the wrong thing. She frowned. 'You must have heard about me before that. *There Goes My Love* was my best picture, but it's way back,' she said. 'Come on inside.'

I followed her down a dim corridor. Jazz music came from upstairs. Louise's apartment was on the ground floor, she showed me into a rather dark living-room full of heavy old furniture. Curtains and covers with sweeping floral patterns were faded from washing. There was an upright piano with yellowing keys and an enormous new television set. 'I can get colour on that thing,' she said. 'But just let me get rid of this trash bucket and we'll have some port. Emma's dressing.'

Flat yet strident, her voice continued from the kitchen. 'Everything's way, way back. I was a star before they started yackety-yacking.' The pail was set down with a clang. 'However, this girl keeps going.' She came back, untying her cloak. 'You're as young as you feel,' she said.

The telephone rang. 'Drat it.' As she picked up the receiver, she added over her shoulder: 'They never stop calling, offering me work.' Into the phone she said loudly: 'This is she!' A pause, then her voice rasped even higher. 'No, I'm a blonde. B-L-O-N-D-E, get it?' Another pause. 'Sure my picture's in your files. It's what? What? REDHEAD? You've got a very old picture, kiddo, that's all I can tell you. Oh, prewar – but definitely. What's the part?' Her nose wrinkled. 'No dialogue? Well, I don't usually take that. I like something with a bit of dialogue. I'm very busy just now you know, week with Magnagram, yes, dialogue part, and – huh? A week Tuesday? You just wait while I look that day up.'

She winked at me and laid down the instrument for a moment. Putting a pencil between her teeth, she picked up a magazine and agitated the pages. 'Friday,' she said, 'out. Monday, out. Day with Triumph Monday. Wednesday, out. Retakes for Magnagram, stand-by call. Tuesday ... !' Letting the pencil fall, she picked up the receiver. 'So happens Tuesday's my only free day. Lucky for you, I'd say. I wear my own costumes, kept them all from way back, everything, you should see my closets, don't worry.'

She hung up. 'They get you down, sometimes I ask myself why I bother.'

I asked her about the agent she was sending Emma to see.

'Oh, Midge,' she said. 'Old friend of mine. Small potatoes, but a girl's got to start somewhere.' Her eyes narrowed suddenly. 'You interested in Emma? I mean – hot pants?'

I denied it quickly.

'Just a friend,' she said approvingly. 'I like that; you don't come across that often in this filthy town. The things I could tell you –'

She broke off as Emma came into the room, wearing a tight-fitting black dress.

'You look different,' I said.

Emma pointed to her hair. 'The fringe has gone.'

'I made her take it off,' Louise said. 'You can't get away with that kind of thing any more.' She gave the girl a shrewd, critical look. 'I made her buy black, too. Blondes look sexy – if you'll pardon the expression – in black. You need more tan,' she said to Emma, walking purposefully round her eyes roving across her bare back, 'but I guess we'll get around to that eventually. Are you nervous?'

Emma shook her head. 'No, but I'm excited.'

'Good. Midge is a very important little guy. If he likes you, you're in. At the top!' Suddenly she stuck her nose into Emma's neck. 'What the hell have you been putting on yourself?'

'*Bonjour Paris*,' Emma said promptly. 'I found it at a drugstore, reduced.'

'Well, go easy on it now.' Louise turned to me with an expansive sigh, like someone at the end of a hard day's work. 'Okay, boy, take her away.'

In her evening dress she stood out on the porch to watch us leave, hand resting on the shoulder of the old man in a wheel-chair.

'She's the most experienced woman I've ever known,' Emma said as we drove towards Beverly Hills. 'And everything is so straight with Louise.'

We drew up outside the agent's office. 'I have to go to the studio,' I told Emma. 'You can call me there when you're through, and I'll run you home.'

She nodded. 'This may be *it*. Wish me luck.'

'Good luck, Emma.'

I watched her go up the steps. At the top, she gave a childish little skip, then remembered herself and carefully smoothed down her tight black skirt. The pneumatically controlled glass door opened in front of her, and she walked on very slowly and stiffly, almost as if she were balancing a book on her head. I felt sure Louise must have said something about poise.

'Hello !'

'Oh, hello, Emma.'

'I guess you're wondering what happened to me yesterday and why I didn't call.'

'Did you get home all right?'

'Are you kidding? Is that your true opinion of me?'

'No, Emma. Of agents.'

'Well, you listen. This one seemed a real nice old guy, and *extremely* interested. He said there's no one quite like me in his whole experience, and I have a Future !'

'Was that all?'

'Not exactly. We went to a bar and started to *plan my career*. Midge said maybe I should start with a bit part on some television show – oh, he can get me the big things right away, of course, but I may not be *ready* for them yet. Well, I was a little disappointed, I explained I wanted to get right into the movies, that's my whole life, but he told me the important thing was to *get myself seen*, and it was all a step in the right direction. Besides, Rome wasn't built in a day. By this time I'd had quite a few drinks and nothing to eat, and we were so *deep* in conversation I hardly *noticed* at first when he was making passes. But it got so *obvious*, I had to say please don't do that, cut it out, I want to go home. So he said he was sorry, how about one for the road, and he'd take me home. And I said okay, and he held my hand, but just affectionately. Finally I said I suppose the whole thing's off now – I mean, wouldn't you rather I took my Future somewhere else? – but Midge only laughed and asked if I really thought he was that kind of person? And all he wanted was to kiss me good night. Emma baby, he said, you and me are going to be friends. Well, you can imagine. I mean, I had no idea people could be so *nice*. Honestly !'

'What did Louise say?'

'Louise is very pleased. She says I played it real smart.'

Several weeks passed. Once I thought I saw Emma in a sports car driving down Hollywood Boulevard, sitting next to Grant, the young actor who rented a room from Louise. I wasn't sure, because she wore dark glasses and a scarf tied round her head. Then, at a restaurant in Beverly Hills, I saw her with a dark thickset pudgy man wearing a napkin like a bib and eating spaghetti. He had large hairy hands with impeccably manicured, gleaming nails. I knew this must be Midge. When I passed their table, Emma smiled brightly – too brightly, and I felt that for some reason our meeting here didn't please her, and she wanted me to go away. I remarked that she had taken Louise's advice and acquired a deep sun-tan. Midge gave an approving wink. I asked how she was getting on, and she said everything was just fine. Midge winked again. As I went out, I saw her pick up a napkin and wipe tomato sauce from his chin.

'Hello?'

My telephone had rung at three o'clock in the morning. I said 'hello?' again, and there was still no answer, only a frightened gasp and then a kind of sob. 'Who is this?' I asked, and after a pause, another sob, a trembling voice said:

'Emma ...'

The voice sounded very far away.

'Emma? What's the matter?'

The next pause was so long that I thought she must have gone away – then I heard a quick, convulsive catching of breath.

'I . . . don't think . . . I can stand it.'

'Emma, can you get a hold on yourself and tell me what's happened?' No answer. 'Where are you?' A gasp. 'With Midge?'

'If . . . if I can get away . . . I guess I've no right to . . . I mean, to ask such a favour. . . .' Her voice melted numbly away.

'What do you want me to do?'

'Nothing . . . but if I can, could I . . . come round and . . . talk to you?'

'Of course. But can't you tell me what's happened?'

'Oh . . . He's . . . given me a terrible beating. . . .'

'Midge?'

'Yes . . . It was terrible.' Even her voice sounded bruised now.

'Are you still with him?'

'No, but . . . he'll be back. He's locked me in . . . in the bedroom.'

'Would you like me to come round?'

'No!' For a moment she sounded emphatic, then dropped back to the weak, flat note of pain. 'I shouldn't have called you.'

'Listen, Emma. If you're in trouble –'

'It's just that he – oh ! – found out. . . .'

'What?'

But the only answer was a long sigh, then silence.

'You still there, Emma?'

'I . . . think so.' She gave a faint giggle.

'Why don't you tell me where you are and let me come round?'

'No, I ... I couldn't even let you in. I'm sorry.'

'What for?'

'I shouldn't have called.'

'Don't be ridiculous.'

'I shouldn't have called.' Her voice grew stronger. 'Don't do anything. Leave me alone. Honestly. Good-bye.'

She hung up.

Midge's number was not in the telephone book, and I couldn't get it through Information. I rang Louise, but there was no answer. Had Midge come back by now, I wondered, and started beating Emma again? Why? Did he hurt her badly, or was she mainly frightened? I went back to bed, not quite sure how disturbed I should be.

In the morning I went to see Louise. In a purple housecoat and a pair of old carpet slippers, she was impatiently sweeping the porch with a push broom. The old man had been wheeled on to the lawn, and dozed in the shade of a pepper tree.

When Louise saw me, her face went cold. 'Emma isn't here any more, you know.' She went on sweeping, but the movements grew slower as I began to tell her about the telephone call. Finally she stopped altogether and leaned on the broom with a peculiar but friendly smile on her face. 'Come on inside,' she said. 'And never try calling me after midnight again – I switch the darn thing off and no one can reach me, come hell and high water.'

She had been doing housework in the living-room, which smelt of wax. A rug was rolled up and a large turkey duster lay on the piano.

'When Emma came to this house, I told her it had a clean reputation,' Louise said in a self-satisfied tone. 'But first she carries on with Grant – and then,' she gave a quick grating laugh, 'she's carried *off* by Midge!'

'She's living with Midge, then?'

Louise nodded. 'She played hard to get for a day or two, then she moved in.'

'Last night she said on the phone that he'd found out something – that's why he beat her.'

'Found out she's still carrying on with Grant,' Louise said promptly. 'And half the world besides, if you ask me. Of course, if I'd known she was only a *child* –'

'I'd say she was more than that.'

Louise sat down heavily on the couch. 'Well, let me tell you something. The day that girl set foot in my house, she was fourteen. Fourteen. And that's what she still is.'

I stared at her.

'Only a child,' she repeated. 'If she's got any sense, she'll make trouble for Midge. I mean, real good trouble.' She gave a little jerk with her head. 'Ever hear of statutory rape, kiddo?' She got up and dabbed with the turkey duster at a photograph elaborately framed in silver.

'See this?' she asked irrelevantly, holding it up. It showed a sandy-haired man with a thin face and small clipped moustache. 'My late husband Seymour. He was the last and best.' Her eyes looked unusually tender. 'Seymour gave me nine glorious years and broke my heart when he died. People ask me why I never marry again. Once you've had a Cadillac, I tell them, you don't settle for a Ford.'

'I suppose not,' I said.

She put the photograph back on the piano, giving it another flick with the duster. 'I know what I'm talking about,' she said. 'Love's the greatest thing in the world. And I've nothing against sex, as long as it's clean. But with a girl like Emma – I told her, you don't get on that way. People never do. Would you like a glass of port?'

I said it was too early.

'Yeah, I suppose it's early.' Sighing, she sat down again. 'Let me tell you something else. In nineteen twenty-five I was in a chorus line on Broadway, tap-tap-tapping away every night. And next to me was quite a cute little kid called Julia Katzander. Well, we both landed up in this town. I got into pictures before she did, but today she's way ahead of me; she's still the greatest. Julie Forbes,' she said. 'You can't get bigger than that. But how do you think she got there, and stayed there? She played it clean, boy. Julie Forbes is a clean woman, and I'm glad to say it's paid off.'

'And I'm glad to hear it,' I said, then asked her for Midge's address. She shook her head and said she didn't have it, but changed her mind a moment later and gave it to me.

At the front door, she put a hand on my shoulder. 'It's a beautiful day,' she said, glancing up at the hazy blue sky, patting her metallic hair, nodding with approval at her nicely-kept lawn. 'But what the hell? I feel like running wild again, I'd like to get out of this doggone town and take another trip to Las Vegas.'

It was an apartment house in the section of Hollywood just below Sunset Boulevard that was fashionable thirty years ago. Now it is becoming like any other quiet suburb, with cars parked bumper to bumper on each side of the street and signs saying APT. FOR RENT in the front gardens. Stucco bungalows have sprung up in the shadow of the old, confidently ornate and solid Spanish mansions with tiled patios, tropical vegetation, arched entrances and shuttered windows. Two children in blue jeans and cowboy hats played on the sidewalk outside one of the bungalows, but down the broad steps from the apartment house patio came, like a ghost, a majestic rich-looking lady dressed as if for cocktails in New York and carrying a chihuahua.

Midge lived on the top floor. As I rang the bell, I could hear the radio playing inside. Emma opened the door, but only a few inches.

'Oh, it's you.' She had a small bruise under her left eye and seemed mildly surprised. 'How did you find this place?'

'Louise told me.'

She giggled. 'I bet she told you more than that. Well, come in!'

She led me through the hall, into the living-room, expertly swinging her little buttocks as she walked. 'The cat's away, but I guess you checked up on that before you came round?'

I nodded. She gave me a rather furtive glance, then looked away. 'About last night,' she said with a faint tremor in her voice. 'I want you just to put it right out of your mind. I must have been crazy to call you up like that. It was just – well, I wasn't used to being hit like that. Quite hard, you know.'

'But now you are?'

'Oh, you've still got that *tone* in your voice. But nothing's as terrible as you think. Honestly.' Standing with her back to the fireplace, in which had been placed a vase of artificial tulips, she looked round at the anonymous modern living-room, white walls, fitted mohair carpet, sleek davenports, venetian blinds. 'Don't you like this apartment?'

'It's very nice.'

'It certainly is.' She opened her eyes very wide. 'Sometimes I have to pinch myself and say, Emma Slack from Galena, you'd better wake up. This can't be *you*, living here!' She pressed a button in the wall and a bookcase slid open, revealing a cocktail cabinet on the other side. 'See what I mean? Let's have a Bloody Mary.'

Happily, she picked up a shaker. 'This morning I had a letter from Aunt Rosalie, that's the older one. I hadn't heard a word from my old aunts, I thought at least they'd try and find out where I was, but not a word. So finally I had to write and tell *them*. Wasn't it mortifying? Anyway, now Aunt Rosalie comes back with a stiff little note saying how they both pray for me every night. I'd told them everything was just great, but from the way she wrote you'd think – well, you'd think my situation was desperate.'

'I'm glad it isn't,' I said.

'Oh, it's fantastic!' She was agitating the shaker vigorously. 'I go inside all the studios now. Why, I'm *inside* practically all the time.'

'Seeing people, you mean?'

'No. Having lunch.'

'When is Midge going to get you a part?'

'We have to wait for the right one,' she said, looking very serious. 'Midge says, at this stage it may be better to *turn things down*. It's very important *what I do first*. Sometimes you can do yourself more harm than good by working just for the sake of working, did you know that?' She handed me a drink. 'Are you writing that script?'

'Yes,' I said.

'You never introduced me to that director. Oh, don't apologize. I wouldn't have accepted the introduction!'

'Why on earth not?'

She smiled. 'I hope I'm not saying anything I shouldn't about a friend of yours, but he's got a terrible reputation. With girls, I mean. Midge says he'd have me in the hay.'

'And one at a time's enough?'

Her mouth dropped open. She looked very offended. 'Well, honestly! What a disgusting thing to say.' Turning her back, she retreated to the window. 'You certainly are taking liberties.'

After a silence, I said: 'All right, Emma. I'm sorry.'

'You certainly should be. Yes.'

She continued to stand with her back to me.

'Are you ever going to speak to me again?'

She turned round slowly. 'Well – you mustn't get personal, you know. I can't stand it.'

I wanted to burst out laughing, she looked so genuinely outraged. Her cheeks were still quite pink. 'I promise,' I said. 'If you'll let me ask one question.'

'All right, but don't make it insulting.'

'It's very respectful,' I said. 'Is it true you're only fourteen?'

She gasped. 'Louise told you?'

'Yes.'

'Then Grant must have told her, Grant's the only one I told. Frankly, I'd appreciate it if you kept this information to yourself,' she went on after a moment of reflection. 'I'm fifteen next month, as a matter of fact, so I'm really growing up, but I find people don't take you seriously unless you're at least seventeen. So it might be embarrassing. I don't want anybody sending me back to school, or anything.'

Now more time passes. I am working at the studio every day. The sound of hammering echoes across the back lot wilderness, and I suppose they must be building something new. It seems a long while ago that they were shooting the science-fiction film, and the war film, and the western; now they are shooting a western, a war film, and a science-fiction film. Yesterday in occupied Paris, a young Nazi fell in love with a girl from Montmartre. This morning they robbed the bank again. This afternoon a visitor from Space strides across the small-town green and peers in at the drugstore window. And while everybody screams, the St Louis Midland Express is being stoked. It leaves tonight for another station, just a hundred yards away, where outlaws will ride in and hold it up.

I haven't seen Emma again; but, living in this world, I think it ought to have a place for her, somewhere.

And now, coming out of the studio commissary after lunch, I notice a sports car parked near the entrance. Emma is sitting in it alone. She wears a close-fitting pink dress and looks in a bad temper.

I say hello.

'Oh, it's you.' Her voice sounds dispirited.

'What are you doing here?'

'Midge was meeting me for lunch but he didn't show up.'

'Why didn't you come in anyway?'

Her mouth tightens. 'I can't sit in that place all by myself and watch nobody take any notice. It's too depressing.' Then she gives me an appealing look. 'Are you busy?'

'I should be.'

'Will you take me for a walk?'

We set off through the parking lot, in the direction of the abandoned harbour town. It is midsummer. The earth looks flaked and dry. Emma doesn't talk at first, but kicks a stone along. Presently she stops, looks back at the studio buildings, and gives a long sigh.

'You're not happy, Emma.'

'Oh, only sometimes.' She shrugs. 'I'm sick of waiting around, that's all. Everything's waiting.'

We walk on. I suppose she has forgotten the first days, and my conscientious discouragements. Probably she doesn't remember the time before Midge, or doesn't think about it, anyway. It is even difficult to remind myself that her first visit to a studio was here, with me. Our connexions seem to be slipping away.

'Midge has never stood me up before!' She giggles. 'Maybe he's getting tired of me. It's a sign, isn't it?'

'What would you do if he turned you out?'

'I've thought about that,' she says blithely. 'I guess I'd have to find a new agent.'

'Suppose you couldn't?'

'Oh, I'm pretty enough. Honestly.' She is losing interest

in the subject. 'I may not *stand out*, but no one's ever said I wasn't pretty.'

We reach the quayside. There is no one around. The boats nod peacefully. In the distance, hammering begins.

'It's clever the way they do all this.' Emma looks up at the artificial canvas sky. 'It makes me *see myself*.' She points at the tilted spotlight, the empty warehouses with moss on the floor. 'It isn't all for nothing, is it? It couldn't be!' she goes on before I can answer. 'I mean, living in that old hotel and waiting for the *moment*, and everything. It couldn't be all for nothing.'

We skirt the quayside. Emma walks more slowly. Presently the hunger dies out of her eyes and she gives a little smile. 'But I get some fun, you know. You know?'

I ask if she ever sees Grant. For a moment she looks vague, then shakes her head. 'Grant? Oh no, I never see *him*. But there's . . .' A coy expression comes over her face, she seems about to impart a confidence, then thinks better of it. 'Midge is taking me to a preview tonight,' she says instead. 'I love previews. He'd better show up for *that*, or we're through!'

We have reached the other side of the harbour, and the land starts to slope down again. The sound of hammering is nearer. Emma takes a few steps forward, glances down the hill, and suddenly almost screams.

'What's the matter?'

Transfixed, she goes on staring. I follow her gaze, and see they are building a new set below us. Part of a street stretches away. At the top of it, the façade of an old Gothic mansion, grey and elaborate, with a cupola. Beyond, a line of stores with shutters. On the other side, a hotel is being assembled, curlicued and porticoed. Cars and trucks are parked nearby.

'You know what it's like?' Emma's voice rises. 'It's *exactly* like Galena!' She clutches my arm. 'I mean, there's even the waterfront behind us, and – well, just for a moment I really thought I was back in Galena again. It came as a shock, after running away two thousand miles!'

She can't take her eyes off it. I tell her we should go back, because I have to work.

'I'll stay and walk around by myself.'

'You'll be all right?'

She laughs. 'You'll never stop thinking the worst is going to happen, will you?'

'Oh,' I say, 'I don't think anything's going to happen.'

'Of course it isn't! Well ...' She holds out her hand. 'I guess I'll see you around.'

'I hope so, Emma.'

'But don't ...' She hesitates. 'Don't call me.'

'Why not?'

'Because – oh, it doesn't matter.' She glances down the street again, gives a little shiver. 'It's a funny feeling. Honestly. I mean, finding yourself back where you came from.' Her eyes are very bright. 'Good-bye now.'

'Good-bye, Emma.'

She starts down the street. I turn back towards the harbour, wondering why she doesn't want me to call her. I suppose that I remind her of doubts, uncertainties, things she doesn't want to think about. What can she be thinking about now?

I look back once. Standing in front of the hotel, she sees me and waves. Then, as she goes on down, her little figure dwindles and vanishes from sight.

Sometimes I'm Blue

TOWARDS Malibu the city falls away at last into a dry landscape punctuated with motels and garages and restaurants on the ocean side of the coast highway, with solitary houses towards the hills. Everything is scattered. It looks as if a hand has opened and dropped litter from the sky.

One of the restaurants, a long wooden shack painted white, is called The Burrow. Beside it, a plot of waste land has been made into a terrace with rough wooden tables and red wicker chairs. A neon sign flashes on and off, day as well as night.

This afternoon, a wind had started to blow in from the ocean. It felt cool. Everyone except myself, I thought, had gone inside. Getting up to leave, I noticed a young man sitting alone at a table behind me; brow slightly furrowed, he watched the surf. He wore an open beach shirt with blue polka dots, a pair of bathing trunks, and had no shoes. You'd have taken him for another handsome Californian boy who spent a lot of time on the beach. His strong tanned, hairy body was sprawled in the chair; he had perfect white teeth and a St Christopher medal on a thin silver chain round his neck. At first glance he seemed to have that impeccable American sexuality and body structure, factory packed and returnable to makers if not in perfect condition. But this was misleading. Two features broke the mould, his deep rapt ultramarine eyes and his extraordinary smile. As I got up he smiled at me, looking very directly at my face. It changed him. The smile seemed his point of contact with the world, a symbol of communication. It had a quick nervous radiance and there was a quiver of anxiety in his eyes at the same time, as if he feared you wouldn't smile back, there was no communication, you hadn't seen or heard.

'Hey!' he called across the terrace. 'Notice anything about me?'

He looked like a disappointed child when I shook my head. 'I got no clothes,' he said, patting the shirt and the bathing trunks. 'This is all.'

'Well, I suppose you've got some clothes back where you live?'

'Come over here a moment, will you?' As I did so, he laughed. 'I've got lots of clothes in lots of places. Clothes in San Francisco, clothes in Beverly Hills, clothes in Texas, clothes in New York too. Right now, I don't feel like going to any of those places. In fact, I don't want to see any of them any more!'

'What about the clothes at your own place?'

'That's impossible,' he said. 'Out of the question.'

'Why?'

'Sit down a moment, will you?' The wind ruffled his hair, he kept brushing a dark lock back from his forehead. 'Eva and I had a big row, I said I'm leaving, I said I'm never coming back. I walked out. Only, I forgot my clothes.'

'A delicate situation,' I said.

He laughed again. 'If you knew more, you'd use another word. Hey, I forgot to introduce myself.' With a brilliant smile, he took my hand and held it tightly. Held it for a long time. 'My name's Steve. Steve Pollock.'

I knew this wasn't true. I'd recognized him when I came over to the table. His picture had been in the newspapers more than once, his name was Clyde and he was the son of Canning Wallace, the Hollywood agent. His father didn't handle many clients, perhaps twenty stars and five or six directors, but they were all expensive and successful. Two of them, of course, were Cliff Harriston and Julie Forbes.

Canning was an influential man in Hollywood, and an air of social exclusivity surrounded him. During the war he had worked for the O.W.I. and made good political connexions in Washington. He had an elegant home in Beverly Hills, a ranch in Texas, where he knew most of the millionaires, and an apartment in the East 50s in New York. He gave dinner parties for famous people; on week-ends his swimming pool glittered. In Washington he was a frequent guest at Embassy Row. It was said he had once flown to London specially to attend a royal garden party. He had been married for many years to an actress who was not very talented but had done quite well through his influence. He was constantly unfaithful to her. Over two hundred guests attended their silver wedding anniversary party.

Only a few weeks after this party, Clyde made his first newspaper headline, and his mother wept at the police station, saying she couldn't understand how he could do such a thing to her. (His father said nothing and wouldn't speak to Clyde for a week.) Clyde had always seemed such a good boy, quiet and with nice manners; they had always been proud of him, by the time he was twelve you could tell how handsome he was going to be. Clyde was such a privileged boy; the wonderful people who came to his parents' home were so fond of him, and often brought him presents. Why should he get drunk and hit one of them in a restaurant, call him a phoney and break his jaw? Mrs Wallace knew that seventeen could be a difficult age, but she also knew many boys who had got through adolescence without ever doing a thing like that. She wept again. (The case was settled out of court, his father paying the hospital bill and an indemnity besides.) They sent Clyde away to the ranch in Texas.

It was just as difficult being seventeen on a ranch in Texas. He went on drinking and fighting there. They brought him back to Beverly Hills, where everyone who came to the house was very kind and said, 'Hi, Clyde!' as if nothing had ever happened. He had a serious talk with his father; Mrs Wallace had advised her husband to be tactful and try to find out *what was going on in Clyde's mind*, but all Canning could discover was that the boy wanted to get a job as steward on a ship, and go round the world. This was naturally out of the question. It had been agreed for a long time that Clyde should become a partner in his father's agency when he was eighteen.

Now Clyde said he didn't want that, he talked about people being phoneys, and Canning grew angry. Mrs Wallace thought they should send him to a psychiatrist, but Canning hated the idea. They decided the only thing to do was *be patient*, and it began to get worse. Clyde came home drunk two or three nights a week. They practically stopped his allowance, but he ran up bills at liquor stores. Then he hit someone else. Then he had his third automobile accident, more serious than the others because a girl with him had her leg crushed, and would always limp as a result. The accident was Clyde's fault; he always drove too fast, and had been doing ninety miles an hour along Pacific Coast Highway.

Canning wouldn't come to court but Mrs Wallace heard her son put on probation for two years, ordered to see a psychiatrist and forbidden to drive or drink. She wept.

'You're Clyde Wallace, aren't you?'

The smile vanished abruptly. He sipped his martini, leaning both elbows on the table. For a few moments there was no trace of good humour in his face, then suddenly it returned. 'Who are you?' he asked, mock aggressive. 'Why are you sitting at my table?'

'I stopped off here for a drink on the way back from Malibu. You asked me to sit at your table.'

'I see.' He sipped the martini again, watching me. 'Does it matter?'

'What?'

'That I'm Clyde Wallace.'

'Doesn't matter to me,' I said, 'though it probably does to you.'

He laughed. 'Hey, there's Walt! He's been trying to telephone his mother.'

A young man, rather short and stocky with worried homely features and a blond crewcut, came up to the table. He looked a few years older than Clyde.

'Walt, how many martinis have I had today? I'm on probation,' he explained to me with a pleased smile. 'No drinking, no driving.'

'You've had six,' Walt said. 'No, five.'

Clyde slapped him on the back. 'Know everything, don't you? Nursemaid,' he said. 'Get me another.'

Walt shook his head and sat down.

Clyde's voice was cold. 'Walt, I asked you to get me another martini.'

'No.'

'Well, you're the boss,' Clyde said, affable again. He reached across the table and tweaked Walt's nose. 'Did you talk to your mother?'

'No.' His face became more worried. 'You see, it's like this,' he told me. 'Usually I have dinner with my mother Saturday night. Last night I couldn't make it, so we said today, Sunday. But she said, call up first in case anything happens. Now she's not there and I don't know whether she's expecting me or not.'

Clyde laughed. 'You're expecting her to expect you.'

'It's a very nice custom, having dinner with your mother once a week. I like it, Clyde.'

'Depends on your mother. Hey, how am I going to get my clothes?'

Walt gave a sigh. I guessed Clyde had asked this question several times during the day. 'I can go or you can go or we can both go,' he said. 'I told you, *you* have to decide.'

Clyde nodded. 'Excuse me, I'm going to hunt a martini.' He walked off towards the shack.

'He has to make his own decisions.' Walt pressed his lips together. 'All his life people have made decisions for Clyde. His psychiatrist told me, make *him* decide whenever you can.'

'Would you tell me what's happening?' I said.

He looked at me with surprise. 'You don't know?'

'I'd never met Clyde till he started talking to me a few minutes ago.'

'Huh? I thought you must be someone he knew. Well, Clyde often does that.' Walt glanced towards the shack. 'Matter of fact, I've only known Clyde a year, though I guess I'm his best friend now, and he started talking to me just the same way. Clyde likes to do that, you know.'

'He told me he'd just had a row with someone called Eva. Who is she?'

Walt became worried again. 'Listen, Clyde can be difficult to handle and – I mean this in a perfectly friendly manner,' Walt said, 'but maybe you shouldn't get mixed up in anything like this. Maybe you should go now.'

'I'm interested.'

'Well ...' His face cleared. 'I guess if Clyde got talking about Eva, it's his way of wanting you to know. Eva Dearborn,' he went on, glancing at the shack again, 'she's – she's married to a big real estate agent. She's around fifty.

Rich. About a year ago, after the trial, she moved in on
Clyde.'

'How do you mean, moved in?'

'After the trial Clyde rented a little beach house. Up along
the coast at Zuma. He met Eva through some friend, and a
week later she'd moved in.' Walt frowned. 'Now she won't
get out. But the point is, Clyde asked *me* to come and live
there too, for a kind of protection, you see. There are three
of us in that house, and it doesn't work out.'

'I should think not.'

'That house is not a good place to sleep.'

I couldn't understand his resignation. 'But it's awful.
There must be some way of getting her out?'

Walt disagreed. Eva was a kind of blackmailer, he said. In
some way she'd convinced Clyde that he needed her. She had
lent him money. She could be violent, and if they really
quarrelled, Clyde might get violent too. That would involve
the police and endanger his probation.

I asked if Clyde's parents knew about it.

'He doesn't see his mother any more. Canning thought he
upset her too much, and it wasn't good for either of them.
He sees Canning occasionally, but I guess Canning's had
enough scandal and he wouldn't do anything.'

'You think Clyde has really left Eva this time?'

'I don't know. If I'd really left somebody, I wouldn't want
to go back for my clothes.'

Clyde came back with a martini in his hand. His face was
sad. 'Hello,' he said to Walt, nodded to me, slipped into the
chair and gazed at the ocean like a small lost boy.

'What's the matter, Clyde?'

Irritably he shifted his chair a few inches away from Walt,
not taking his eyes off the ocean.

'You can tell me, Clyde.' Walt waited, looking at the
ocean too, as if trying to see what Clyde could see.

'Has a person any *right*?' Clyde burst out to the surf, the sky. 'Any right to come into your own house and live there and tell you what to do?' He swung round and faced us. 'I mean, she should leave *me*! But she's there waiting for me, I drove back past the house an hour ago, and saw her car. The way I look at it is,' he spoke very slowly, 'I consider a guy should be able to go into his *own* house, fetch his *own* clothes and tell a girl she mustn't stick around any more. He should be able to do those things.'

'You're absolutely right,' Walt said.

He waved his hand impatiently. 'She said, she actually said, "if you and Walt go fishing tonight, we're through!"'

I glanced at Walt for confirmation of this. Clyde noticed, and his eyes gleamed. 'I swear it!'

Walt nodded. 'Clyde likes to go fishing, so we arranged to go fishing, we even invited Eva along. She said no, she felt tired, but all right you go. No scene. She was quite nice about it. Then suddenly after lunch Clyde and I are talking about going fishing, and she screams at him. "You go fishing, Clyde, and we're through." She really screams at him.'

'What did Clyde say?'

Clyde sat up straight, watching for our approval. 'I said, "then we're through." And she said, "don't ever come back." I said, "Eva, this happens to be my house, don't *you* ever come back!" She says she'll kill me. I walk out, but I forget my clothes.' He looked at Walt. 'Can I stay at your place tonight?'

'I told you, Clyde. Stay as long as you want.' Walt turned to me. 'Eva has a gun.'

Clyde lay back in his chair, playing with his St Christopher medal. 'Get me another martini, will you?'

'You shouldn't have any more.'

'Why?'

'It's not good for you.'

'Nothing's good for me, so who cares?'

'Stop pitying yourself, Clyde.'

'It's not pity, it's fact number one.' He scratched his bare stomach. 'Cold and hard.'

'I don't believe it.'

Walt had gone rather pale. Clyde stretched across the table and ruffled his hair. 'Oh, you're so wonderful. You're the only part of my life that counts for anything.' He grinned. After a moment, Walt grinned back. Then the brightness went out of Clyde's face again. 'What are you waiting for? Get me another martini.'

Silently Walt got up and went into the shack.

I said: 'You'd better not drink any more.'

He gave me a disgusted look. 'Are you another one with a Tolstoy complex?'

'Why do you say that?'

'Listen, have you read *War and Peace*?'

I shook my head. 'I've tried several times, but I've never been able to finish it.' Clyde glowered at me. 'That's just me, I'm not saying anything against it.'

'You'd better not.' He put his hand on my wrist. 'It's pretty good. In fact, it's pretty great. I read a book about Tolstoy too; that man was practically a saint. There should be more men like that.'

'All the same, I haven't got a Tolstoy complex. How can I, since I've never read him properly?'

'You're as clear a case of the Tolstoy complex as I ever saw.' He leaned across, smiling up into my eyes. 'You see, Tolstoy – well, *he turned it all down.*' Clyde waved at the shack, the neon sign, the cars passing along the highway. 'Civilization,' he said quietly. 'Tolstoy said, give everything you have to the poor. He said, learn to love people, especially the poor. He was good. He believed in saving people because he loved them. I don't mean sex,' he smiled at me again, 'but – humanity. Now, the point is, you're sitting here, watching, listening, turning it all down and wanting *me* to be saved.'

'I'd like to see you saved,' I said. 'That's a very ordinary reaction, nothing more.'

'It's a semi-Tolstoy complex. And the point is – give up. It's too late here, it's phoney. Maybe if I can get through this probation I'll go to Mexico. Or Italy. Where they live simply. Where there's no dollar sign.' He took a wad of money from his shirt pocket and held up a twenty dollar bill. 'Here's the sign,' he said. 'Well, learn to love the poor. Give it away.'

With a quick gesture he seized my hand, put the bill in my palm, and closed my fingers over it.

'I don't want it,' I said.

'I owe it to you.' He pressed his hand more tightly over mine.

'What for?'

'Oh, for this conversation. A lot of people get up and walk away from me, you know.'

'Well, don't start paying them not to.'

He laughed and let go my hand. The bill lay on the table between us.

'Nobody wants twenty bucks? No starving widow? No hungry child?' Clyde took it between thumb and forefinger. 'Here's the sign,' he said, and tore it up.

Fragments floated on the breeze to the middle of the terrace, and scattered. Walt came back with a martini in his hand. He set it down in front of Clyde, who gave no sign of noticing it.

'We ought to get those clothes,' Walt said.

Clyde shook his head with a brief convulsive movement, as if a fly had brushed against it. Tired of the subject, of every subject, he stared at the ocean, then lay back and closed his eyes.

Walt said in a low voice: 'This is a bad day.'

A little later, I was walking with them both on Malibu pier. It was four o'clock. The wind was still rising, heavy surf broke against the shore. Boats waited to go out later. A few people fished from the pier railings, most had given up. At the far end, a group of fishermen stood chatting outside the little café. Juke-box music played against the wind.

Outside the booth with a look-out tower where the fishermen sold bait and tackle, hung an enormous seabass over two feet long. Clyde stared at it.

'Some bass,' he said presently. 'How much does it weigh?'

'Forty-five pounds,' said a fisherman in the booth, and came forward with an even bigger one in his arms. 'Why, hello Clyde.' He hung up the fish. 'This one's fifty-nine.'

Clyde patted it. 'Some bass. You catch them both, Frankie?'

The fisherman nodded.

'You going out again tonight?'

'Seven o'clock. Want to come along?'

'No, I can't,' Clyde said. 'I got too much to do. Look at that bass,' he said to Walt. 'I'm cold,' he added. He went over to the side and leaned on the railing, staring down at the ocean. 'Smells good here, doesn't it?'

'Yes,' I said.

'Salty and good. Wind freshens it up. You know there's no air in this damned town?' He looked across to the hills, his face indignant. 'That's another thing wrong with it, it's airless. All that stuff around you that you can't see – it's dead.' He sighed. 'Just sometimes a patch of it comes alive. Like now. And last night I walked past some houses, smelt jasmine.'

He leaned down towards the ocean again. 'This is the Pacific,' he said. 'Peaceful. Never throw yourself into a peaceful ocean, you wouldn't believe you could drown.'

'The surf's pretty high.'

Clyde listened to it for a moment, a gust of wind made his hair stand up, then it flopped back over his forehead. He clapped me on the shoulder. 'You're right. Think I should jump?'

Walt came over. 'I'm hungry.'

'You always are,' Clyde said. 'You're a hungry kid.'

'I didn't have any lunch.'

'Neither did I.'

'You've been drinking, that makes a difference.'

'Well, you go and drink – or eat. Take my car.' Clyde gave him a push. 'Go on, shove off.'

'Clyde, don't be like that.'

'Like what?' Clyde pushed him again.

'Like that, Clyde.'

'But that's *me*. Mean.' His eyes shone. 'You ought to know that, you're my buddy.'

'Sometimes I wonder why.'

Clyde laughed. 'So do I. But you're the only part of my life that counts for anything.' He threw his arms round Walt and hugged him. 'You're wonderful.'

'You're pretty great yourself.' Walt broke free, looking flushed. 'I'm hungry,' he repeated.

'Okay,' Clyde said, very amiable. 'Let's feed Walt.' He gave him another push, more violent, and forced him back to the railing. 'Let's feed Walt to the fishes.'

They struggled. Walt's face was grim.

'I'm laughing,' Clyde said. 'This is a joke, Walt.'

He tightened his arm round Walt's neck. Walt jabbed his elbow into Clyde's stomach and thrust him back.

'Clyde, will you stop that?'

'Oh, excuse me,' Clyde said and walked off to the men's room.

Walt leaned against the chipped white wall of the fishermen's booth and closed his eyes. He was breathing quickly, he pressed his hand against his forehead as if something threatened to break out of it. 'What shall I do?' he asked. He opened his eyes and gave a nervous smile.

I said: 'How exactly did you meet Clyde?'

'At some bar, a few weeks before he had that accident. He was drunk, I helped him get home.' Walt closed his eyes again. 'It went on from there.' He opened his eyes and looked at his feet. He shifted them. 'I'm a very ordinary sort of guy, you know.'

I nodded.

'Don't I strike you as an ordinary normal sort of guy?' He glanced sharply at me.

'*You* do, but not your situation.'

'Situation?' he echoed. 'A person and a situation are the same thing.'

'Not necessarily. What you get out of counts just as much as what you get into.'

'You think I should get out of this?'

'Do you want to?'

He shifted his feet again. 'You trying to make me admit something?'

'Why should I? It was simply because you asked me what you should do.'

'I see him every day,' Walt said, half to himself. He looked at me again. 'There's almost no one else now. His psychiatrist said I must be careful. He said, Clyde wants you to enter his own madness.'

'I don't like the sound of Clyde's madness. Instead of entering his, why don't you try and make him enter yours?'

'You think I'm mad?' Walt scratched his head. 'I thought I struck you as normal?'

'Oh, it's all relative,' I said. 'What does the psychiatrist say about Eva?'

'He says she's basically a mother substitute, and when Clyde's ready to break with it, he will.'

'There's really nobody to help him, is there?'

'There's me,' Walt said. 'Clyde tells me I'm the only one, you know. And I've kept him out of trouble. I drive him around, and watch him, and try to stop him drinking too much. And it's a funny thing,' he said, a tear in the corner of one eye, 'I guess I care about Clyde more than anyone else in the world. I'd do anything for him. I've never felt this way about any guy before.'

Clyde came back, whistling.

'Walt, we have to get my clothes,' he said in a brisk cheerful voice. 'How shall we do that?'

But first it was another bar. 'Hey, I feel like driving!' Clyde said as we left the pier. Walt managed to dissuade him, but as soon as we got into the white Porsche Clyde was urging him to do a hundred miles an hour along the highway. 'Let's go, Walt, let's really go.' Walt shook his head. 'Walt! Come *on*, Walt!' The car kept to a steady fifty-five. 'Let's have some speed, for God's sake, Walt!' All the time he was fiddling with the radio knob, switching from station to station. As we did sixty, Tchaikovsky's *Romeo and Juliet* blared out.

Walt whistled under his breath.

'Your whistling is spoiling my enjoyment of the music, Walt.'

'I'm sorry.'

At Zuma, we passed the beach house. A car was parked outside.

'She's still waiting,' Clyde said. 'Turn around.'

'Why don't we do it now, Clyde?'

He shook his head. 'I need a drink first.'

'It's better if you don't.'

'Will you turn the car around, Walt?'

We headed back towards Malibu. A calypso was coming from the radio now. There were two cars in front of us, one in each lane.

'You can pass them, Walt. Pass them between the lanes.'

'Too dangerous.'

Clyde shrugged, then pointed to a bar ahead. 'Stop there!' he ordered.

'The owner doesn't like you.'

'Ralph? He's crazy about me.'

We went into the bar and sat at the counter. Beyond it was a dining-room; people at the booths were drinking cocktails. A man in a white tuxedo played the piano. Nearly everyone stared at Clyde in his beach clothes and bare feet.

'Hi, Clyde,' said the barman, friendly but nervous. 'What's it going to be?'

'Champagne, champagne for everyone. It's my birthday.'

'Well, congratulations, Clyde. How old are you?'

He looked morose. 'I don't know a thing like that.'

'A man knows his own age, Clyde.'

'Forget it.' Clyde gave him a glowing smile. 'It's not my birthday.' The barman laughed dutifully.

'But you still want champagne?'

'Sure. The best. Imported.'

A tall blonde girl in a white dress entered the bar, looked round, sat down at a booth by herself. Clyde watched her intently.

'Who's that broad?' he asked the barman.

'Which one?'

'The blonde with the crazy figure.'

The barman glanced at her. 'She comes in here a lot, Clyde, with her husband. Waiting for him now, I guess.'

Clyde laughed. 'You mean you can't fix me up?'

'She's married, and waiting for her husband.' Walt sounded tense. 'Don't make trouble.'

'And don't look so jealous.' Clyde swung round and whispered something in his ear. Walt went very red. 'Oh, I forgot you don't like threesomes. Hi, Ralph! That's a beautiful suit, I'm crazy about it,' Clyde said as a portly man in a bright orange linen suit and black suede shoes came up to the bar counter.

'You really like it?' Ralph stroked the lapels. 'Fantastic tailoring,' he said with a complacent smile.

'That's what I call a suit with real class,' Clyde said, and gave me a wink.

A voice called over the loudspeaker: 'Telephone for the boss!' Ralph hurried away. 'Good to see you again, Clyde.' He smiled over his shoulder and waved, but his eyes were cold.

The barman opened a bottle of champagne.

'Get yourself a glass,' Clyde said.

'Why, thank you, Clyde.' Glasses were filled. 'Your health, Clyde.' The barman raised his glass. 'And happy birthday, whenever it is.'

A fisherman had sat down on the stool next to mine. Clyde leaned across the counter. 'Get yourself a glass, Harry!'

'I'll stick to beer, Clyde. I'm strictly a beer man, remember?'

'Then let me buy you a beer. How's fishing?'

'Too darned much of it.' He yawned. 'Out all last night, back at seven this morning. At one the boss calls up and asks me to mend a boat, can you beat it? Now I have to go out again at seven. You forget what it's like to sleep in bed.'

'Yes,' Clyde said. 'Did you see these seabass on the pier?'

'No, who caught them?'

'Frankie. A forty-fiver and a fifty-niner.'

Harry gave a whistle.

'Ralph!' said Clyde as the proprietor came back to the bar. 'That's a terrible suit. You look grotesque in that suit. You should take off that suit before you make an idiot of yourself in front of everybody.'

'I'm sorry you feel that way, kid.' Ralph was icily calm. 'I happen to like it.'

'What do you like about it?'

'Just about everything. I like the colour.'

'How can you say that, Ralph? The colour's terrible. You should never wear that suit. That suit is a mess. Who dreamed it up, for God's sake?'

'I did. Designed the whole thing myself. Had gold buttons put on.' Blandly he held up a cuff.

Clyde hid his face in his hands. 'Take it away, you're blinding me.'

'You are the only person who ever said a word against this suit. Excuse me,' Ralph added as the loudspeaker summoned him to the telephone again.

Clyde gave a sigh. 'People should be truthful with each other. I mean, it's nicer when people are truthful. It stings a bit, but it's nicer. Take my uncle, the only truthful man in my family was my Uncle Lester.'

'How's your father?' the barman asked.

'Great,' Clyde said without a flicker. 'A great man, you know. Busy. Big deals all the time. Always hits the spot.'

'That's fine.'

'It's beautiful. Stick with the old man and you can't go wrong.' He was pouring out more champagne. 'But my Uncle Lester hadn't a penny when he died.' He leaned across the counter again. 'Harry, do you worship the dollar sign?'

The fisherman grinned. 'I'm going out to work tonight, aren't I?'

'Sure. But my father made more money last week than you made last year. You're saying the wrong prayer. Stick with the old man,' Clyde repeated, 'and the door to success swings open before you even knock on it.' He looked up as Ralph came back to the bar. 'That's a beautiful suit. I'm crazy about it.'

The proprietor's mouth tightened. 'Glad you like it, Clyde.'

'I'm crazy about it. And I'm crazy about you, Ralph, I love you very much.'

'I'm not built that way.' Ralph smirked. 'Better find yourself a girl.'

As he walked away, Clyde called after him: 'That's a lousy pianist you have here, better get rid of him before he closes up this wretched joint. I guess Ralph doesn't like me,' he said to the barman.

'Sure, he likes you.'

'When he sees me come in here, his face falls to the ground. He'd like to kick my face in, but my father's a big man around here. A lot of people feel that way about me, you know.'

'You're all wrong, Clyde. The boss likes you very much. He told me.'

Clyde shook his head. 'People should be truthful with each other.' He turned to me and smiled. 'You see what it's like?' His eyes were very soft and pleading. 'I'm not really drunk. I'm just playing it that way. I like to watch the cagey smiles on cagey faces. I'm really *turning it all down*.' He winked, and tapped his forehead. 'In here.' He beat on the counter. 'Let's have some more champagne.'

'No,' Walt said.

Affectionate, Clyde put his arm round Walt's neck. 'No?'

'No. We have to fetch those clothes.'

'You're right.' He slipped off the stool, then looked at me. 'You coming?'

Clyde was silent at first, as we drove to the house at Zuma. He didn't turn on the radio or ask Walt to go faster. Once he jerked his thumb back in the direction of the bar. 'All phoneys in that place, except Harry.'

He brooded. The sun was going down and the dazzle on the water made a cloud in the sky look like a rainbow, prismatically streaked with green and blue and pink.

'That's a good sign,' he said. 'I like that cloud. I feel this is going to be my lucky day. Are you superstitious?'

'No,' I said.

'You should be. Superstition's crazy. Believe in it, and you don't have to worry about the world any more. Superstition explains everything. They had a war, millions of people got killed, because some idiot broke a mirror.'

We turned off the highway into a gravel track. The coast arched into a small promontory, and Clyde's house was the first, standing at the base of the land's curve. It was small and wooden, painted blue. A car was parked outside.

Clyde didn't get out at once. Frowning, he lit a cigarette.

'What's the matter?'

He looked at me, and shook his head. 'You stay here. I can't let you come in this house.'

'The presence of a stranger might help,' Walt said.

'Nothing helps.' He was still frowning. 'You got a pocket knife, Walt?'

'Why?'

'Maybe we should slit up one of the tyres on her car, so she can't come after us.'

'You know what she'd do. She'd tell the police. You've got to keep cool, Clyde.'

'I'm cool. You cool?' he asked me.

'The coolest.'

He smiled. 'Come on, then.' He got out of the car, went towards the house, turned back. He opened the door of the other car.

'Tell you what we'll do. We'll turn on her lights and let her battery run down. She can't prove she didn't do that herself.'

He turned on the lights of the car, watched them for a moment with satisfaction.

'Looks good,' he said.

The house was built below the level of the track. I followed Clyde down a flight of wooden steps at the side. Directly below, the ocean broke loudly against rocks and spray leapt into the air. Clyde swayed a little as he walked down, holding on to the balustrade.

The front door was open and led directly into the kitchen. Through a doorway on the left was the living-room. A television set was turned on there. I supposed the bedroom lay beyond the living-room.

Walt went into the living-room. Clyde signalled to me to stay with him, and opened a closet door in the kitchen wall. Rows of suits hung inside. He looked at them and seemed dazed. Finally he took out a white seersucker suit and handed it to me.

'Hold this.' A trunk stood in the corner, he opened it and took out a pile of shirts. After a moment he put them all back, closed the trunk and sat on it with his head in his hands. 'Her stuff takes up all the closet space in the bedroom,' he said. 'She's got a lot of stuff.'

'Don't let that worry you now, Clyde. Choose a shirt.'

He nodded, got up and opened the trunk again.

As I stood holding the suit, I glanced through the doorway into the living-room. The doorway was low; I could see the legs and body of a woman sitting in a wicker chair, but I couldn't see her face. She was watching the kitchen, not the television set. Sunburnt legs were crossed and very still, a pair of moccasin slippers on the feet, one dangling precariously.

Walt came out of the living-room, carrying the telephone on a long wire. I looked inquiringly at him, but he shook his head – telling me, I imagined, to stay with Clyde – and took the telephone out to the porch.

When I looked back at Clyde, he was putting on a white shirt. He took the suit away from me and started to hang it up in the closet. Then he brought it back to me.

'No, that's okay.' He still seemed dazed. I started to lay the suit on the table and he said: 'Hold on to it, will you?'

Outside, on the porch, Walt was telephoning.

It was very strange, and time had become suspended. I had no idea how long I had been standing there, holding Clyde's suit, when he jerked my arm suddenly and snatched it away from me. He put on the trousers, then swore and took them off again.

'Forgot my underpants.'

Walt came through from the porch, carried the telephone into the living-room. I heard him say: 'You okay, Eva?' She didn't move or answer. The loose slipper had fallen off and lay on the floor.

Clyde had put on his trousers, and stood in front of a mirror, very carefully combing his hair.

'You only taking one suit?' I asked.

'Is all I need.'

'What about the rest?'

He didn't answer. Walt came in and said to me: 'She wants to meet you.'

I walked through the doorway and saw her face. A shock

almost of disappointment at first, because it was so ordinary:
short, rather bulky body with a round face, small eyes, small
bunched mouth, cheeks a little puffy. A white linen beach
hat was crammed on the top of her head. Her skin was very
tanned.

A quiet but abrasive voice asked: 'You some kind of
writer?'

'Yes,' I said.

'What kind? Movies?'

'Sometimes.'

She laughed curtly. 'Times are bad, huh?'

I nodded.

'We-ell . . .'

She hardly looked at me while she spoke; she didn't smile
or change her expression, which had something glazed and
withdrawn about it. Now she put a finger to her mouth and
bit off a broken piece of nail. The deliberately inelegant
gesture told something about her. Eva was rich and money
was power to her. Nothing else mattered, you didn't have to
be attractive or charming.

She spat out the nail. 'Pictures are lousy, that's the
trouble. But if you're talented, you'll get so rich here you'll
die. You'll die anyway,' she added with a laugh. 'However,
this town can use talent.' Outside, a heavy wave broke on
the rocks and spray rattled the windows. 'That's what I
keep telling Clyde. It's no good just being a handsome kid
and having a famous father if you're *nothing*. It doesn't
work that way any more. Excuse me, I have to go in there.'
She pointed to the kitchen as if she had a cake in the oven
that needed attention. 'Sit down and watch television.'

It was quiet and unemphatic, but an order. I sat on a chair
opposite the set while Walt removed the telephone again
and went out to the porch.

From the chair I could see three things: the ocean surf

through the window on the left, its sound blotted out by the television set, then the set itself, and a full-length wall mirror just beyond it. Eva was reflected in the mirror, standing with her back to me in the kitchen. Wandering round, Clyde was sometimes reflected, sometimes not.

I turned down the sound from the television set and sat in the chair again. Now I could hear the ocean, like an enormous heartbeat.

For a while Eva didn't say anything. She stood watching Clyde, who had strewn clothes all over the kitchen. He was staring at suits and shirts, confused by their disarray. She moved closer to him, the beach hat level with his shoulders.

As he went back to the closet, she said: 'You leaving?'

'Yes, I'm leaving.'

'Those socks don't match.'

Evidently he was wearing odd ones; he muttered something and his reflection disappeared.

'Can't even dress yourself, can you?'

No answer.

'Are you drunk?'

No answer.

A laugh. 'I can tell them about this drinking of yours, you know.'

His reflection came back. I could see him changing socks.

'So you're leaving.'

'Yes, I'm leaving.'

'But I won't let you!' Louder, this.

'You can't stop me, Eva.'

She snapped her fingers. 'Like that I can stop you.'

Clyde picked up a pair of shoes.

'You can't do anything without me, Clyde. You'll see. Anything you try to do, you just won't be able to. You didn't go fishing, did you?'

'No, I didn't.'

'You see? I told you not to, you didn't go.' Quietly:
'That's the way it is, Clyde.'

He moved out of sight; she followed him. All I could see
was the litter of clothes. Clyde's voice came in a sudden
desperate shout: 'Eva, will you get out of my life?'

Silence, except for the ocean. I glanced away, at another
shower of spray as it hit the window, at the old Jeanette
MacDonald film on television. On the porch, Walt was still
telephoning.

On the wall behind my chair I noticed about a dozen
framed photographs, all of Clyde as a child, with his father.
The earliest picture must have been taken when Clyde was
about four, the last when he was twelve or thirteen. Canning
was tall, erect, always wearing a conscious paternal smile.
On a fishing trip, at Miami Beach, on horseback in Texas,
he smiled. Even then it was the antithesis of Clyde's, radiant and questioning. There were no pictures of Mrs Wallace.

'*Eva!* Let go of me, Eva!'

They were reflected in the mirror again, struggling. I
could see their bodies interlocked, hands reaching up.

'You hit me, Clyde, and I'll call the sheriff!'

'I don't *want* to hit. Just – ' He broke away from her,
disappeared again. She watched him, then sat on the table.
I could see her face: stony, expressionless.

'Listen to me. I'm the only one who really cares about
you. The only one in the world, Clyde.'

'I don't want you to care.'

'Someone's got to.' She crossed her bare feet. 'Someone's
got to love you.'

'I've got people to love me.'

'Who?' Silence. 'Just tell me who!' Silence. Her voice
rising fiercely: '*You couldn't even go fishing!*'

She got up from the table. For a while I couldn't see

either of them again. When their reflections came back, they were struggling. Eva had a stool and was trying to push it in Clyde's face, or bring it down on his head. He managed to get it away from her, then walked to the mirror and began knotting his tie.

'There's no one else.' She was beginning again. 'Your father won't help, your mother never tried. They wish you'd never been born.'

'I've got people.'

'Walt? You mean Walt?' She laughed. 'Walt's just queer for you. You know that. And you're driving him crazy, he won't stand it much longer, he'll walk out on you soon. Oh, you're the loneliest person I ever saw.'

His voice sounded weak and tired. 'Okay, I'm lonely. Yes, I'm lonely.'

'This is a terrible town when no one cares about you. You'll never get well in a place like this. I can take you anywhere you want to go. Don't you want to go to Mexico? Italy?'

'I don't want to go anywhere with you.'

'You don't mean that. You know I love you. I've done more than anyone else.'

'More than anyone else to drive me out of my mind.'

'You don't mean that. Why should I bother with you, Clyde, if I don't love you? I'm rich. I've got people, lots of people.'

'Fine, give a party.'

A pause, then: 'Clyde. Just look at me, Clyde, and tell me one thing.'

He turned away, arranging a white handkerchief in the breast pocket of his coat. She went after him and swung him round by the shoulders. 'Look at me, damn you! Tell me you don't owe me anything. Go on, tell me that if I hadn't been here, you'd still be standing on your feet.' She shook him. 'Tell me you wouldn't be in jail, or lying in the gutter, or smashed up in some car?'

He looked at her, but he didn't answer.

She laughed. 'You've admitted it. I can squash you under one foot and I can sit you up on the moon. That's why I love you, and that's why I despise you so much you make me sick!' She gave a small, curious grunt of rage. 'All right, I've finished with you. You're leaving.'

She let go of him, and his whole body trembled. 'Eva ...' His voice became almost a whine. 'It's true. You love me. You're the only one who cares. I'm sorry, Eva.'

He started to take off his coat.

'Oh, *please*,' she said. 'You're leaving. Let me help you on with that thing.' She slipped the coat back over his shoulders. 'You look so pretty. But you owe me fifty dollars.'

'I'll pay you.'

'Now. I need it now, Clyde.'

'Why?'

'I didn't get to the bank this week. So will you pay me, unless I have to ask your father? Considering how much you owe me, Clyde, I think it's very nice of me to settle for fifty dollars.'

He took a wad of money from his pocket. 'I know why you want me to pay you. You want to see how much money I've got.' Looking at her with hatred, he put three twenty dollar bills in her hand. 'Keep the change, you may need it.'

Walt came back from the porch with the telephone.

'I'm all through.' Clyde smiled. 'Let's go.'

Eva was sitting on the table again, very still. The beach hat was slightly askew. She looked at Clyde, neat in his seersucker suit, black tie and white shirt. 'You know what it'll be like, don't you? Remember the times you came home and said you were blue? I always made you feel better.' She ran her forefinger down Walt's face. 'Can *you* make Clyde feel better?'

'What about all that stuff?' Walt asked, pointing to the clothes still lying about the kitchen.

'Oh, leave her to clean up the mess,' Clyde said and went out of the front door.

I said good-bye to Eva. She nodded. 'Bye, Eva,' Walt said. She nodded again, sitting very stiffly on the table, eyes watching until we turned the corner and went up the steps. Surf pounded against the rocks.

Clyde kept on looking at himself in the driving mirror. He straightened his tie. Smoothed down his shirt collar. Wiped a tiny smut from his forehead.

'You did it,' Walt said. 'You got your suit, walked out, did everything yourself. You look good in that suit, too.'

'It's a very good suit,' Clyde said.

'You chose the right shirt and tie.'

He nodded. 'Yeah, it looks good.'

'How do you feel?'

'I don't know. You like these shoes?'

They were hand made, of light grey suede.

'Sure,' Walt said. 'They look good with the suit, too.'

'The whole thing looks good,' Clyde said.

'Walt,' I asked, 'what were you doing all that time on the telephone?'

'Trying to reach my mother. First time, the line was busy. I wanted to let her know I couldn't make it for dinner, the way things were shaping up.'

'You can make it,' Clyde said. 'It's only six o'clock.'

'Really?' I said, still feeling that something had gone wrong with time, it couldn't have been only three hours ago that I first saw Clyde sitting on the terrace of The Burrow in his beach clothes and bare feet, watching the ocean. We were caught now in the end of another beach day. A long line of cars headed back towards Hollywood. The wind had dropped, the sun was low over the ocean, the landscape lay in a cool blurred light. We stopped at a traffic signal, and you could hear several radios playing at once in the cars, loud wistful voices seasoned the air with all the daily dreams and complaints of love.

'We should stick together this evening,' Walt said.

'I want to do something.' Clyde brushed back a lock of hair from his forehead. 'I'm all dressed up, aren't I? A new man?'

'We'll celebrate your freedom,' Walt said.

Clyde frowned. 'But I'm not free.'

'Free of Eva.'

'It doesn't feel so good now.' He gave a shiver. 'It feels all empty and lonesome. Why should it be like that?'

'I'm here,' Walt said. 'It won't feel lonesome with me.'

'I don't know.' Clyde looked at me as if he'd never seen me before in his life. 'Where do you come from, where do you fit in?'

'I've been trying to figure that out,' I said.

'Let me know if you solve the problem.' He shivered again. 'Where does anyone fit in? Hey, I want to get out!' he said as we passed the pier.

Walt slowed down. 'What for, Clyde?'

'I want to take a walk on the pier.'

The car stopped and he jumped out, standing uncertainly on the edge of the highway.

'You really want to go on the pier?'

'That's what I said.'

Walt took his arm. 'I'll help you across.'

'Friends are wonderful people,' Clyde said, 'but they never leave you alone.'

I watched Walt steer him through the lines of fast traffic. At the entrance to the pier they stood talking for a moment, then Clyde pushed him away and walked off by himself.

Walt came back to the car, sat in the driver's seat with his head bowed. 'I have to settle this thing, don't I? I'm not even living my own life any more.'

I couldn't think of anything to say.

'I should have a career besides looking after Clyde.'

'What did you do before you met him?'

He laughed. 'Never really got started. One year I worked in a factory, nuts and bolts. Then I was a swimming instructor. When I met Clyde I was a driving instructor.'

'Does Clyde pay you?'

'Driver's rates. Tips, sometimes.' He paused. 'The first time I met him I liked him so much, even though he was drunk.'

'What did you see in him, Walt?'

'The first time I saw him, I knew there was a real nice guy in Clyde. And he has *ideas*. He wants to live right, he can tell a phoney a mile off. Only thing is, he can't do anything about it.'

'Do you think he ever will?'

'Wouldn't it be great?' Walt said. 'I mean, wouldn't it be great if things started to go right for him at last? I hate this town like Clyde does. I want to get away. We keep on talking about going around the world, wouldn't it be great?' He fell into silence. Then he said: 'Clyde can be a terrible person, show you no respect. I think that's what hurts, even though I don't respect myself.'

'Why?'

He shook his head suddenly. 'I've never wanted to go with

a guy before. Honestly.' Another silence. 'I know the way I feel. I know it's wrong, I'm ashamed.'

'You shouldn't be.'

'Don't say that, don't entitle me to consideration. That kind of thing is wrong.' Walt got out of the car. 'Let's go and find Clyde.'

'Maybe you should drive me to The Burrow first, and I'll get my car. I should be going.'

'Don't go.'

'Why?'

He shrugged. 'I don't know. Maybe . . . I want to be with Clyde, but I don't want to be alone with him just now. It's too tricky. Can you understand?'

'Yes, but sooner or later –'

'I know that, and it's going to be sooner. You can take so much and I've taken it, and I'm going to settle this thing with Clyde. Everything else has been settled,' he said with a rueful smile, 'so this might as well be the day.'

Clyde was standing at the end of the pier, leaning over the rails and looking at the ocean. He had bought a plate of potato chips, ate one in his fingers from time to time. His hair was untidy again. He had loosened his tie and undone the top button of his shirt.

We came and stood quite close to him, but he didn't look up.

'Hi,' Walt said in a lame voice.

He turned round slowly. 'Hi, Walt. Who are you?'

'You okay?'

'No.' Clyde spoke to the ocean. 'I'm blue.'

'You shouldn't be. You walked out on Eva, like you always wanted to.'

He ignored this. 'Walt, there's still time to go fishing. Like to go fishing?'

'You can't go fishing in that suit.'

'Well, answer this question,' Clyde said. He smiled. '*What happened? How did we get here?* Make sense.'

'It doesn't matter what happened. Doesn't matter why we're here. All that matters is where we go now.'

'You're a fool. I can't move from this pier without knowing why I got here.'

'You always liked the pier, you like to go fishing. That's all.' Walt moved towards him. 'Come and have dinner, Clyde.'

Clyde held up his hand warningly. 'Don't come any nearer.'

'What's the matter?'

'I don't know yet. I've been standing here, looking at the ocean, trying to figure out this goddamned day. Oh, look!' he said suddenly.

Two fishing boats had started out.

'There's Harry.' He cupped his hands over his mouth. 'HARRY!'

The boat was too far away for Harry to hear, it moved on through a faint glow of sunset. Clyde called again, then beat the railing with his fist.

'There was a clear time,' he said. 'Once it was clear.'

'It'll come again,' Walt said.

He gave an irritated shrug. 'You know how I feel? Like this pier. I mean, look at this great ocean. It's always there, isn't it? It doesn't feel, the ocean doesn't know anything, but it's great and big and blind, and it lasts for ever. Look at this pier, this stupid little pier, sticking out in this great ocean!' He beat the railing again. 'It isn't even steady, it hasn't got a chance.' He looked at Walt. 'You didn't make sense. Do we have to go to some phoney bar?'

'We can eat at some quiet little place.'

'I'm not hungry.' He watched the boats again, moving further away.

'Clyde, will you listen to me?'

'I'm listening.' He spoke to the ocean.

'I need a little more consideration.' Walt's voice trembled. 'You can take so much.'

'Take it or leave it,' Clyde said.

'You don't mean that.'

'You're talking like Eva.' He smiled, but he sounded angry. 'Get this. I don't mean *anything*.'

'I don't believe you, Clyde.'

'Jesus God !' the cry echoed out across the ocean. 'Everybody looks at me, says they don't believe it, says I don't mean it, tells me what to do.' With a quick rough movement he took Walt's head in his hands, and twisted it around to face the ocean.

'What do you see?'

'The ocean. Let me go, Clyde.'

Clyde's grip tightened. 'Don't say anything, just answer my questions. So you see the ocean. What's the name of the ocean?'

'The Pacific ocean.'

'Very good.' He gave Walt's head another sharp twist. 'Now look this way. What do you see?'

'You. Clyde Wallace.'

'Say that name again, will you?'

'Clyde Wallace.'

'Not so good.' He let Walt go. 'You see nobody.'

'Now *you're* talking like Eva.' Walt rubbed his head.

'Sometimes she made sense.' He sighed, and spoke very quietly. 'I think I'm sorry for just about everything I've ever done. And for everything I'm going to do.' Then he shouted suddenly. 'Walt, get the hell out of here !'

Walt stared at him, not moving.

'Stop hanging around!' Clyde shouted. 'Get the hell out of here! Split!'

'Okay.' Walt's face was very taut. 'Good-bye, Clyde.'

I started to go after him, but he brushed me away. I said: 'Clyde, you shouldn't have done that. Ask him to come back.'

He smiled faintly, watching Walt as he walked away down the pier. Walt looked back once, but Clyde didn't appear to notice. He went on smiling.

'Ask him to come back, Clyde.'

'You know what's on my mind?' He stood with his back to the railing, and loosened his tie further. 'It's funny, I'm thinking about the day my Uncle Lester died. I was fifteen. I had to go to his bedside and say good-bye. There was a nurse and my mother and father talking about something when I came in. My uncle had a stroke, his face was paralysed, the nurse said he couldn't hear. I went in and took his hand and said: "I'm real sorry, Uncle Lester. I shall miss you." I watched his face, and you couldn't tell anything, but he never took his eyes off me, and somehow I felt he could hear. "I always liked you a lot, Uncle Lester," I said, "I want you to know I always *appreciated* you. Also, I shan't forget you when you're gone." My mother came over. "That'll do, that was very nice, Clyde." I looked at her and said, "But I meant it." "I know you meant it, it was very nice," she said, "but he can't hear you." "Maybe he can," I said, "and if there's a chance he can hear me, I want him to know how I feel. He doesn't get much appreciation, you know." My father tried to make me come away. "This is hardly the time or the place for an argument, Clyde," he said. "Indeed no," the nurse said. "I'm afraid the patient has just passed on." Then I was angry with them. I told my mother and father they'd wasted this valuable time when I could have finished explaining to my Uncle Lester how much I appreciated him. And I knew my mother and father didn't really want me to appreciate him, they never liked him because he was never much good at anything. But he was the only one...'

After a pause he added: 'I don't know why I'm thinking about the day my Uncle Lester died,' and moved away. He leaned on the railing and watched the boats, small and distant now.

'Well, good-bye,' I said.

'You going?'

'You don't want me to stay, do you?'

'What's the difference? Well, good-bye.' He shook my hand. 'Nice meeting you. Really.'

He let go my hand very slowly, smiling in my face with the same open, anxious radiance as on the first time that afternoon when he'd called to me across the terrace of the café. It felt like days ago.

I looked at his deep friendly eyes with laughter wrinkling the skin round them; and for a moment it was like looking at nothing. I supposed that if I were Walt or Eva or a psychiatrist or a disappointed father or a wilting mother, I would see something there, something I wanted, or could pity or mould or entreat. But all I could think of was that plastic material which looks like soft pale clay; you take it into your hands and press it into any shape you like, and when you have finished playing with it you let it go back to what it was before, vacant and inanimate.

'I must call Eva,' he said, turned and waved cheerfully as I walked away.

Walt is standing at the entrance to the pier, near the white Porsche. Lines of cars still flow past along the highway. Hands in pockets he looks up at the hills. Above the pier the land slants down abruptly, a sombre bluff overlaid with scrub still blackened from a fire.

'My car's in town; can I ride with you?'

Mine is parked a hundred yards down the highway, at The Burrow. Before we start to walk, we both look back at the pier. Clyde is still gazing at the ocean. The boats are small dark specks heading for the horizon.

Walt turns away slowly. 'I feel bad because he'll have to drive himself home. If a cop catches him he'll be in trouble.'

'Eva'll come and get him,' I say.

'How do you know?'

'He said he was going to call her.'

We walk for a moment in silence. 'Did he say anything else?' Walt asks, his face sad. 'Did he say anything for me?'

'No.'

'It's over, anyway. Even if he calls *me* tomorrow and tells me he's sorry, it's completely over. I've been thinking, maybe I'll find a boat and sign on – as a steward or something. I want to get on a boat. I wasn't born here, did you know that?'

'No. Where were you born, Walt?'

'You wouldn't have heard of it.' For some reason he hesitates. 'A town called Lima in Ohio. My father ran a drugstore.'

'When did you leave it?'

'Five years ago, when I was twenty. I didn't want to spend my life in Ohio; a friend of mine had come out here already; he said California is the place. Well, I got this job in a factory and I was crazy about California, the climate and everything. I don't know a lot of people but I'm quiet. Did I tell you my father died last year? Mother's just out here on a visit, we have some cousins ...' His forehead creases with anxious lines. 'I guess I was okay till I met Clyde. Since this year with Clyde, everything's started to look different.'

We have reached my car. Walt stops with his hands on the door, looking at the highway, a restaurant on the other side, its neon sign winking below barren hills, cratered where the earth has slid away. 'It's my own fault, I guess. I don't respect myself any more.'

'You must stop saying that.'

He shakes his head. 'No, I have to fight it.'

We drive off. Dusk is falling and the ocean looks very calm.

'My father used to play checkers in the evenings,' Walt says. 'I never could stand the game. They've had a lot of rainstorms in Ohio recently.'

This is the last remark he makes for some time, until we turn off the highway. As we leave the ocean behind, he glances at it. 'You really think he'll go back to Eva?'

'He has to go back to somebody. There's a kind of person – well, he needs somebody to give him an identity. Otherwise he's pretty blue.'

'That's a terrible way to live. You think Clyde was always like that?'

'I don't know.' I've been wondering about it during the drive. 'His father must have given Clyde an identity quite early on. Then he threw it away, but before he could find a real one, if he had it, everyone crowded around with offers. Eva's was the best. The strongest, anyway.'

Walt is gazing ahead, at the winding road. 'I think I must have been crazy. I mean, living in that house with Eva too, and the bars, and the people who hate Clyde so politely in bars, and whizzing along that highway, and then you know the way Clyde teases. ...' He switches on the radio. 'There were times when I just wanted to *run*.'

'I can imagine that.'

'Now I want to get on a boat.'

'There must be something about that ocean,' I say. 'Every-one wants to go on it.'

'There's something about every ocean.' A popular song comes from the radio. Walt's tense homely face is suddenly relaxed. 'Clyde said it, didn't he? He said the ocean doesn't change, and he said it lasts for ever.'

A few minutes later, we have said good-bye. 'Nice meet-ing you.' Walt shakes my hand. 'I guess I'll take my mother out to dinner after all.' I am left, I don't know why, with an electric certainty that neither Clyde, Walt nor myself, who have suddenly met for a few hours on this late summer day, dropped like the landscape as if from a hand in the sky, will ever see each other again.

News from the Slide Area

SUMMER is always reluctant to go. Sometimes it makes a false departure and comes back for Christmas. For a few weeks now, signs have presaged the end. One night it rains gently. A wind from the ocean swiftly wraps a sparkling afternoon in fog. Electric storms break out over the desert at night, salvoes of thunder are heard and prongs of lightning flash like exclamations in the sky. Every day at the beach, the young lifeguards sit in their towers. By the end of summer they are deeply tanned, yet somehow autumn creeps into their eyes. Each time they scan the ocean with its swimmers waiting for surf to ride, it seems like a last glance before saying good-bye.

While summer fades, the city still spreads and grows. Much of the growing you wouldn't notice. You pass a truck in the night, drawing a new frame-house; there are always plenty of these, set down and lost in the general sprawling pattern. But sometimes a landmark disappears, like the old pier between Santa Monica and Venice. Replacing the shabby arcades of obsolete peep-shows and makeshift booths is a bright new pleasure-cape, clean and synthetic. Neptune's sculpture presides over an artificial lake with coloured fountains and large aerated bubbles. Walk past it while the music plays, taking the moving stairway that lifts you above tree-like chandeliers with outstretched branches of light, and step into an elevator. It doesn't move, but in the centre of it a transparent column fills up with water, to make you think you're going beneath the sea. You find yourself in a vast dim cavity called Neptune's Kingdom. You walk round a tank with glass walls. It represents the ocean bed, but there is no water, only an illusion created by the play of light. Stuffed barracudas and other outsize creatures spin slowly round on wires. Neptune watches from his throne. Coral, marine growths and shells, all too brightly tinted, litter the depths. Less than half a mile away from this dry electrical kingdom is the Pacific itself, pale and streaked with patches of seaweed. At this moment it is secretly swallowing up ton after ton of disinfected garbage.

For other kingdoms have been created. Beyond Venice, there used to be a desolate stretch of sand dunes and waste ground, planted here and there with oil derricks. Then came a regiment of black squat cylindrical tanks. The face of the landscape changed; factory chimneys, scaffolding, machinery, wire fences, converged upon the empty beaches. Everything feels silent, looks unattended, but inside the tanks the city's garbage is being chemically purified, then rushed along an underground channel and poured into the ocean.

To the north, cupped in the mountains, are missile bases. KEEP OUT. Constructions point skywards from a bulldozed desert. Old newspapers and empty cans of beer lie on the ground. Higher up, new houses are being built. The view should be good.

So the refuse is purified and pumped; the missiles are loaded; the lifeguard watches from his sunny tower; stuffed fish ponderously circle a waterless cage; and, in his frame-house, a man wakes up to find he has a neighbour.

'Yes, mister, it's a strange world,' Rosa Veen says. 'But I like it. Ever since I came out here – and it's seventeen years now – I'm always thinking of the future. That's partly because it's my business. But there's something else. The past is out of place here, mister. You just don't feel it, you only feel the future.'

Rosa, I suppose, is a witch. The little plate on her door

says, CONSULTATIONS. She advertises occasionally in the classified section of the newspapers, under Personal Advisers. *Rosa Veen solves prob. By Appt.* The city is full of sorcerers : clairvoyants, astrologers, palmists, psychic readers, diviners by the ancient oriental methods. They do almost as well, I should say, as psychoanalysts. Astrologers are the most fashionable; they control film stars, write columns in the press, give Capricorn and Virgo parties. Rosa is one of the humble prophets, who work in little rooms in every section of the city and offer Help for two or three dollars, like the wise men and women in primitive villages. Everyday she receives Vibrations in her parlour above a Chinese laundry in Hollywood.

A comfortable, sloping woman of about sixty, Rosa speaks in a cracked and uneducated voice and walks with a limp. You want to frame her in a rocking chair, on a porch, or bent over a stove, baking potato bread. Her parlour is very simply furnished. A couch with faded upholstery and anti-macassars, a captain's chair, a braid rug. And a card table, with two chairs, at which business is conducted.

'Who sent you to me, mister?'

'Zeena Nelson. Do you remember her? She came to you quite a while ago, after her sister died.'

Her forehead wrinkles. 'Oh, the murder. Yeah, I remember that. Did they ever catch the man who did it?'

'Not yet.'

'Well, I guess they're still working on it.' Rosa places herself at the card table, smoothing the cheap plastic cloth, and I sit opposite her. I notice a china ashtray with the figure of a naked woman painted on it. An Indian mask hanging on the wall. A jar of peacock feathers. And a potted tea-plant, rather withered.

'The junk don't mean anything,' Rosa says. 'It's just little gifts from people I helped.'

She asks me to hold out my left hand, palm upwards. She presses her own left palm down on it three times, breathes heavily, then leans back in her chair. 'Uh-huh,' she says. She stares at the plastic tablecloth. 'Say, mister. You could have been a doctor.'

'I suppose I could.'

She watches me narrowly. 'Or a lawyer.'

'I suppose so.'

She sighs. 'But you ain't.'

I agree. She sighs again. Through the window I can see a palm tree and a billboard advertising filter cigarettes.

'Say, mister.'

'Yes?'

'Your kind of work ain't exactly regular. It comes and goes. And there's inspiration in it, too.'

'That's pretty good.' I decide we might as well settle this quickly. 'I'm a writer.'

'There you are, then.' She stares at the tablecloth. 'I'm getting an M.' She draws it in the air. 'A big M. You know somebody whose name begins with an M?'

'Several.' *Marguerite Osterberg-Steblechi.* But Rosa's not a spiritualist.

'This is a feller. Young. Gives me a funny feeling.'

'Go on.'

'Like it's very hot. Sun.' *Mark Cusden.* 'This feller lives in the sun.' She watches me. 'And I'm getting an island, too.'

Now she startles me. I tell her about Mark, and ask if she can get any more vibrations.

She nods. 'Yeah, I'm getting more. I'm getting a pain.' She gives a little frown. 'Sort of a shooting pain.' She touches her head. 'And then dragons and sharks come out of the sea. And terrible bright colours. And then it's all right again.' She looks relieved. 'But that shoot of pain, and the things that come out of the sea – he should watch it!'

A pause. I try to think of nothing; but that's impossible. A line of names, places, memories, forms in my head, as long as the traffic block outside.

'Say, mister. Here's a D. A girl whose name begins with a D. I'm getting the whole name ... Della? Delia?'

'I don't know anyone called Della or Delia.'

'Think again, mister.'

'I'm sure I don't.'

Rosa gives me a reproachful look. 'Well, I'm getting her. Della or Delia. She's pretty, too.'

'Can you describe her?'

'She – I guess she's a blonde. Maybe she's a model, there's a lot of photographs of her around.'

'I'm afraid you've drawn a blank.'

'Well, you think it over.' Rosa gets up, goes slowly over to the window and closes it. 'Too much noisy traffic, it interferes. You think over this Della or Delia. A lot of people tell me I've drawn a blank, then they call up later and say, "Rosa, you were right!" So you think it over.'

'All right.'

She sits down again. 'You going to ask me about happiness, mister?'

'Are you getting some?'

'Happiness is a funny thing.' She nods several times. 'When I was a girl of twenty, I wanted a husband more than anything in the world. And I got one. And I was miserable. Had a son. Son died. Then I broke my leg, it wouldn't heal. Then I discovered my Gift, left my husband and came out here.'

I ask if her husband is still alive.

Rosa shrugs. 'Could be. Bumming around some place, if he is. But I'm happier than I've ever been, mister. And I couldn't imagine it turning out this way. I don't get around too well, I live alone and offer Help at very reasonable charges. I tell everyone this. There's always hope, but you never know just how anything'll turn out. It's all mixed up ... I'm getting a C.'

Cliff? Clyde Wallace?

Rather uncannily, Rosa shakes her head. 'No, this is a woman. Not a spring chicken, either.'

Carlotta.

'A big woman.'

I can't think of anyone else.

'You know a big woman, mister, who's been kind of upset? I'd like to comfort her, that's how I feel. Why, they've turned her out of her own home!'

Carmen Lynch. Of course. Timmy telephoned a few days ago to say that she'd had a row with Roeling, and was leaving. I asked Timmy if she'd found a new situation. He told me she was going to be companion-chauffeur to a rich widow in Beverly Hills.

'There you are, then.'

No doubt of it, Rosa's a witch. 'How do you do it?' I ask.

'It just comes to me, mister. I get the Vibrations.'

'It's extraordinary.'

'Yeah, that's what the psychiatrists say. I had seven of them come down once, and some doctors. I tell them it's like doing sums in the head. Two and two makes four, you know. That's all I can tell them.' Another pause. 'Now here's a man and a woman, old people, standing by water. And some graves. Then some mountains.'

'No, that doesn't mean anything to me.'

'When you were a kid, mister?'

I try to find an association for this image, but I can't. 'Is it good or bad?'

'Couldn't say, mister. It's there, that's all.'

'I can't place it.'

'Well, maybe this is something came up that shouldn't. How about N? You know an N?'

'I once had an aunt called Nancy.'

'This is a feller. Ned?'

I shake my head.

'Shoo!' says Rosa, rather sharply. 'There's some Vibrations around here that don't belong. Is your father dead?'

'No.' She seems to be losing her way. I think of getting up to go.

'Say, mister! I knew there was another young feller – I'm getting him. Very good-looking, I'd say, blue eyes; when he smiles you want to kiss him, you really do. But I don't know about him. He's struggling, mister, like he wants to get out of a cage. And the ocean's mixed up in it.'

Clyde. She's found her way back. 'Do you think he'll get out of the cage?'

'I don't know. I'd like to help him, that's how I feel, but I don't know . . .'

I pay her three dollars. 'Thank you, mister. Did I Help?' 'You almost scared me sometimes.' 'Good luck, mister. And don't worry. There's a lot of trouble in this world, and most of us get our share of it – but don't anyone try to tell me there's no hope! Hope's our daily bread, mister. Don't forget to cut yourself a slice of it when you wake up in the morning.'

Going down the stairs, passing the laundry, I don't know whether it is disturbing, or important, or hopeful, that these scattered life-waves should come together and tremble, for a few moments, on the antennae of a homely old cripple.

Two days later, I am walking past a movie theatre on Hollywood Boulevard. It is showing a pair of horror films, *Attack of the Ant Women* and *High School Ghoul*. Furred and fanged, monsters scowl from glaring posters at the sun-lit street. A girl's face is twisted in a scream. On a board out-side the theatre are photographs from the films. In *High School Ghoul*, I recognize a face: round, childlike, wide-eyed, with blonde hair. She is evidently the heroine. In one scene she cowers against a blackboard in an empty class-room at night, while the monster advances between a row of desks. In another, she is being consoled by a handsome teacher.

It is the face, unmistakably, of Emma Slack. I look at the posters. The leading lady of *High School Ghoul* is called Delia Blow. 'You think over this Della or Delia ...' I re-member Rosa Veen, and the world spins. Is my father dead? Do I know someone called Ned? When I was a child, did two old people lead me to a riverside cemetery? No; all this at least turns out to have been somebody else's world. Yet one of Rosa's Vibrations has echoed as mysteriously as if a guitar left on a chair suddenly twanged by itself. I forgot about Emma a long while ago. When she disappeared down the hill on the studio back lot, it struck me as final. If I ever saw her again, it would be years later and she'd have a hus-band and four children, as the palmist at Dubuque said.

Now I want to find her again, and decide to try the same apartment since it is only five minutes away. On the quiet residential street, nothing seems to have changed. A bunga-low is for rent. Two boys in cowboy hats play on the side-walk. A woman disappears into one of the Spanish man-sions.

I ring the bell, and Emma opens the door.

'Well!'

She looks exactly the same. A little taller, perhaps. After all, she is still growing. 'Welcome, stranger!' she says. 'But what have you turned up for?'

As we go into the living-room, I explain about Rosa. She

listens very intently, mouth dropping open. 'It's *Fate*! Honestly. Of course I believe in them all, I've always believed in astrologers and fortune-tellers and everything, so I shouldn't be surprised.' She gasps. 'But I am. Just think of someone who I've never met, knowing everything about me!'

'Are you still Emma?' I ask. 'Or should I call you Delia?'

'Well, I'm Emma to myself. They call me Delia on the set, but somehow I haven't got used to it. At first I tried saying to myself before I went to sleep at night, "Emma Slack you're Delia Blow, Emma Slack you're Delia Blow," but it didn't work.' She presses the button in the wall, the bookcase slides open to reveal a cocktail cabinet. 'Would you like a Bloody Mary?'

'Thank you, Emma.'

'I'm getting quite fond of them.' She picks up a shaker. 'Have you seen my picture?'

'Not yet. I only knew about it fifteen minutes ago.'

Emma sighs. 'A lot of people don't know about it yet. That's the trouble. As Midge says, there's not much for a girl in a monster picture.'

'All the same. Emma, it's wonderful. You're a star in your first film!'

'I suppose so. But it wasn't exactly what I expected. I mean, my name's up there but I don't *feel* like a star. Nobody's ever recognized me in the street, though I walked up and down outside the theatre quite a lot. And it all happened so *quickly*! It seemed like they'd finished the picture almost as soon as I knew I'd got the part. When they said they'd pay me four hundred dollars a week, I was terribly excited – but it was only for a week.'

'Still, it should lead to something.'

'To another monster picture.' She giggles. 'I start *Curse of the Ghouls* next week.'

I raise my glass. 'Well, here's to Delia Blow.'

'Oh, thank you. But do you really like that name?'

'It's easy to remember. Did Midge invent it?' She nods. 'How is Midge?'

'Fine.' She sounds rather indifferent. 'We're married, you know.'

'No, I didn't.'

'Yes. It was Midge's idea; he kept on asking, and in the end I thought – what's the difference?'

'I suppose you had to get your aunts' consent?'

'They were very pleased. They thought it might make me settle down.' Her eyes cloud over. 'But I'm beginning to wonder.'

'What?'

Emma looks grave. 'I've been in this place more than a year now. And in a way I guess a lot has happened. I mean, I've been in a monster picture, and I'm going to be in another.' She doesn't mention getting married. 'But although I've got in the movies now, nobody cares. I thought once I get in, that's it! But I've been to see my monster picture five times, and I listen to what people say when they come out, and they never talk about *me*. Only about the monsters. Nobody asks, who's that pretty blonde girl? Sometimes I get discouraged, you know.'

'Maybe,' I suggest, 'you've got a better part in *Curse of the Ghouls*.'

'No, it's exactly the same. Not the kind of thing to make you stand out. I'd have turned it down, honestly, but Midge got my salary upped a hundred dollars. Will you give me the address of that fortune-teller?'

'You want to consult Rosa?'

'I certainly do. I'm going to ask if she sees any way out of monster pictures for me.'

I warn her not to expect too much, because Rosa grows vague when you mention the future.

'I've got to try. I can't stand it. I've been to three astrologers and a palmist already. One of the astrologers thought he saw a way out. He found a connexion with music in my horoscope. I ought to sing, he said. So now I'm taking lessons. It might lead somewhere, I guess, and it's about time I knew where I was going.'

Emma is standing by the window. Behind her, a panoramic view of the city. Lights are coming on. I suppose that one of them, in all the twinkling miles, catches her name on the monster poster.

Now it has officially happened. We didn't know, when the sun went down yesterday evening, that it was the end of summer; but the sky has been overcast since morning, and it rains. 'Today,' says a radio announcer, 'is the first day of autumn.' He makes it sound final. Toward sunset, the sky clears, but rain is expected again during the night.

The beach has a peculiar charm at this hour. It has been empty all day, the sand looks clean and there is no litter. A few people have come down to stroll or swim. On the stone breakwaters, gulls perch.

Zeena walks by herself, along the shore. I thought I'd find her here; she hadn't answered the telephone, she wasn't in The Place. 'She came in for a few minutes, then wandered out the way she does,' the barman said.

'Hello darling.'

I tell her I've seen the story in the newspapers. SEX FIEND CAUGHT! 'Have the police been in touch with you?'

She nods. 'Oh yes.' And walks a few steps. 'I saw him today.'

'The killer?'

'Don't call him that, darling. I know he's confessed, he killed Hank and four others, but if you'd seen him you wouldn't use such a *professional* word.'

'What was he like, Zeena?'

She lights another cigarette. 'They were leading him into somebody's office at the station. It was only for a moment. He didn't know who I was. And you know what I thought? It sounds ridiculous, but it flashed through my mind at once – I *don't know what Hank saw in him*. Not a bad-looking face, but something frail. Awfully thin. And troubled. I asked the police if he'd said anything about Hank. All he said was, "yes, she was one of them". He didn't seem to care.'

'It says in the paper he's surprisingly well educated but a classic schizoid type.'

'Does it, darling? Of course I realized at once he was quite mad. It's a madness that comes and goes, isn't that the worst kind? I can't help wondering how he lived in the intermissions, knowing the curtain had to go up again, sooner or later.' Zeena stops, looks at the ocean. 'It's done me such good to pity him!'

We stroll on together. There's almost a springiness in her walk. 'Is that what you felt when you saw him?' I ask. 'The pity?'

'A wave of it. Like a shot in the arm. I walked out feeling absolutely great. And so lucky!' She smiles. 'Darling, I used to think I was a very depressing character – just an old tosspot, dragging along somehow. But then I remember that boy. And Hank ... When I got home, I didn't open the store. I just looked around and had an inspiration. I'm going to sell the whole junkheap and start a Mexican restaurant instead.'

'That sounds a wonderful idea,' I say. 'But can you cook?'

'No, but I'll learn. And honestly darling, with Mexican food it really doesn't matter. Just make it hot, that's all. It's the best kind of food for all the people I know, because it's so cheap and you can't tell what it is. I'll stay open all night and close at dawn.' Her eyes grow misty. 'Everyone'll hear about it, and everyone'll come!'

I leave Zeena by the shore, lighting a cigarette, and walk back to my car. The air feels moist, it'll rain again soon, but the whole sky is a rich glow of sunset. I find myself remembering how the summer began. The cliffs weakened under heavy spring rains, rocks and stones rolled away, then whole sections crumbled and fell. Houses skidded down with them. There were some deaths. For several miles the coast highway was closed. The newspapers rumoured that a long geological survey would be undertaken. Had the highway been cut too deep into the cliffs? Would the land go on falling? Perhaps the area would have to be abandoned and a causeway built out over the ocean. Meanwhile, the ruins were shovelled away, FOR RENT signs went up on beach houses, a few bars and restaurants closed. After three months, the highway was opened again without explanation. Driving along, you saw jagged hollows and craters scarring the cliffs. They looked almost volcanic. WATCH FOR ROCKS. The sun grew stronger. Cars massed along the highway, the long pale stretch of pleasure beaches became filled with people. And the slides were forgotten, nobody talked about them any more.

'Well, there's no point in scaring people. Remember those old ladies who went over the edge? I told them then it wouldn't be the end of it, but I told them not to scare any-body.' The engineer who said this was stocky and unruffled. He had thickly-rimmed spectacles and a briar pipe. The city authorities had consulted him after the houses fell down.

'We'll handle the whole thing quietly, in our own way. That's what I told them.'

'Then how serious are the slides?' I asked.

'I guess you could call the last one a little serious.' He puffed at his pipe. 'Quite a bit of land fell away that time. Took quite a few houses with it.'

'People, too.'

'Sure. People, too.'

'Shouldn't something be done?'

'We need more information.' The engineer's pipe was drawing badly. He lit another match. 'We want to see what happens after the rains next year.'

'You mean, wait for the same thing to happen again?'

'So what else can you do?' The engineer shrugged. 'Make a big project out of it and spend a lot of money? Scare a lot of people and take their business away? It's not worth it. Time's on our side.' He gave a reassuring nod. 'Maybe the foundations *are* shaky, maybe we'll have another slide after the rains next year, but it's a slow, easy process. It'll take years and years before you notice a real difference.'

'A few houses more or less don't really matter,' I said.

'Well, that's not exactly the way I'd put it.' He shrugged again. 'You know what I think? People should be a little careful and not live too near the edge, that's all.'

THRILLERS
STAR

0352397012	Georges Arnaud THE WAGES OF FEAR	50p
0352300167	Niven Busch THE TAKEOVER	50p*
0352398361	Max Caulfield BRUCE LEE LIVES?	45p
0352300523	Henry Denker A PLACE FOR THE MIGHTY	75p*
0352300337	Robert Flood THE HIT MAN	65p*
0352398906	Robert Hawkes NARC: THE DELGADO KILLINGS	50p*
0352398213	NARC: THE DEATH LIST	50p*
0352398558	NARC: THE DEATH OF A COURIER	50p*
0352398590	Burt Hirschfeld MOMENT OF POWER	75p*
0352300914	William Woolfolk THE OVERLORDS	75p*

THRILLERS
TANDEM

0426141709	R. L. Brent LIQUIDATOR 1	30p*
0426145844	LIQUIDATOR 2: CONTRACT FOR A KILLING	35p*
0426150503	LIQUIDATOR 3: THE COCAINE CONNECTION	35p*
0426143493	Nick Carter AGENT COUNTER-AGENT	35p*
0426173473	ASSAULT ON ENGLAND	50p*
0426168976	AZTEC AVENGER	45p*
0426173635	BERLIN	50p*
0426125622	A BULLET FOR FIDEL	40p*
042617304X	CAIRO	50p*
0426173554	THE COBRA KILL	50p*
0426169182	DEATH OF THE FALCON	45p*
0426174003	THE DEATH STRAIN	50p*
0426173988	THE DEFECTOR	50p*
0426173392	THE EXECUTIONERS	50p*
0426157125	HOUR OF THE WOLF	40p*
0426173201	THE HUMAN TIME BOMB	50p*
0426157206	THE KREMLIN FILE	40p*

Not for sale in Canada.

0426173120	THE LIVING DEATH	50p*
0426173716	THE MIND KILLERS	50p*
0426168704	OUR AGENT IN ROME IS MISSING	45p*
0426126262	THE RED GUARD	40p*
0426168895	THE SPANISH CONNECTION	45p*
0426125460	SPY CASTLE	40p*
0426174194	TIME CLOCK OF DEATH	50p*
0426147286	Max Franklin NINETY NINE DEAD	35p*
0426150422	Michael T. Kaufman THE NICKEL RIDE	35p*
042615181X	Allan Morgan BLOOD – THE CAT CAY WARRANT	35p*
0426147014	BLOOD – THE SPANDAU WARRANT	35p*
0426172914	Michael Maguire SHOT SILK	50p*
0426146131	Jim Robinson TOGETHER BROTHERS	35p*
042614533X	Michael Stratford ADAM 12 – THE SNIPER	35p*

CRIME
STAR

035239837X	"Joey" HIT 29		60p*
0352300019	KILLER		50p*
0352398639	Donald Rumbelow THE COMPLETE JACK THE RIPPER	(NF) (illus)	60p

CRIME
TANDEM

0426170725	Elizabeth Lemarchand THE AFFRACOMBE AFFAIR	45p
0426170806	ALIBI FOR A CORPSE	45p
0426170644	DEATH OF AN OLD GIRL	45p

WAR
STAR

0352300116	Walter Gibson THE BOAT	35p

WAR
TANDEM

0426170482	Wing-Co. Ronald Adams READINESS AT DAWN	50p*

*Not for sale in Canada.

0426170563	WE RENDEZVOUS AT TEN		50p
0426164679	M. G. Comeau OPERATION MERCURY		40p
0426165128	Captain Theodore Detmers THE RAIDER KORMORAN	(NF)	45p
0426150694	J. M. Flynn THE RAID ON REICHSWALD FORTRESS		35p
0426170210	E. P. Hoyt SEA EAGLE	(NF)	50p
042617013X	Georg von Konrat ASSAULT FROM WITHIN	(NF)	60p
0426164911	Theodor Krancke and H. J. Brennecke POCKET BATTLESHIP		50p
0426149122	Gordon Landsborough BATTERY FROM HELLFIRE		40p
0426176464	BENGHAZI BREAKOUT		60p
0426170997	DESERT MARAUDERS		50p
0426166949	THE GLASSHOUSE GANG		50p
0426161254	LONG RUN TO TOBRUK		45p
0426149041	PATROL TO BENGHAZI		40p
0426149203	Lee Parker DONOVAN'S DEVILS – BLUEPRINT FOR EXECUTION		35p*
0426156676	DONOVAN'S DEVILS – THE GUNS OF MAZATLAN		35p*
0426165047	Heinx Schaeffer U-BOAT 977		45p
0426170059	A. V. Sellwood THE WARRING SEAS	(NF)	55p
042616475X	Brigadier Durnford-Slater COMMANDO		45p
0426164830	Michael Crichton-Stuart G. PATROL		45p
0426162722	Graham Wallace RAF BIGGIN HILL		50p

SCIENCE FICTION
STAR

0352398655	Joanna Russ PICNIC ON PARADISE	50p*
0352398469	Kilgore Trout VENUS ON THE HALF SHELL	50p*

SCIENCE FANTASY
STAR

0352398523	W. W. QHE: PROPHETS OF EVIL	50p

*Not for sale in Canada.

SCIENCE FANTASY
TANDEM

	Edgar Rice Burroughs	
0426148401	OUT OF TIME'S ABYSS	35p*

The Fantastic Gor Series

	John Norman	
0426144961	ASSASSIN OF GOR	45p*
0426167821	CAPTIVE OF GOR	60p*
0426147952	HUNTERS OF GOR	45p*
042617531X	MARAUDERS OF GOR	60p*
0426144880	NOMADS OF GOR	45p*
0426167740	PRIEST-KINGS OF GOR	50p*
0426124235	RAIDERS OF GOR	40p*
0426143736	TARNSMAN OF GOR	35p*

Planet Of The Apes

	David Gerrold	
0426147448	BATTLE FOR THE PLANET OF THE APES	35p*
	John Jakes	
0426147529	CONQUEST OF THE PLANET OF THE APES	35p*
	Jerry Pournelle	
042614760X	ESCAPE FROM THE PLANET OF THE APES	35p*
	George Alec Effinger	
0426156757	ESCAPE TO TOMORROW	35p*
0426160371	JOURNEY INTO TERROR	35p*
0426151739	MAN THE FUGITIVE	35p*
	Jane Gaskell	
0426159667	ATLAN	60p
0426164326	THE CITY	45p
0426159586	THE DRAGON	45p
0426159314	THE SERPENT	60p
	John Jakes	
0426167074	BRAK THE BARBARIAN	45p*
0426167236	MARK OF THE DEMONS	45p*
0426167155	THE SORCERESS	45p*

OCCULT (NF)
STAR

	Dion Fortune	
0352398922	THE DEMON LOVER	60p
0352398930	THE SEA PRIESTESS	60p

*Not for sale in Canada.

	"Heather" and Hans Holzer	
0352398434	CONFESSIONS OF A WITCH	50p*
	John Whitman	
0352300841	THE PSYCHIC POWER OF PLANTS	60p*

OCCULT
TANDEM

0426150716	THE TAROT GIFT PACK	£2.50
	Michael Harrison	
0426158512	THE ROOTS OF WITCHCRAFT	50p
	Ronald Holmes	
0426168461	WITCHCRAFT IN BRITISH HISTORY	60p
	Al Koran	
0426174860	BRING OUT THE MAGIC IN YOUR MIND	50p
0426175581	THE MAGIC OF THE MIND IN ACTION	60p*
	Editors John Symonds & Kenneth Grant ALEISTER CROWLEY – THE COMPLETE ASTROLOGICAL	
0426166868	WRITINGS	50p

HORROR
STAR

	Ramsey Campbell	
0352300647	DEMONS BY DAYLIGHT	50p
	Editors Christopher Lee and Michel Parry	
0352398094	CHRISTOPHER LEE'S "X" CERTIFICATE	60p*
	Manly Wade Wellman	
0352300655	WHO FEARS THE DEVIL?	50p

HORROR
TANDEM

	Alfred Hitchcock	
0426149475	THE BEST OF FIENDS	40p*
0426149556	LET IT ALL BLEED OUT	40p*
	W. H. Hodgson	
0426134184	CARNACKI THE GHOST-FINDER	35p
	Jessie Douglas Kerruish	
0426160533	THE UNDYING MONSTER	50p*
	Clifton Adams	
0426160967	OUTLAW DESTINY	45p*
0426160886	TRAGG'S CHOICE	45p*
	Benjamin Capps	
0426160614	THE WHITE MAN'S ROAD	50p
	I. A. Greenfield	
0426071301	THE CAREY BLOOD	35p*
042614998X	THE CAREY GUN	35p*

*Not for sale in Canada.

0426071492	CAREY'S VENGEANCE	35p*
	Fred Grove	
0426169859	BUFFALO SPRING	45p*
0426175743	THE LAND SEEKERS	50p*
0426175662	SUN DANCE	50p*
	James Lewis	
0426157478	A FISTFUL OF DYNAMITE	35p*
	Joe Millard	
0426160452	CAHILL	35p*
	D. B. Olsen	
0426141113	THE NIGHT OF THE BOWSTRING	30p*
	Lewis B. Patten	
0426161092	THE RED SABBATH	45p*
	Herbert Purdum	
0426161173	THE SABER BRAND	50p*
	Martin Ryerson	
0426145178	THE GUNFIGHTER	35p*
	Bret Sanders	
0426147367	HAWK BLOOD BAIT	35p*
0426142500	HAWK VENGEANCE GUN	30p*

THRILLERS
STAR

	Georges Arnaud	
0352397012	THE WAGES OF FEAR	50p
	William F. Buckley Jr.	
0352396962	SAVING THE QUEEN	60p
	Niven Busch	
0352300167	THE TAKEOVER	50p*
	Max Caulfield	
0352398361	BRUCE LEE LIVES?	45p
	Henry Denker	
0352300523	A PLACE FOR THE MIGHTY	75p
	Robert Flood	
0352300337	THE HIT MAN	65p
	Robert Hawkes	
0352398906	NARC: THE DELGADO KILLINGS	50p*
0352398213	NARC: THE DEATH LIST	50p*

WESTERNS
TANDEM
"Alias Smith & Jones"

	Brian Fox	
0426166515	APACHE GOLD	40p
0426166434	CABIN FEVER	40p

*Not for sale in Canada.

0426140907	DEAD RINGER	35p*
042617769X	DRAGOONED	50p
0426140826	OUTLAW TRAIL	35p*

"Dollar"

	Joe Millard	
0426131274	BLOOD FOR A DIRTY DOLLAR	30p*
0426135490	A COFFIN FULL OF DOLLARS	35p*
	Brian Fox	
042614015X	A DOLLAR TO DIE FOR	35p*
	Joe Millard	
0426140079	FOR A FEW DOLLARS MORE	35p*
042613935X	THE GOOD THE BAD THE UGLY	35p*
	Joe Millard	
0426136454	THE MILLION-DOLLAR BLOODHUNT	35p*

"Gunsmoke"

	Jackson Flynn	
0426156595	CHEYENNE VENGEANCE	35p*
0426150260	DUEL AT DODGE CITY	35p*
0426146808	THE RENEGADES	35p*
0426146999	SHOOTOUT	35p*

Louis L'Amour

042613821X	CROSSFIRE TRAIL	35p*
0426138139	KILKENNY	35p*
0426138562	SHOWDOWN AT YELLOW BUTTE	35p*
0426138481	UTAH BLAINE	35p*
	Michael Gleason	
042615018X	McCLOUD: THE CORPSE MAKER	35p*
	David Wilson	
0426156838	McCLOUD: A DANGEROUS PLACE TO DIE	35p*
0426145259	McCLOUD: THE KILLING	35p*
0426164598	McCLOUD: PARK AVENUE EXECUTIONER	40p*

*Not for sale in Canada.

Wyndham Books are available from many booksellers and news-agents. If you have any difficulty please send purchase price plus postage on the scale below to:

Wyndham Cash Sales, or Star Book Service,
123 King Street,   G.P.O. Box 29,
London W6 9JG.   Isle of Man,
                          British Isles.

While every effort is made to keep prices low, it is sometimes necessary to increase prices at short notice. Wyndham Books reserve the right to show new retail prices on covers which may differ from those advertised in the text or elsewhere.

UK AND EIRE
One book 15p plus 7p per copy for each additional book ordered to a maximum charge of 57p.

OTHER COUNTRIES
Rates available on request.

NB These charges are subject to Post Office charge fluctuations.